RADICAL
ENCOUNTERS

Visit us at www.boldstrokesbooks.com

What Reviewers Say About Radclyﬀe's Books

Lammy winner "...*Stolen Moments* is a collection of steamy stories about women who just couldn't wait. It's sex when desire overrides reason, and it's incredibly hot!" – *On Our Backs*

Lammy winner "...*Distant Shores, Silent Thunder* weaves an intricate tapestry about passion and commitment between lovers. The story explores the fragile nature of trust and the sanctuary provided by loving relationships." – *Sapphic Reader*

Shield of Justice is a "...well-plotted...lovely romance...I couldn't turn the pages fast enough!" – Ann Bannon, author of *The Beebo Brinker Chronicles*

A Matter of Trust is a "...sexy, powerful love story filled with angst, discovery and passion that captures the uncertainty of first love and its discovery." – *Just About Write*

"The author's brisk mix of political intrigue, fast-paced action, and frequent interludes of lesbian sex and love...in *Honor Reclaimed*...sure does make for great escapist reading." – *Q Syndicate*

Lammy Finalist *Justice Served* delivers a "...crisply written, fast-paced story with twists and turns and keeps us guessing until the final explosive ending." – *Independent Gay Writer*

Change of Pace is "...contemporary, yet timeless, not only about sex, but also about love, longing, lust, surprises, chance meetings, planned meetings, fulfilling wild fantasies, and trust." – *Midwest Book Review*

"Radclyffe has once again pulled together all the ingredients of a genuine page-turner, this time adding some new spices into the mix. *shadowland* is sure to please—in part because Radclyffe never loses sight of the fact that she is telling a love story, and a compelling one at that." – Cameron Abbott, author of *To The Edge* and *An Inexpressible State of Grace*

Lammy Finalist *Turn Back Time* is filled with… "wonderful love scenes, which are both tender and hot." – *MegaScene*

"*Innocent Hearts*…illustrates that our struggles for acceptance of women loving women is as old as time—only the setting changes. The romance is sweet, sensual, and touching." – *Just About Write*

In Lammy Finalist *When Dreams Tremble* the "…focus on character development is meticulous and comprehensive, filled with angst, regret, and longing, building to the ultimate climax." – *Just About Write*

"*Sweet No More*…snarls, teases and toes the line between pleasure and pain." – *Best Lesbian Erotica 2008*

"*Word of Honor* takes the reader on a great ride. The sex scenes are incredible…and the story builds to an exciting climax that is as chilling as it is rewarding." – *Midwest Book Review*

By the Author

Romances

Innocent Hearts

Love's Melody Lost

Love's Tender Warriors

Tomorrow's Promise

Passion's Bright Fury

Love's Masquerade

shadowland

Fated Love

Turn Back Time

Promising Hearts

When Dreams Tremble

The Lonely Hearts Club

Night Call

The Provincetown Tales

Safe Harbor

Beyond the Breakwater

Distant Shores, Silent Thunder

Storms of Change

Winds of Fortune

Honor Series

Above All, Honor

Honor Bound

Love & Honor

Honor Guards

Honor Reclaimed

Honor Under Siege

Word of Honor

Justice Series

A Matter of Trust (prequel)

Shield of Justice

In Pursuit of Justice

Justice in the Shadows

Justice Served

Erotic Interludes: *Change Of Pace*
(A Short Story Collection)
Radical Encounters
(An Erotic Short Story Collection)

Stacia Seaman and Radclyffe, eds.:
Erotic Interludes 2: *Stolen Moments*
Erotic Interludes 3: *Lessons in Love*
Erotic Interludes 4: *Extreme Passions*
Erotic Interludes 5: *Road Games*
Romantic Interludes 1: *Discovery*

RADICAL
ENCOUNTERS

by

RADCLY*ff*E

2009

RADICAL ENCOUNTERS

ISBN 10: 1-60282-050-3
ISBN 13: 978-1-60282-050-0

This Trade Paperback Original Is Published By
Bold Strokes Books, Inc.
P.O. Box 249
Valley Falls, NY 12185

First Edition: February 2009

CREDITS
Editors: Ruth Sternglantz and Stacia Seaman
Production Design: Stacia Seaman
Cover Design By Sheri (graphicartist2020@hotmail.com)

Acknowledgments

A number of these short stories have appeared individually in anthologies from such publishers as Alyson, Bella Books, Bold Strokes Books, Cleis Press, Intaglio, and Pretty Things Press. They are presented here as an entire collection for the first time, along with four never-before published works ("At Your Service," "Character Study," "Helplessly Hers," and "The Lesson Planner").

Many thanks to my editors, Ruth Sternglantz and Stacia Seaman, for assembling and fine-tuning this collection. Applause for another bold and beautiful cover from Sheri.

And to Lee, for never tiring of the stories. *Amo te.*

Radclyffe 2009

Dedication

For Lee
From the First to the Last

Contents

AT YOUR SERVICE

My employer Lila Cronin, heiress to a newspaper fortune and legal advisor to some of the most powerful men in the state, came out of the club a little after one in the morning on the arm of a woman half her age. Lila's companion for the night, decked out in leather pants, black body-hugging tee, and a studded jacket tossed over one broad shoulder, had the swagger of a woman who knew she was attractive. Despite her cocky attitude, I could tell even from across the street she was totally taken with Lila. I wasn't surprised. Lila always got what she wanted, in the courtroom and the boardroom and the bedroom. But it wasn't Lila's money that made her so successful with women of any age. She was just hot. A little above average height, with a willowy figure, splendid breasts, and a curtain of long dark hair that fell around her pale oval face like a frame on a Modigliani. Her large dark eyes and sculpted features completed the haunting image.

I stepped around the front of the limo and held the rear door open for them. Lila didn't look at me, but she brushed her fingertips over my chest as she passed me to get in. As soon as I was settled behind the wheel, I heard the click of the intercom and then Lila's voice.

"Drive to the sector," she said.

She didn't need to say more. I knew where we were going—not far from the industrial section where old warehouses had been turned into exclusive clubs, some so exclusive that there were no signs to announce their presence. Only those in the know, like Lila, were admitted. And of course, those invited for the pleasure of the members. Ten minutes away, the deteriorating buildings had yet to be reclaimed. Streetlights were dark, victims of the elements and vandals. The roads were cracked and potholed. The neglected blocks provided shelter for the homeless in squats and abandoned vehicles. The dark alleys and empty lots offered privacy for the transactions of the flesh that had become the area's main business. Women and men congregated on corners and in doorways, offering their services to those who cruised the streets in search of transitory pleasure.

I followed the prescribed route, one I had driven many times before, into the heart of the sex sector. I drove slowly, as was required, and as I drove, I had no choice but to listen.

"I'm going to tell you exactly what I want you to do," Lila murmured. "And if you're very good, and do as you're told, I'm going to let you make me come."

"That's what I'm here for," the stranger replied, her voice a husky alto. "To make you feel good."

"Do you like thinking about making me come?"

"Oh yeah. I've been thinking about it for hours."

Lila sounded totally in control, but the stranger was already breathing hard. Lila was probably playing with her, kissing her neck, the curve of her ear, her throat, while her hands roamed over her body, caressing her breasts, fondling her nipples, stroking her stomach and thighs. I imagined Lila's hands, her mouth, exciting the young woman's muscular body as I gripped the steering wheel tightly and stared at the road through dry, unblinking eyes.

"Open my blouse. Touch my breasts," Lila said. "That's right. Take my nipple in your mouth." She caught her breath, the only sign of how excited she must be. "Worry it with your teeth while you suck it."

I heard a zipper sliding down. Lila, opening her new lover's pants. Lila would want to tease her clitoris now.

"Oh Jesus," the stranger muttered.

"Your clitoris is very hard," Lila purred. "I'm going to caress it, but you mustn't come."

The stranger groaned, her breath harsh and panting in my ear.

My stomach clenched and I heard the stranger grunt *oh Jesus* again and I wondered how long she'd last. They usually didn't make it very long once Lila started on them. I kept the speedometer rock solid on twenty miles an hour as we drifted through the streets. My pulse hammered between my legs. My breasts tightened, my nipples ached.

I heard the sounds of frantic sucking and low, hungry moans. The stranger would be devouring Lila's breasts now as Lila stroked and squeezed and excited her clit.

"Are you enjoying that?" Lila asked lazily. "You certainly feel like you are. You've gotten very wet and very large."

"I want to come," the stranger said hoarsely.

Lila laughed. "Of course you do."

Lila tapped on the tinted glass that separated the front seat from the rear compartment, and I rolled it down. "Yes, ma'am?"

"She would like to come. Do you think I should let her?"

"That's up to you, ma'am."

"Perhaps I should let you decide. Turn on the monitor."

I activated the small screen in the middle of the dash that relayed the image of the backseat from a concealed video camera mounted in one corner of the rear compartment. Lila and the stranger were tangled in an embrace, their bodies turned on the seat to face one another. Lila's blouse was unbuttoned, her breasts exposed, the dark-haired stranger sucking at one as her strong, wide fingers fondled the other. Lila caressed her new lover's damp locks, guiding her head from one breast to the other. Lila's hand fluttered inside the crotch of the open leather pants. The leather-clad hips rose and fell in frantic entreaty.

"Very good, darling," Lila crooned, "lick my nipple and then pinch it. Mmm, yes. Now the other breast."

Lila's voice had gotten lower and breathier. The attention to her nipples must be making her clitoris ache. I passed a hand under my uniform jacket and over my breasts, squeezing the pebbled tips. My hips lifted reflexively off the seat, but I tensed my thighs and held the speed steady.

"Should I pinch her clitoris just like she's pinching my nipples?" Lila asked, and I knew the question was directed to me.

"Only if she's doing a good job," I said. "Otherwise, she shouldn't be rewarded."

"Mmm, she *is* making my clitoris twitch every time she pinches my nipples. I think I'll squeeze her a little."

I heard a whimper follow close after. Lila was a skilled and relentless masturbator, and I imagined her young paramour was desperate to climax by now. I also knew Lila wouldn't let her. I watched the monitor as I drove, and saw Lila's lover press her hand between her legs, over Lila's gyrating hand.

"Please," the stranger groaned. "Please just a little harder right there. I'm almost coming."

"She doesn't deserve your touch," I said and Lila immediately withdrew her hand. The stranger's face contorted as she gasped, open mouthed against Lila's breast, her crotch pumping empty air. "She should be punished."

"Did you hear that, darling?" Lila yanked on her lover's hair, forcing her face up. "Should I punish you?"

"Anything," the young woman begged. "Just touch my clit again. I'm so close now."

Lila kissed her hungrily. Even on the small monitor, I could see her plunging her tongue into the woman's mouth, sucking and biting her tongue. Lila roughly fondled the woman's breasts through her tight T-shirt, her nails digging into the prominent peaks of her nipples, pinching and twisting. The woman's dazed expression turned into a grimace of pleasure and her body stiffened as if an electric current had forced all of her muscles to contract at once.

"I'm coming," she cried out in shocked pleasure. "Oh God, I'm coming."

The young woman bucked and writhed, moaning her release into Lila's mouth until at last she slumped next to Lila, her chest heaving. Her eyes were closed, her mouth slack, as if all of her energy had been sapped by her orgasm.

"She needs to suck your clit," I said. "For not asking."

"Pull to the curb and power down the rear window," Lila instructed.

My stomach tightened but I did as I was told. Turning off the engine, I watched the monitor and saw Lila kiss the young woman again, then grasp her shoulders and push her down onto the floor, between her legs. Lila shifted toward the open window and I couldn't see or hear her for a few moments. Eventually she straightened and our eyes met in the monitor just as the front passenger door opened and a young, short-haired blonde wearing tight black jeans and a short black leather jacket open over a white lace top climbed in.

"I'm going to let her make me come now," Lila said to me over the speakers. Lila smiled almost cruelly, raising her hips to draw her dress up her thighs. She stroked the dark head, then guided it to her center. Her lids flickered. Her young lover had started to lick her. "You will watch, won't you?"

"Yes." I grasped the steering wheel with both hands as the blonde pressed close to me and unzipped my pants. She didn't speak. I knew she wouldn't. Lila would have instructed her not to speak to me. A red light blinked above my head to the left. The second video camera had just been activated. Lila was watching me on a monitor set into the partition dividing us. The blonde pushed her hand inside my pants and caressed my clitoris with her fingertips.

"Her clit's really swollen already," the blonde reported, sliding her fingers along it. "And hard. I think she's going to come if I do what you said."

"No, she won't," Lila said, her voice low and heavy. "She knows better." She looked down at the head rocking from side to side between her legs. "Not so fast, darling. You mustn't try to make me come right away." Her eyes closed for a fraction of a second. "That's better. Just kiss it. Yes. Very good. Now suck very gently."

Lila moaned and my clit jerked. The blonde was watching the monitor now too and breathing heavily. Her fingers raced up and down my clit, and I think she forgot she wasn't supposed to make me come.

"Not so hard," I whispered to the blonde, because I was getting close to orgasm. I wasn't supposed to talk to her, and I hoped Lila wouldn't hear, but I couldn't hold back much longer if she kept doing what she was doing.

"Is she making your clit come?" Lila asked me eagerly. She cupped her breast and rolled her nipple. "Is she making you lose control?"

"No," I gasped, trying to shift my hips away from the stimulation. I felt the pre-orgasmic tremors start in my clitoris and fan out between my legs. I made a face, fighting the pressure building in my clit, and Lila must have seen I was getting ready to come. She grasped the dark head between her legs with both hands.

"Now, darling," Lila demanded of the young woman. "Suck me harder now. All of me. That's right. All the way down. Oh yes. Hold me in your mouth and suck."

"Oh fuck," the blonde next to me whimpered. "She's so hot.

I wanna come." She stared at the monitor, then at me, all the while whipping my clit from side to side with her fingers. "Come on, baby. Come with her."

"There, darling. There! I'm coming in your mouth!" Lila cried, looking right at me.

My hips shot up until my thighs jammed into the steering wheel. "Squeeze me. Squeeze my clit now. Make me come. Hurry."

"Yes, yes," the blonde chanted and she plunged her other hand into her jeans.

I felt her shuddering and heard her coming but all of my attention was on Lila. Her face erupted in pleasure and she surged forward, riding her lover's mouth. Her eyes glazed over but she never took them from mine as I called out her name and spilled into the blonde's hand.

Lila sagged back against the seat, looking supremely satisfied. The blonde slumped next to me, her hand twitching on my clit. I kept a death grip on the steering wheel. My clit, still jerking with the last of my orgasm, started to get hard again. Silence stretched, the only sounds our rapid breathing until after a moment, Lila opened a compartment in the back and took out a thick white envelope. She handed it to her young lover, who had dragged herself back up onto the seat next to Lila. I removed a similar one from a pocket in the door next to me. I gave it to the blonde.

"Thank you," I said.

She laughed and buttoned her jeans, then grasped the envelope. "I should be thanking you." She slid back across the seat and grasped the passenger door handle. "Anytime you're in the neighborhood, look me up."

Then she was gone. With my pants still open, I started the engine and drove just below the speed limit back to one of the well-lit main streets, where the dark-haired stranger got out. I waited, idling at the curb, until she got into a cab and disappeared. Then I pulled into traffic.

"Home?" I asked. Our monitors were still on. I could see Lila and she could see me. Lila nodded.

"Did she take good care of you," Lila asked, lazily caressing her nipples with her fingertips.

"Yes."

"Did you come in your pants while she played with your clit?"

"Yes."

"Would you like to come again?"

"Yes."

"You'd like to put your hand in your pants right now and make your clit come, wouldn't you."

"No."

"Why not? It's still hard, isn't it?"

"Yes. For you, yes."

"How shall I make you come?" Lila mused. "Shall I fuck you while I suck your clit? That would make you come right away, wouldn't it?"

"Yes."

"Or shall I masturbate you while I work my fingers in your ass so you come extra hard?"

"Whatever way pleases you." I met her gaze, my labored breath loud over the speakers. "I'm at your service."

CINNAMON SECRETS

I smelled her first.

A sweet, spicy scent that cut straight through the miasma of odors that were so familiar I didn't notice them any longer—popcorn, cotton candy, and roasted peanuts. This was a playful, seductive aroma that captured my attention like a whisper of hot breath in my ear. Seeking the source, I gave the metal spike tethering the tent line one more hearty smack with my sledgehammer, then turned around and rested the broad iron head on the ground between my legs. The thick wooden handle nestled against my crotch.

She was standing just behind me, studying me as if I were one of the sideshow attractions, a quizzical look on her face as her dark eyes swept me from head to toe. Her nose wrinkled just the tiniest bit, creasing her otherwise flawless olive-skinned face with an expression not of condescension, but concentration. Her frank appraisal caught me off guard, and I felt myself blushing, wondering how I looked to her in my work boots, threadbare jeans, and sweat-stained sleeveless T-shirt that I'd ripped down the front a couple of inches for ventilation. I wasn't used to women cruising me quite so openly—at least not in a hell of a long time.

I wasn't wearing a bra, and though I'm not particularly endowed, when I felt my nipples tense under her continued scrutiny, I was sure she noticed. Even on a sultry August night in the middle of a dusty fairground, though, she looked as cool as a cucumber in one of those flimsy flowery things that my mother used to call sundresses. Her smooth, tanned legs were bare, her red painted toenails peeked through open-toed sandals, and, incongruously, she had a small white daisy tucked behind her left ear. Her shoulder-length ebony hair was pulled back and tied with a pale yellow scarf, and all in all, she looked as if she should be sitting on a veranda on a Bayou plantation a hundred years ago. I smelled that little bit of sin again and watched her take a bite of a big red candy apple.

"Hi," I said, watching her perfect white teeth chisel two matching crescents in the shiny scarlet surface. Juice oozed from the hard white meat inside and little flakes of the candy shell melted on her full lips, deepening them to a moist fiery crimson. I felt a twinge inside my jeans. Jesus, I was getting hard.

"I know this sounds ridiculous," she said, "but don't I know you from somewhere?"

I didn't answer because I was watching the tip of her tongue snake out and catch the tiny droplets of cinnamon and apple before they slithered down her chin. It was so unconscious, so natural, I couldn't help but imagine just exactly how it would feel if she licked the juice from my—

"I'm so sorry," she said stiffly, her face flaming, "I have no idea why I said—"

"No, wait," I blurted out when she started to walk away. "You do. Know me. I mean, you've seen me. At least, I've seen you." I stopped, realizing that I sounded like an idiot. And I held out my hand and told her my name. "I'm an EMT. You've seen me in the ER. You work the night shift at County, right?"

"Of course!" She smiled, absently sucking at a few streaks of red liquid candy that had dribbled onto the back of her hand. "Without the uniform, I didn't place you at first. I'm…"

"Christy…I know." Boy, did I know. Every time we transported a patient to her ER at night, I noticed her. She looked great even in scrubs—tight little butt, high full breasts, and long, long legs. I didn't think she'd ever noticed me, though. Usually she was too busy getting report or triaging to do more than toss me a glance. At least that's what I'd always thought. The fact that she had paid me enough attention to recognize me now made me feel good. Better than good. It made me pleasantly horny, just a nice little buzz between my thighs. Unconsciously, I rocked my hips, and when the handle of the hammer bumped my clit, it zinged a bit harder.

"So, you volunteering here?" Christy asked, indicating the tent with the red cross stenciled on the side.

"Yeah." I grinned. Inanely, probably, but she had a fabulous mouth which was at the moment nibbling at the edges of that candy-coated apple. I couldn't take my eyes off the way she licked at it. Every little swipe of her tongue shot right to my crotch.

She looked me right in the eye, turned the apple to a new spot, and took another bite. "I love these things," she said after she swallowed and tongued her lips again. "But I always make a mess." She raised her hand to show the wooden stick that speared the core of the apple. Rivulets of thick ruby syrup trailed down onto her fingers. "I'm going to have to find some place to wash up."

"Come to the equipment trailer," I said hastily. "We've got a john."

"You sure?"

"Yes." Boldly, I held out my hand for her free one. "Come on. It's around back behind the tent."

I led her through the maze of tent ropes, trash barrels, and empty benches to the small trailer that housed the emergency medical equipment and our personal gear. I was the only one on shift at the moment, so we were alone when we stepped into the dim compartment. I switched on the light over the small sink, which gave us just enough illumination to see each other by. The space was crowded, and when I turned back to where she stood just inside the door, we were so close I could feel her breath on my neck. It tingled with the taste of cinnamon. I didn't move and neither did she. Not until she leaned back against the inside of the door and held up the apple.

"Want a bite?"

Oh, man, did I ever. I slid one step closer until my thighs just grazed hers, braced my hands on the doorjamb on either side of her shoulders, and leaned my head down. "Hold it still," I said.

"Okay." Christy settled her free hand on my hip. "Go ahead. But no hands—just your mouth."

With my eyes locked on hers, I slowly opened my mouth, pressed my lower body a little harder against her, and bit down on the rim of the apple where she'd last taken a bite. My bottom lip brushed the wet surface of the fruit as my teeth scraped over the stiff covering. I closed my lips ever so slowly, edging my hips forward at the same speed until my crotch settled into the vee between her thighs. I gave my head a little shake and broke off a section. I ended up with a portion of it extending beyond my lips.

"That's an awfully big piece." Her voice was breathy, and she reached around to my ass and squeezed. "You should share."

I kept the sweet-tart fruity concoction between my teeth and let her pull the other half into her mouth. Our lips met, the candy apple joining us, and we both sucked on it. My head was getting light from not breathing, and the steady rush of blood into my clit was making it ache. I could feel her nipples like small stones crushed against mine. Finally I bit through my half and she sucked the other part into her mouth. I swallowed it fast; so did she. And then our mouths were fused again, free of everything but the taste of cinnamon and sex.

I heard a thump, but my tongue was in her mouth, chasing after the juice and the spice, and I didn't register what it was. I got one hand between us and clasped her breast. She was swollen and heavy in my palm, and when I flicked her nipple, she moaned. The sound made me want to come. Christy pulled her mouth away and held up her empty hand between us.

"Still a mess."

She was breathing fast, her breasts rising and falling with each uneven gasp. My stomach was in knots, my clit like a rock, and there was no way I was letting her move. I shifted my hand from her breast to her wrist and pulled her fingers into my mouth, sucking the melted candy from her skin. Her eyes glazed as she tilted her head back against the door, watching me lick her through half-lowered lids. Her fingertips played over my tongue as I slid up and down the length of her fingers. I worked my thigh between hers and she rode me to the same slow rhythm as my mouth on her flesh. When her fingers were clean I went after her mouth again, releasing her wrist and dropping my hand to the outside of her thigh. I slipped my fingers under the light cotton dress as my tongue probed her mouth for the taste of cinnamon. She bit my lips like I was her candy apple.

The silk between her thighs was soaked. I traced a furrow in the thin material with my fingertip, slow-stroking the bump of her clitoris each time I passed. Her fist opened and closed on my ass, picking up speed as she pushed harder and harder against my hand. My palm was slippery with her juice. I edged her panties aside. She was swollen and wet, full and ripe—her scent as sweet and mouthwatering as the candy-coated apple that lay abandoned on the floor between us. I fondled her, teasing inside her opening and then up and down her slick cleft, flicking her clit with each pass, until I felt her legs stiffen and her back arch. Then I stopped.

"No, noo," she groaned, grabbing my wrist and squeezing her legs around my hand. "I'm almost coming. Rub my clit, baby…baby, rub it nice."

I skimmed inside her mouth, then sucked her lips, gathering the last little bit of cinnamon on my tongue. Then I slid to my knees and pushed her dress up at the same time. I pulled her panties aside and closed my mouth on her sex, working her clit in and out between my lips. She shuddered and whimpered, and then I licked her, catching her drops on my tongue and teasing the essence from her pouting lips. This time, when her clit turned rocklike beneath my tongue, I didn't stop. I circled the tip, flicked the shaft back and forth, and tugged it deeper and deeper into my mouth as I slid two, then three fingers inside her.

"Fuck me," she whispered. "Fuck me. Suck me suck me, do it hard. I'm gonna come."

I looked up at her face as I worked her clit, thrusting my fingers slow and deep, watching her head roll from side to side against the door. Eyes closed, she dug her fingers spasmodically into my shoulders and chanted over and over, "That's it that's it I'm coming, I'm coming coming…you're making me come…"

I tasted the rush of her orgasm, sweet and rich, just before she jerked against my face. She tightened down around my fingers, releasing a single high cry of pleasure and surprise. She rode my hand and my face, coming hard. I shook uncontrollably with the pressure in my belly, and I jammed one hand between my legs, rolling my clit between the folds of rough denim.

I shot off, doubled over, shivering through my orgasm with my forehead cradled against her trembling thighs. When I could finally focus, I saw the apple lying on the floor between my knees, the sweet red candy melting in the heat.

Every time I've made love to her since, I've tasted the sweet cinnamon secret she saves just for me.

PRIVATE CALLER

"Hello?" I said absently, most of my attention on the report I was reviewing.

"Do you know what I'm doing right now?"

I glanced at my watch. It was later than I thought. Almost 8 p.m. I was most likely the only one left in the office, which, considering that I was the boss, was probably appropriate. I leaned back in my chair and smiled at the sound of my best friend's voice. "Well, Sylvia, I imagine you're doing something very exciting, like—"

"Oh I am," the breathless voice said. "I'm lying outside on the patio, nude, and I'm imagining you beside me while I touch myself."

"Jesus, Syl," I said, sitting forward sharply. Sylvia and I had once had a sweaty, frantic, fabulous night of passion on a narrow bed in a cramped dorm room. That was before she met Alan, the love of her life, and settled down with him to raise children and do whatever it is married straight women do. "Are you hitting the champagne again?"

"Oh no, I wouldn't want to numb my senses. Not when I want to come as much as I do right now."

I heard the hitch in her voice and I knew with absolute certainty that she was masturbating. And I also knew it wasn't my friend Sylvia. My mind went blank for a few seconds. I'd never had a phone call like this before. I stared at my desk console, saw that my personal line was blinking, and checked caller ID. Private number. Jesus.

"Who?"

"God...it makes me so wet to think about you fucking me. So deep inside I—"

"I'm sorry, you've got the wrong number." Why the hell was I apologizing? I was on the receiving end of a dirty phone call. Still, perversely curious, I strained to hear her voice, trying to place it. But I couldn't.

"No," she said, sounding dreamy and needy at the same time. "It's you, Avery. It's you…oh, I'm going to come soon…touch me there oh yes…ohh—"

I slammed down the phone, shaking, and stared at it as if it might come to life and bite me. I'd never heard anything like that in my life. So…so…sexy. Jesus, she'd sounded so sexy. I stood up abruptly and paced in front of my desk, the sound of her voice, her excitement, burning the surface of my brain. My clit thumped with every step, but I refused to admit that I was aroused. Finally, I searched the outer offices and then walked up and down the hall looking for a light, some sign of where she might be. She knew my name. I had to know her. There was no one. I went back to my office but I couldn't work. An hour later I went home and had a stiff drink. That night I dreamed of a woman whose face I couldn't see, writhing beneath me while I fucked her until she came with her nails raking my back. When I woke the next morning my clit was hard and I came in the shower and pretended it was just like any other day.

The first few times my phone rang in the office, my heart pounded as I answered it. I almost expected—hoped—it would be her. After a while I realized I was being foolish and vowed to forget about the strange call. And I did, for all but a few fleeting moments each day.

A week later I returned from a business trip and stopped by the office on my way home from the airport to check my mail. My secretary had already left and it was quiet in the building. Just as I sat down at my desk, the phone rang.

"Avery Campbell."

"Do you know what I'm doing?"

I caught my breath and gripped the phone so tightly my fingers ached. "Who are you?"

"I'm lying naked on my bed. The windows are open and I'm surrounded by the toys I like to fuck myself with. I love to slide something big inside when I'm ready to come. I imagine it's your hand and I come so hard."

I saw it, every movement, felt her cunt close around my fingers. "Look, I'm not going to play—"

"Did you…oh that's so good…did you…have a good flight?"

I was listening hard, trying to place the voice, and I heard a choked moan. My stomach spasmed and I felt a flood of come between my legs. I couldn't help myself, I had to know. "What are you doing?"

"I'm playing with my clit. I like to pinch it…until I have to come." Her breath shuddered. "My nipples are super sensitive and sometimes I stop to squeeze them. That makes my clit harder."

Mine was like a stone between my thighs, but I kept my free hand firmly on my desktop. I would not be seduced by a voice. But I couldn't force myself to hang up the phone.

"It feels so good," she crooned. "So good when you rub my clit, when you lick me…oh yes, lick that spot…you'll make me come…"

"Don't come," I heard myself say, not believing I'd actually spoken.

"Oh, I want to. Please, I want to come for you."

"Not until I'm inside you." I hunched over the desk, my eyes closed, straining to hear the smallest sound, completely focused on her and her pleasure. "Do you have a cock there?"

"My favorite," she whined. "B-but I can't wait."

She was gasping, muttering broken words, moaning steadily. "Stop it," I said sharply. She whimpered. "Get that cock. The big one. Our favorite. The one that makes you come all over it when I fuck you. Do you have it? Do you?"

"Yes. Yes…but I…please, I'm going to come soon."

"Not until I'm inside you. Put my cock between your legs. Hurry. Do it."

I stopped breathing. I heard a cry, a wild sound of anguished pleasure and knew she was starting to come. I shot to my feet, shouting, "Can you feel me fucking you? Can you? Can you?"

"Yesssss," she screamed as she orgasmed, and I quietly disconnected.

"Jesus Christ." My shirt was soaked with sweat. My crotch was just as wet and I wondered if I'd come. I might have. My clit was throbbing the way it did right after I climaxed, but I couldn't remember it. It had all been her. All I could feel was being inside her while she came. I'd never been so aroused, or so satisfied. "Oh fuck."

What had just happened? And who the hell was she?

I sat down and stared at the phone, willing it to ring. *Call me back.*

Please call me back. I needed to hear her voice. I craved it like a touch. I wanted to make her come again.

A day passed. Another. And another. The phone rang. It was always business. I took care of it with the part of my mind that was capable of functioning at top efficiency no matter what was happening around me. But my body remained poised, coiled like a tight spring, for the sound of her voice to set me off. My clit was always hard. My cunt was always wet. I didn't masturbate, even when I lay awake tense and throbbing every night. Once I jolted awake, just after dawn, emerging from some erotic dream that left me hovering on the edge of orgasm. My clit was twitching and my brain was too slow to prevent my hand from squeezing the hot need between my thighs and I came sharply, straining to hear the sound of her voice.

By the time a week had passed, my body was a time bomb and my mind reverberated with the mantra, *Call me, Call me, Call me.*

I worked later and later every night, even later than I needed to, waiting for the call. When the phone rang close to ten one night, I snatched it up and listened in breathless silence.

"Do you know what I'm doing?"

"Tell me," I ground out.

"I'm sitting…" Her breath caught. "Sitting on the couch with your cock inside me…"

I closed my eyes to shut out everything except her. "You're sitting in my lap with my cock buried in your cunt."

"Yesss."

"I'm squeezing your nipples while we fuck. I've got a nice easy rhythm going, in deep and then almost all the way out, taking my time. Feel it?"

"Oh God yes." Her voice was wispy and thin. I knew what she was doing. I could see her fucking herself while she worked up her clit.

"Stop touching your clit. I'll do it when it's time."

"Please," she groaned.

"Shh. Slowly. Take my cock all the way in."

"I'm going to come on your cock." She said it as if it were a miraculous discovery.

"Yes," I growled. "You are. But not yet."

"I want to."

"Hold still. Hold my cock inside and breathe. Just breathe and feel me buried inside you."

"You feel so good." She moaned. "I want to come."

"I know." The blood thundered in my head and I saw red behind my closed lids. The muscles in my arms and legs ached with tension. I wanted to fuck her until she came screaming around my cock, clawing at my shoulders, biting my neck, disintegrating with pleasure. "Is your clit hard?"

"So hard…please…I need—"

"Fuck your clit." She shouted my name and I lost it. "Fuck my cock! Fuck it. Fuck it. Ah, fuck. I'm going to come inside you."

She sounded as if she was crying and then her voice was rising, catching, tearing, and she was screaming, "I'm coming I'm coming oh God God I'm coming so hard."

I groaned and an orgasm skittered around the edges of my barely conscious mind. I knew I was coming but I didn't care. I was inside her and she was coming and that's all that mattered. Eventually I realized I was sprawled on my desk gasping, the phone still pressed to my ear. Faintly, I heard whimpering and crooning and little satisfied cries. I sucked great gulps of air, seeing her curled up with my cock still buried to the hilt inside her.

"Sleep tight, baby," I whispered and hung up the phone.

One week. Two weeks. Three. I was going crazy. I picked up the phone a dozen times a day and all I heard was a dial tone. I couldn't eat. I couldn't sleep. I couldn't work. I wanted to come all the time and I couldn't. My secretary finally asked me if I was sick. I told her it was the flu. How could I tell her I was dying for a woman I'd never seen?

I fucked a stranger I picked up in a bar, but when she came I kept listening for the sound of her voice and it wasn't enough. I made her come again, and again, and again and again until she begged me to stop. It wasn't her. I couldn't come.

It was midnight, some night, when the phone rang. I stared at it, not believing what I heard. It stopped ringing. I sobbed and held my head in my hands. The phone rang.

"Please," I whispered when I picked it up.

"Do you know what I'm doing?"

"Please."

"I'm waiting."

Fury, joy, need poured through me as I sprang to my feet. "Where?"

"In the lounge down the hall."

I dropped the phone and ran. The office was empty, the hall a hollow tunnel of dim fluorescence. The echo of my footsteps raced to catch up to my wild need. I shoved through the lounge door into near darkness, but I didn't need to see her. I could hear her breathing. At last. Quick, shallow gasps of anticipation.

I was beside her in a second and my hands, my mouth, were on her neck, her breasts, her mouth. Her naked flesh was hot and yielding and when I kissed her, she sucked on my plundering tongue like a starving beast. I wanted to fuck her immediately. I wanted to be so far inside her she could never disappear again. My want was only a beat away from wrath and I knew I could hurt her. I could fuck her and leave her wanting and still never be free.

I turned her in my arms until her back was against my chest. I palmed her breasts while I bit the soft triangle between her neck and shoulder, twisting her nipples until she whimpered and sagged against me. I sucked her earlobe like it was her clit while she covered my hands and squeezed my fingers hard around her breasts.

"Do you know what I'm doing?" I whispered as I guided her by memory to the sofa that stood in the middle of the room. I pushed her forward until her belly was against the rear of the sofa, then put one hand on the back of her neck and forced her to bend over. I felt her brace herself with her arms against the cushions as I slid my free hand between her legs from behind. She was wet, raging hot, and I slipped easily inside her.

"Do you know what I'm doing?"

"Oh, yes," she cried, pushing back hard against my fingers. "You're going to fuck me until I come. I've waited so long. Please. Please hurry please."

I filled her, but I wasn't ready to give her what she wanted. I listened to her moan as she circled her hips, recognizing the sounds she made when she needed to come. Forcing back the urge to pound myself inside her, I gently slid my thumb into her ass. She made a high keening noise and I sensed her reaching for her clit.

"No!" I released her neck and jerked her hand away from her cunt.

"I need to come," she panted. "Please. Just let me touch it."

"No."

I started to fuck her, front and back, slow deep strokes that made her cry out each time I buried myself. I bent over her back, my face against the curve of her neck, and fondled her breasts. I was close to coming but I didn't care if I did or not. I listened to her excitement grow, her cries becoming long, wavering wails of pleasure.

"My clit...hold my clit," she moaned. "I can't come unless you do...squeeze it...ooh please..."

She was so hard her clit stood straight up, and I pinched it and pulled it the way I knew she liked. Her body stiffened and she turned to fire inside.

"You're making me come," she screamed, pushing her hips back to impale her spasming cunt on my fingers. She clamped down hard and gushed into my hand and I struggled to hold her while she shuddered and cried.

Then we were both on the floor and I was cradling her in my arms while she sighed and kissed my neck and made all the contented sounds I'd been living to hear.

"Good?" I murmured, still fondling her swollen breasts.

"Mmm, a really really hard one," she said in a faraway voice.

A minute passed while I savored her satisfaction. Then she stirred and kissed my neck again. "I have to go to work soon."

"Tomorrow night," I said. "Do you know what you'll be doing?"

She cupped my crotch and squeezed my cunt until I gasped. "Yes. Do you?"

"I'll be waiting for your call."

NICK OF TIME

When the phone rang, I knew I shouldn't answer. Part of me craved a diversion, and that's exactly why I hesitated. I didn't have time to be distracted. Zero hour, D-day, the Moment of Truth—whatever the phrase for "the clock is ticking and you're running out of time"—was written in big bold letters across the blank screen of my computer monitor.

Second ring. I clenched my jaws, determined to be strong.

Third ring. I ground my teeth.

Fourth ring. I pressed both hands hard against my thighs.

Fifth ring. Sweat broke out on my forehead.

Sixth—I snatched up the phone.

"Hello?"

"Did I catch you in the middle of a workout?"

"Nope, I'm at my desk."

I leaned back and closed my eyes, picturing my best friend Carly. At 10:00 at night, she'd probably be curled up on the sofa with a book, her long runner's legs bare and her riotous red curls disheveled because she unconsciously twisted the long locks around her finger as she read. We'd met on our first day of college at freshman orientation and had been practically inseparable ever since. We'd pledged the same sorority, ended up sharing a room, and throughout most of that year shared pretty much everything, even dating the same guys, although not at the same time. All that changed one night in the middle of commiserating about the unsatisfying state of our love lives because neither of us had been able to find anyone who could kiss, or do anything else to our satisfaction. We were sitting cross-legged on her bed, facing each other, wearing what we usually wore to bed. Big, long, loose T-shirts and nothing else. I can't remember which guys we had been complaining about, but I distinctly remember Carly stopping in mid-rant and staring at me as if she'd never seen me before. Or maybe seeing me for the first time.

"You know, you have a fantastic mouth."

"What?" I said stupidly.

"Your lips," Carly murmured, leaning forward so our knees touched. She braced her hand on my bare thigh as if she needed to keep her balance and traced my bottom lip with the index finger of her other hand. "They're a beautiful color and so full." She dipped her finger ever so slightly inside, and without thinking, I caught it with my teeth. She made a little sound of approval in the back of her throat, and I felt weak and hot, as if I'd been running for hours.

I'd seen her naked. I'd touched her casually hundreds of times. I had told her things I'd never told another human being. There were things I didn't know about myself, or hadn't yet admitted, but Carly— Carly, I knew. But until that moment, I had never noticed there were tiny flecks of gold around the edges of her hazel irises. I hadn't imagined that her fingertip running along the inside of my lip could feel as if she was stroking me deep inside. I had never once dreamed that the heat of her body could consume me when we weren't even touching.

"Carly, what—"

"Shh," she whispered. "You know."

Her lips were hot and wet, and when her tongue slipped gently into my mouth, I whimpered helplessly, wanting things I had no clue how to express. She took my hand and guided it beneath her T-shirt to her breast. Her nipple tightened against my palm, and she shivered and gave a little cry. That tiny, vulnerable gesture gave me the courage to follow my desperate desire.

I guided her back onto the bed, following until I was lying on top of her, my thigh between hers, my hand traveling from one breast to the other, squeezing and fondling, exploring her with breathless wonder. I kissed her and got lost in her softness, in the sweet taste of her mouth— too lost to realize what her breathless cries meant until she clutched my shoulders and arched beneath me, her legs twisting around mine.

"I think I'm coming," she gasped.

I remember holding my breath, my heart pounding so fiercely I thought it might burst and not caring if it did, so long as I lived long enough to watch her face while she came. She kept her eyes open and I couldn't have looked away if someone had held a gun to my head. She let me see everything in her eyes—her need, her fears, her pleasure. I've never known anyone braver, before or since. I didn't take a breath until she started to laugh.

"Oh my God," Carly half laughed, half sobbed. She wrapped her arms around my waist when I tried to pull away. "Oh my God, that was unbelievable."

My leg was still between hers and she was wet and hot and beautiful. I was—I don't really know what I was, because I'd never felt anything like that before. Terrified, exhilarated, aching, in awe. Carly nudged me with her knee and I shuddered. Grinning, she turned her hand over and slid it between us, down my sweat-slick belly and between my legs. My head snapped back when she closed her fingers around me, and I thought I might pass out.

"Just hold on," Carly whispered as she held me and stroked me until I couldn't hold on anymore. Then she held me and stroked me as I lay quivering in her arms.

"Do you think this means…?" Carly whispered after a long time, and I answered, "I don't know."

I wasn't ready, but Carly was, and I'd never known Carly to run away from anything. So she ran toward her truth while I stumbled along behind. I took too long and she found a girlfriend. There have been a lot of girlfriends in the six years since then. For both of us. But the one constant in my life has been Carly.

"You don't sound like you're working." Carly's voice called me back to the present. "You sound breathless."

I hadn't been before, but I was now. I concentrated on sounding normal. "Actually, the correct term would be trying to work."

"You're stuck?" Carly asked incredulously.

I never suffered from writer's block, and she knew it. It wasn't writer's block precisely, it was…boredom. "Not exactly. I'm just having trouble getting motivated."

"What are you writing?"

I sighed. "I promised Vanessa a selection for her next anthology."

"The fantasy thing?"

"Yeah, that's the one."

"When is it due?"

"Uh…" I glanced at the time on my computer. "In about two hours."

Carly burst out laughing. "I can't believe you waited this long. You always get everything done weeks in advance. It's disgusting."

"I know," I said miserably. "I've been putting it off."

"Why?"

I shrugged and then realized she couldn't see me. "It's weird. Every time I sit down to write, my mind goes blank."

"No fantasies, hmmm?" Carly teased.

I laughed. "Oh, I've got plenty of fantasies. But this isn't supposed to be true confessions."

"You just need to get primed. Do a spinoff of one of yours." Her voice held a note of challenge. "Come on, let's practice. What's your favorite fantasy?"

"Forget it, Carly. I don't do autobiographical erotica."

"I didn't say write it. I said tell me. Or are you chicken?"

"Chicken?" I heard a muffled sound as if the phone had been dropped. "What are you doing?"

"Getting comfortable on the couch. Stretching out so you can tell me a story."

I'd sat on that couch dozens of times, watching television with her, eating popcorn and sharing a bottle of wine. Sometimes she fell asleep. Sometimes we both did and woke up leaning against each other, as comfortable in each other's space as a long-term couple. I pushed back my swivel chair and propped my feet on my desk. I always worked in sweats, so I felt pretty relaxed too.

"Maybe I should write about one of your true-life adventures," I goaded.

"Like you'd know."

I'm not sure exactly why I said what I said next. I could tell she wanted me to do something, say something, but I wasn't sure what. She was always a step ahead of me, and I was tired of trying to catch up and always getting there too late.

"Well, there's the night Lucy Carmichael went down on you in the middle of a pledge party."

I heard a gasp, then total silence, and I started to worry.

"Carly?"

"How did you know that? I never told anyone."

I suddenly realized I'd made a big mistake. As close as we were, there were still secrets between us. And I had just told Carly that something she thought had been a secret, wasn't. I searched for a plausible story. But this was Carly, and though there might have been things I hadn't told her, I wouldn't lie.

"I watched you."

"Where?" she whispered.

I closed my eyes, picturing the dark room with a bed in the middle piled high with coats. There was just enough moonlight to see my way around the furniture as I crossed toward the bathroom. The party was in full swing downstairs, and when I'd finally gotten fed up with watching Lucy fall all over Carly, I decided to take a break upstairs. Just as I reached a hand inside the bathroom, feeling along the wall for the light switch, the bedroom door behind me banged open and two women stumbled in. Almost by instinct, I ducked into the dark bathroom. And then I recognized Carly's voice. I peeked around the corner and saw she was with Lucy.

"Whoa, hey, in a hurry?" Carly laughed as Lucy threw her down on the bed.

"God yes," Lucy gasped, tugging at Carly's jeans. "I've wanted to taste you all night long."

Carly twisted her fingers in Lucy's hair. "Come on up here and taste some of this first."

Lucy climbed up Carly's body and attacked her mouth. I considered trying to sneak out while they were groping each other, but I was afraid they would see me and I was embarrassed to admit I'd been watching this long. I was even more humiliated that I couldn't look away. I knew what Lucy was tasting as she plunged her tongue into Carly's mouth, how good Carly's body felt moving beneath her. I imagined the heat and the small sounds Carly made in her throat and I couldn't stop staring, desperate for some glimpse of her face, terrified I would see her look at Lucy the way she'd looked at me once. With such stark honesty I'd wanted to weep.

"I can't wait," Lucy groaned, pushing away and grabbing Carly's legs. She twisted them until Carly was lying half on top of the pile of coats with her legs dangling over the side of the bed, and then she knelt, forcing Carly's legs apart.

When Lucy buried her face between Carly's thighs, Carly pushed herself up on her elbows and looked down in the moonlight, watching Lucy make her come. I hid in the shadows and saw Carly shiver with each small movement of Lucy's head. I clenched my hands, my body rigid, listening to Carly's sobbing breaths, her broken moans of pleasure, knowing from the sounds that she would come soon. She struggled on the edge for long minutes, her chest heaving, her legs trembling.

"Oh, I can't get there," Carly groaned, "and I need to so bad."

I'll never know why I slid into a sliver of silver light, but she stared across the chasm into my face, her mouth opening wide in a silent scream of pleasure as her back arched and she came instantly. I slipped out of the room, her cries following me into the night. That night and every night thereafter.

"I was in the bathroom," I confessed.

"You were really there?" Carly whispered.

"Yes."

"I always thought I'd imagined it. Seeing you. You never said."

"Sorry," I muttered. "I thought you might be mad."

"How could I be mad when you made me come?"

"I wish," I whispered.

"You wish what?" she said, sounding confused.

There was still time for me to laugh it off. There had always been time enough for that.

"I wanted to be the one making you come." I took a deep breath. "In fact, it's one of my favorite fantasies when I want to get off."

"You think about me when you make yourself come?"

"Sometimes, yeah. A lot of times, actually."

Carly laughed, a lazy throaty chuckle. "Wanna tell me what you think about when you're rubbing your clit? Is that how you do it? You rub it until you get all wet and it gets stiff and you come?"

"Mostly." I was already wet and stiff, and hearing her talk about it made it impossible for me to think of anything else. I slid my hand into my sweatpants and touched the top of my clit with one finger. A jolt of pleasure shot down my legs, and I started a little tiny circular motion, just enough to keep the feeling going.

"I like a vibrator myself," Carly said. "Do you ever use one?"

I flashed on an image of her lying on her bed, her legs spread wide, her head tilted back, making herself come on the vibrator. I rubbed my clit a little harder. "Not too often. It makes me come too fast."

I heard a thunk. "What was that?"

"I'm getting out the vibrator I keep in the end table," Carly said. "Sometimes when I'm reading and I get turned on, I need a quickie."

I groaned and switched to squeezing my clit.

"So tell me what you think about me when you're coming."

"When I first start getting my clit hard," I said, "I think about you naked and about us kissing. I think about the way your tongue fills my mouth and me sucking on it." I pushed a finger lower and stroked between my lips and over the underside of my clit. It ached in that need-to-come way. "While we're kissing, I'm playing with your nipples."

"I love when you pull on them," Carly whispered, her words slow and careful, as if she was concentrating very hard.

"Are you teasing your clit with the vibrator?"

"Uh-huh. Just for a second…every now and then."

I leaned my head back and masturbated my clit faster. The pressure was building in my pelvis, but I was good at holding off. I could push myself to the edge over and over, backing off each time until my whole body twitched and I'd come no matter how hard I tried to stop. "Don't come until I get to the part where I'm licking you."

"I'll wait," Carly gasped. "Tell me what you're doing to me."

"I'm playing with your clit until it's as hard as it can get—"

"You make me have to come so bad…" she whispered.

"I pull your legs over the side of the bed and kneel on the floor between them." I hooked my thumb over the top of my clit and held it with two fingers underneath, starting to jerk it slowly. "And then I swirl the tip of my tongue around the end of your clit."

Carly whimpered and I knew she had the vibrator right on her clit.

"You sit up to watch me make you come, and I push my tongue lower where you're sweet and hot. I want to stay there, inside you, but you can't wait."

"Oh, soon."

"You rub against my face and tell me to lick…" My clit started buzzing and I knew I only had a few more seconds. "I usually come as soon as you tell me to lick…oh, fuck Carly…I—"

"Lick me…lick me hard…lick me so I come in your mouth."

I held my breath and stopped moving, every fiber focused on Carly. I saw her eyes, wide and stunned with pleasure, felt her body shudder, heard her voice catch on a cry of pleasure, and another, and then another. I forgot to breathe for so long, spots of light danced behind my eyelids, but still I waited. Waited for one more thing.

Carly laughed. "Oh my God, that was incredible."

"Yes," I whispered, caressing my clit until my hips rose and I flooded my hand with come, "it was."

"So," Carly said teasingly. "Was that better than the fantasy?"

"Oh yeah," I said, stretching my cramped legs. I toyed with my clit, keeping it hard, and wondered if I could get off again so soon.

"You're not the only one who's had that fantasy, you know."

"Really?" I sat up and forgot about wanting to come again. She had that serious note in her voice and I needed to pay attention.

"Really. In fact, there's a whole other part to it we didn't get to yet. The part about what I do to you."

I waited for her to say more, and when she didn't, I realized it was finally time for me to go first. "Maybe I should come over and you can tell me all about it."

"Maybe you should come over and I'll show you."

I grinned. "What about my deadline?"

"Vanessa will cut you some slack. You can write about all of this first thing in the morning."

"Yeah, but it's supposed to be a fantasy, not real life."

"So? Who's to know?"

"Carly's so right," I thought as I pulled on my jeans, "who's to know?"

LONELY TOWN

There's nothing quite so lonely as a Saturday night in a strange town on the far side of midnight. In the last twenty-four hours, I'd crossed more than just time zones and thousands of miles—I'd shed one reality for another, let my ordinary life slip away like an unneeded cloak until I arrived halfway around the world a different person. No one knew me other than as the persona I allowed them to see. No one met me at the airport, because I wasn't scheduled to appear until the next morning. Until then, I was only a name on a program and a face on a flyer.

Too tired to sleep and too restless to read, I decided to go for a walk, ignoring the concerned expression on the night clerk's face as I crossed the lobby and stepped out into the dark. As was true in so many cities in the middle of the night, traffic was sparse and pedestrians rare. Nevertheless, the sidewalks were well lit by a combination of street lamps, neon reflections from store signs, and a surprisingly bright gibbous moon.

I walked in the direction that the cars were headed, the steady thud of my booted feet on the empty pavement a welcome accompaniment, like the beating of another heart in a darkened room. As soon as I turned the corner, I saw the bold, black letters of the stark white marquee a block away. *Grand Hotel*. Why not? What better way to spend the last hours of anonymity than with the woman who was famous for her secretiveness and seclusion. As I approached the theater, I caught movement out of the corner of my eye and turned to see a woman crossing the street at an angle, her path on an intercept with mine. With the lights behind her and her body shrouded in a long military-style coat that came to just below her knees, I could see little of her face and nothing of her body. I knew without doubt, however, that it was a woman by the singularly fluid grace of her movements. She drew near with a purposeful stride as if she were late to meet me and eager to catch up. I slowed to wait, as if our rendezvous were prearranged.

"Are you going to the theater?"

Her voice was husky, with a lilting accent that tinged her English with a hint of Scandinavia. Closer now, I could see that she was indeed blond, her eyes blue or green, too muted in the half-light for me to be certain. Her coat billowed with each step, exposing long legs in pale denim and a shirt unbuttoned far enough to reveal that she wore nothing under it.

"Yes. Do you think it's too late?"

"No," she replied, extending her hand. "I think we're just in time."

I took her hand as if I had a hundred times before.

Her fingers were long, slender, and cool. Her palm was soft, but with a faint ridge at the base of each finger suggesting that she worked with her hands. I stole another glance at her face, thinking that with her arched cheekbones and full jaw she might have been a model. But there was nothing studied or posed about her. She was at ease in her body in a way that those who made their living with theirs were not.

"Have you seen it before?" I asked.

Her full mouth curved into a secret smile. "Many times."

She moved even closer as we walked until her shoulder and thigh touched mine, the way a lover's would, with familiarity and possession. I struggled not to close my fingers tightly around hers as a surge of desire caught me unawares and made me stumble.

"Are you all right?" she asked.

"Perfect," I replied, only then realizing that it was true. At the first touch of her hand, I'd forgotten the disquieting sensation of being halfway around the world and a stranger to everyone, even myself. The parts of myself I'd left behind slowly reappeared, sliding into the empty places effortlessly until I remembered who I was and why I had come.

"Two, please," she announced as she passed several oddly colored notes through the semicircular hole in the Plexiglas to the bored-looking young man in the booth.

"Oh no," I protested, belatedly realizing that we had reached the theater while I had been lost somewhere between yesterday and tomorrow. "You must let me pay."

She laughed softly. "It is, as you would say, my treat."

I blushed furiously, not at all certain that she meant it the way I took it, but her words brought another flood of arousal from my depths. She cocked an eyebrow at me, then swept her fingers lightly over my cheek and down my neck until her hand cupped my throat. She leaned close, there in the bright lights of the ticket booth, and skimmed her mouth over mine. "We should go in."

"Yes," I breathed, wanting nothing more than more of her mouth.

The lights went down just as we stepped into the theater, and she guided me through the blackness into the back row, to the far corner seats. There was no one in front of us or to the side. In fact, the other figures in the room were merely faint reminders that we were not alone. Distant images of Garbo and Barrymore flickered on the screen, their words a faint hum beneath the roaring in my ears.

Her coat fanned out behind her as she shrugged it from her shoulders, and when she extended her arm along the seat behind my back, the tips of her fingers grazed my shoulder. Each fleshy circle was a burning coal that penetrated the cotton to my skin. I leaned against her, and when my breast pressed to her side, my nipple tightened into a pebble of tingling nerves. She curled her arm and drew me closer, shifting to put her mouth against my ear.

"No one can see."

It wasn't true, but the illusion of invisibility beneath the otherworldly light in the cavernous space was enough. I tugged the shirt from her jeans and rested my hand on her belly. Her stomach tensed as I slowly rubbed my palm over the soft skin, pressing harder as the moments passed, my eyes on the screen but every sense tuned to her. The muscles beneath my fingers quivered and grew rigid, and with a faint moan, she shifted in her seat and spread her legs wide, her knee brushing mine. I knew she would be naked under the denim. The fingers that curved around my upper arm trembled. I could stop, but what would be the point? From the instant she'd taken my hand and I'd let her, our destination had been clear.

It was my turn to skim my lips over her ear, my breath a teasing kiss. "Are you hard already? Can you feel the seam brush against your clit, just like my lips caressing the tip?"

"Yes." Urgent and low.

My hand moved up, pushing fabric aside to cup her breast, grasping a nipple—already standing up, hard and sensitive, waiting. I squeezed gently. Once more. And again, harder, twisting a little until her body stiffened and another soft gasp escaped her. Her hips lifted, her heart skittering beneath my palm. I lowered my mouth to the other breast, biting through the soft cotton to tug on tender flesh. The gasp became a moan—hers or mine, I wasn't certain. My clit jerked insistently, keeping time with her racing pulse, and I finally dropped my free hand to my crotch and rubbed the stiff prominence through my pants.

"Open your jeans," I murmured against her neck as I drew my tongue along the curve of that beautiful jaw. Her breath, shallow and fast, drowned out the sound of Crawford's haughty inflections. I glanced down, saw her rip at the button and zipper, and squeezed the fabric between my thighs hard around my own aching need. My clit twitched, my vision blurred, and I had to ease off or come. I tortured her nipple a little more with my teeth to take my mind off the pressure in my clit.

Her eyes, suddenly bright and clear in the murky light, held mine.

"Please."

I stopped touching myself and pushed my fingers down the front of her pants as she rocked her hips, urging my fingers to find her. God, I wanted to take her fast—to make her come on my fingers, in my hand. I rested my fingertips just above the base of her clitoris, pressing down ever more firmly while circling up and down the stiff length, making it throb as the blood built inside. I knew how it felt, how it hurt in a way that could only be pleasure. Then, one hand stroking through that liquid heat below, I grasped her neck with my free hand and turned her face to mine. I worked my tongue into her mouth, the way I wanted to be working inside her. Turning in the seat, I threw one leg over hers. Clit pounding as I rode her leg, I sucked on her tongue the way I wanted her sucking on me. She bucked on my hand and moaned into my mouth and I forgot why I was waiting. Her need and mine conspired to undo me, and I surrendered willingly.

I pushed my hand deeper into her pants, my wrist tenting the denim until the zipper bit into my skin. Unmindful of the pain, I slid my fingers into her and angled my arm to get higher, crushing her clit, wet and hard, into my palm. Half lying on her now, my tongue in her mouth, my fingers buried inside, I took her hard and fast, beating her clit with the heel of my hand on each thrust. She pulled away from the kiss and closed her teeth on my neck when she started to come, muffling her cries with my flesh. She clamped down around my fingers as her hips jerked up, her rigid body barely touching the seat, and I felt a breathless, heart-stopping wonder as she came. I was ready to come, needed desperately to come, but in that moment, the only thing that I knew was her pleasure. Only when she slumped back into the seat with a last, long moan did the fury of my desire overtake me. I closed my hand around her still-pulsing sex and lowered my forehead to her chest. Dimly I was aware of her holding me as I shuddered and thrust against her tensed thigh. I choked on my own sobs of pleasure as a dam burst inside me and every barrier dissolved. I came in the arms of a stranger who knew me more intimately in that moment than anyone else in my life.

We dozed through the rest of the movie. I blamed my torpor on jet lag, but the truth was that I liked the way she held me. When the credits rolled, we straightened our clothing and left before the others. The streets were completely empty, and we walked in silence the few short blocks to my hotel. In the darkness beneath the awning, she leaned down and kissed me, the same knowing brush of lips with which she had first greeted me.

"Good night," she said softly.

I watched her walk away until the billowing edges of her coat became only the shifting shadows of the night. Then I turned and walked inside. It was not the Grand Hotel, and no grand passion awaited me here. But when I finally laid my head upon the crisp, white pillowcase, I felt her body next to mine and her breath against my cheek. I closed my eyes, knowing I would not sleep alone.

ZOCALO DARE

Traipsing through a crowd of people on a hot Sunday afternoon is not my idea of a good time. I shouldn't have worn the heels. Or the leather skirt. Even the white bikini-style halter top that tied with a single strap behind my neck wasn't a good choice. The only thing that saved the outfit was the fact that while I was getting a sunburn, it was making my girlfriend hot. And jealous. She wouldn't admit to that, of course. But the minute we skirted around the barriers on Pine Street that the cops had set up to block the street to traffic so the vendors could set up their tents, she grabbed my hand. Being that she's not one for public displays of affection, I was kind of surprised. Then, as we dove into the throngs of gays and dykes and inched our way from booth to booth, occasionally stopping to peruse the merchandise or fill out raffle tickets for a free weekend at a bed-and-breakfast in Rehoboth, she draped an arm around my shoulder. I gave her a curious look. "What gives?"

"Nothing."

She had that short, snarly tone that told me she was pissed about something. Her eyes get really dark—black—when she's angry, and they were like ink now.

"You wanted to come to the Pride Festival, remember?" I, on the other hand, had wanted to stay home by the pool with a cool drink. I hadn't found the celebrations very interesting or exciting since Showtime and First Union started showing up. Gone were the days of Dykes on Bikes and fags in nuns' habits. Sigh. "So now you got me here, and you're all pouty."

"I don't fucking pout."

I almost laughed, because for such a tough butch, she's adorable when she pouts. And she was pouting. "So what's the matter?"

"I didn't expect every dyke within a hundred miles to have eyes glued to your ass."

I almost turned around to see if I had a little chain of eyeballs trailing from my skirt, but I could tell she really wasn't in the mood for joking around. "I haven't noticed anyone cruising me."

I meant it, and she must've been able to tell, because her flinty expression softened. She stroked my bare shoulder, then leaned close and kissed the side of my neck, just below my ear. It was sweet, and I murmured appreciatively. But she also knew that the particular spot she was currently nibbling, ever so lightly, was directly connected to my clit. She was reminding me just where I belonged. I got the message.

"Are you sure you wanna be here?" My voice sounded husky, and it was totally beyond my control. It'd been like that since the first time I'd seen her across the room at a party. She'd looked remote and a little bored, leaning against the wall with a bottle of beer in one hand. She'd also looked hot in tight black jeans and a T-shirt that flattered her rower's shoulders. When she'd caught me staring, she'd grinned with just enough insolence to make me turn my back and walk away from her. Those sexy dykes who just know they make women drool are always trouble. The next thing I knew, she had me pinned to a wall in a dark corner with her mouth on my neck and her hands up my skirt. I hadn't minded a bit.

I rubbed my palm over her tight belly. I always think about those guys who tame alligators when I do that. "Change your mind?"

"I did want to check it out," she said, her mouth moving on my neck, "but now I'm thinking I'd rather be at home where I can lick you in all the places that make you squirm."

My clit twitched. Damn her. She owned me and she knew it, but every now and then, I liked to remind her that I'm not as easy as she thinks. Today was one of those days, and I was determined to make her wait. Even if it killed me.

"Uh-uh. You got me down here, and now I want to see what's going on."

I didn't wait for her reply but rejoined the milling crowd wandering through the narrow cobblestone streets. Ten seconds later I felt her right behind me, her palm in the middle of my bare back. I didn't try to shrug her off. I'm not that strong, or that crazy. Besides, I love it when she touches me. We strolled with the flow, up and down the streets in the four-square-block area devoted to the festival. Nearing the intersection of Pine and 13th, I saw a crowd gathered across from the gay bookstore. Curious, I headed in that direction. As I drew closer, I heard a rhythmic slapping sound, like a flag snapping in the wind. People stood four deep, necks craning to see whatever was happening on the corner. I'm not tall, but I'm wily. With my girlfriend in my wake, I insinuated myself between the bodies until I could see what all the commotion was about. When I got my first glimpse, I stopped so quickly my girlfriend rammed my ass with her crotch. Naturally, she stayed put and simply wrapped both arms around my middle, holding me against her front.

"Wow," she breathed in my ear.

Wow indeed. Ten feet away, a person—gender unknown—leaned over a leather-covered bench while a chick in knee-high patent leather boots, garter belt, fishnet stockings, and black lace panties with matching bustier beat his or her ass with a wooden paddle. With every blow, the bare butt twitched and a low moan floated on the air. The center of each round cheek blushed red. Watching the surprisingly well-defined muscles in the chick's forearms bunch each time the paddle fell and seeing the rhythmic jerk of the flagellant's hips followed by a breathy moan had my clit twitching again. I was lost in the rhythm of it all when suddenly it stopped. I caught my breath and realized for the first time that my girlfriend's hand cradled my left breast, her thumb flicking my stiff nipple. I also realized I was wet. When I reached back, cupped her crotch, and squeezed, she groaned softly and set her teeth into the back of my neck.

Aha.

"Anyone else want to try?" the dark-haired dom asked the crowd in general. "If you're a novice, I'll be gentle."

My girlfriend tongued the spot she'd just bitten, then sucked it. She does that when she's hot. I wasn't sure exactly what had my girl so turned on, but if it was this little item in black leather, I was going to be certain that it wasn't her for much longer.

"Yeah," I said, stepping forward so unexpectedly my girlfriend lost her grip on me. "I'll go."

From behind me, I heard my girlfriend's grunt of surprise. I looked back, smiled sweetly, and said, "Stand someplace I can see you, baby."

"If you're new," the chick said with just the tiniest hint of condescension, "we don't have to do it on the bare. You can take it on your skirt. It won't hurt as much."

Ha. You wish I'd let you top me. Without a word, I turned my back and hiked my skirt up to my waist. I was wearing a black silk thong that I figured showed enough of my ass to prove my point. Then I leaned down on my elbows on the bench and got myself comfortable. If I bowed my back, which handily put my butt in the air, I could look up and see my girlfriend's face a few feet away. Her eyes were that dangerous black again and riveted on me. One hand was clenched at her side, and the other was hooked over the pocket of her jeans, her thumb tucked inside, her fingers just touching her fly. Everybody else was looking at my ass, and it was as if she and I existed in some parallel universe, just the two of us. I started to smile, then caught my breath at the searing pain that lanced across my ass. I gasped, I couldn't help myself. She'd caught me by surprise, the bitch. I never moved my eyes from my girlfriend's.

The next blow smarted just as much, but I was a little bit more prepared. It hurt, and that was a fact. The backs of my thighs tingled, and I couldn't help but clench my butt—I don't know if it helped or not, and by the third blow I had tears in my eyes. My vision was just a little bit blurry, but not so much that I couldn't see my girlfriend's hips twitch each time the paddle fell. Her fingers were shaking as they moved lower on her crotch.

Four. I pulled my lip between my teeth and moaned softly. It still hurt, but the fire had become a glow that was spreading through the thick muscles of my ass into the valley between my thighs. I felt moisture soak the thin strand of thong in my cleft, and my clit gave a little series of warning twitches. The pain, the pleasure—it was all happening at once, and I couldn't sort it out. Didn't want to—I just didn't want it to stop.

Five. I gave a little cry and heard my girlfriend groan. Her lids were heavy, her lips slightly parted, and I saw her fingertips digging into the denim between her legs. She was trying to get at her clit.

Mine didn't seem to need to be touched. Each time the paddle fell, the pressure in my clit grew as if I were milking it between my fingers. The skin of my ass was on fire, but it was nothing compared to what was happening inside me.

Six. I mouthed the words, I want to come.

My girlfriend's thighs shook as she palmed herself through her jeans, twisting and jerking the material in her fist. She didn't look as if she cared who saw her.

Seven. I was moaning nonstop, my pelvis making little jerky thrusts as if I was fucking someone underneath me. My clit felt like it was ready to explode. I hoped so. I wanted it to. All I could feel was my heart beating out the end of it. God, God, I wanted to shoot it.

Eight.

She's making me come, I whispered—or maybe I screamed it. *She's making me come.*

Nine. My girlfriend's fingers, white against the black denim, squeezed down on her clit, and her hips jerked as if she'd taken the blow. When the paddle cracked down, the pain shot through my ass and into my clit, and I came in a rush, wailing in surprise.

Ten. My girlfriend grunted and came and I roared into another mind-blowing orgasm right on top of the first.

I don't remember very much about the next few minutes, except whimpering faintly as I leaned against my girlfriend's broad chest. Her heart hammered beneath my cheek, and I felt her body tremble. Faintly I heard the chick with the paddle ask if anyone else wanted to go. She sounded a little breathless. Good.

"Did she hurt you, baby?" my girlfriend crooned as she smoothed her hand over my hair and pressed her lips to my forehead.

"Yes," I murmured, nuzzling her neck, my arms around her waist. My ass still throbbed, and so did my clit, point and counterpoint. God, I was so ready for more.

"You want me to hurt her?"

"Some other time." I pressed my hips into her crotch. "Take me home so you can lick me in all those places that make me squirm."

"I've got a better idea," she said in that dark smoky tone that means she's hot for me.

"Oh yeah?"

"I think I'll start by kissing all those hurt spots. Then I'll lick them."

Oh yeah, the payoff was definitely gonna be worth it in the end.

TOP OF THE CLASS

Allie punched in the first three digits of Cindy's phone number and then hesitated. With a sigh, she pushed the off button and surveyed the mountain of clothes that had sprouted in the middle of the bed as she'd tried on and discarded outfit after outfit. Somehow, the excuse that she couldn't go out because she had nothing to wear felt thin, even to her.

"I can't believe I let them talk me into something as stupid as this." She fingered the leather chaps she had purchased one summer for a horseback camping trip. Smiling, she recalled that the concept had been a little bit more glamorous than the actual event, but it had still been fun. Of course, most of the clothes she'd purchased for the eight-day excursion never saw any further use. "And they're not going to tonight, either."

Eyeing the black leather pants and mesh top with a shake of her head, she scooped up the whole pile and dumped it on a chair, then marched to the closet and pulled out what she usually wore for a night out with friends—jeans and a scoop-necked, ribbed white T-shirt. All right, so it was true that the simple attire always got her plenty of attention. The jeans hugged her high, tight ass, and with no bra under the form-fitting T-shirt, her breasts just screamed for a warm palm to cup them. The thought of fingers playing across her tight nipples caused her belly to twitch. "Okay. Okay. So maybe they're right and I do need a little recreational sex, but vanilla will do me just fine."

A glance at the clock told her she had less than ten minutes before Cindy and Jeri arrived to pick her up. She still wasn't certain how she'd let them talk her into going with them to Chances, the local leather bar. Just because she'd played that stupid Truth or Dare game at Jeri's birthday party and had even more stupidly told the truth about one of her favorite fantasies was no reason to repay her honesty by dragging her out to a club where she would only feel out of place.

"So come on, Al, tell," Cindy prodded. "What's your favorite jerk-off fantasy?"

"What makes you think I—"

Cindy and Jeri hooted her down, and Allie grinned.

"Okay, okay. Truth." She sighed. "I want to top this incredibly hot butch and have my way with her."

"So why haven't you?" Cindy asked.

"I haven't a clue how to go about it. Afraid of being turned down, I guess."

"Yeah, but," Jeri chimed in, "if you didn't have to worry about any of that…what would you do?"

"I'd tie her up and torment her and then fuck her silly."

And after that, they'd badgered and cajoled until she'd agreed to at least go with them, just to see.

"So, I'll stay for a drink or two to keep them happy, and then I'll beg off," Allie muttered as she leaned close to the mirror to apply her eye makeup. "At least then they won't call me a chicken any longer."

At the sound of her doorbell ringing, she shouted down the hall from her bedroom, "I'll be right out!"

Hastily, she grabbed her keys and pulled open the door. "Oh!"

The woman standing on her front porch looked like she'd stepped directly out of Allie's favorite wet dream. Short thick dark hair, cobalt blue eyes, a lopsided grin, and even, white teeth. The package was spectacular, and the wrapping even better. Long lean legs sheathed in skintight black leather, a matching vest over nothing but flesh, and a suggestive swelling below the wide studded belt that signaled a surprise tucked behind her fly. Her bare arms and stomach were tight with muscle. A silver bar pierced the top of her navel, and a tribal band tattoo circled her left biceps.

Allie resisted the impulse to touch her just to see if she was real.

"Allie?" Gorgeous Creature inquired.

"Yes?" Allie replied in a high, thin voice she barely recognized. She cleared her throat, feeling foolish. "Can I help you?"

Again the megawatt grin, this time accompanied by a subtle shrug of broad, strong shoulders that set off ripples of pleasure in the pit of Allie's stomach.

"I'm Ryan." Fantasy Lover extended her hand. "And I'm yours for the evening."

Allie stared. Heartbreak Material was obviously a nutcase. "There's been a mistake."

Ryan smiled as if she'd heard that one before.

Allie hurried on, "I was just on my way out." She started to close the door. "If you'll excuse me."

"Cindy and Jeri won't be coming, so there's no need to hurry."

The little voice of reason in Allie's head screamed, Close the door! but the part of her brain ruled by Id won out. She leaned against the half-open door. "How do you know them?"

Ryan slid two long, tapering fingers into the slit pocket on the front of her vest and teased out a folded piece of paper. She held it out between her fingers. Clever fingers. "The work order."

"I'm sure there's…" Allie took the note, skimmed the few lines, and laughed in disbelief. "They paid for you to be my…slave?"

"If you desire." Ryan nodded toward the paper. "Apparently they thought you would prefer that. However, if you would like to reverse the scene, that can be arranged."

"I'm going to kill them," Allie muttered under her breath. Still, she was beyond intrigued, and there really didn't seem to be anything overtly crazy about the woman standing in front of her. Well, if you didn't count the fact that she…hired out…as a sex slave. She looked Ryan up and down. "And if I want to be the slave, do you just… switch?"

"I can," Ryan said seriously, "but you might prefer a replace—"

"No!" Allie spoke so quickly that she surprised them both. Blushing, she added hastily, "I mean, this…arrangement…seems fine."

"I'm glad."

Allie studied Ryan's face, certain that she had heard gentle sincerity in her voice. But then, nothing about the situation was real. So what did it matter how she sounded? "You're serious?"

"Yes, quite."

"Are you…is this…safe?"

Ryan nodded. "If you mean me, yes. If you mean anything that might happen, the answer is also yes. I'm experienced, and you can trust that I won't allow anything to happen that either of us would regret."

Allie released the door, and it swung open as she leaned her back against the doorjamb, her arms crossed just below her breasts. The very idea of having sex with Ryan, a perfect stranger, was perversely exciting. She was hot. But every time Allie thought of actually dominating her, of being free to do anything she wanted with her, she felt a thrill that was entirely new. It went beyond physical excitement. It was as if every cell in her body buzzed with sexual anticipation. "And you'll enjoy it?"

Ryan bowed her head, dropping her gaze from Allie's for the first time. "It would be my pleasure to serve you."

"I don't know wh—"

"Perhaps you wish to bring me inside where it is more private. So you may examine me and determine if I please you. Mistress."

Allie's breath caught as heat raced over her skin. She knew if she thought about what she was doing, she'd close the door and leave Ryan standing alone in the dark. And she'd never know if her fantasies were any more than that—unrequited dreams. She'd imagined just what she'd do so many times—she'd only been waiting for permission. She stepped inside. "Follow me."

Then Allie turned and walked to her bedroom. She did not look back when she flicked on the small lamp just inside the door, but she knew Ryan was behind her. She could smell her. The thick, hot odor of desire. She sensed as soon as Ryan had lowered her gaze that she was saying Allie was in charge, and Allie didn't intend to pass up this chance to do what she'd been dreaming of.

"Kneel by the bed," Allie said, pleased by the quickly muffled gasp. She slowly circled Ryan's kneeling form, all of her senses inexplicably heightened. She saw the tiny hairs at the back of Ryan's neck flutter as she passed and heard the breath rush in and out of Ryan's chest. Seeing all that power and beauty harnessed and waiting, hers to command, drove the last whispers of resistance from her consciousness. Everything in the room receded from her awareness except Ryan and the steady rush of blood into her pulsing clit.

She stopped and traced her fingernail along the edge of Ryan's jaw, over her chin, and down her throat. "Take off your vest."

Wordlessly, Ryan unbuttoned her vest and dropped it on the floor. Her breasts rose proudly, tight cones tipped with hard, dark nipples. Allie grasped one and twisted slowly. With a groan, Ryan tipped her head back, her eyes half closed.

"Oh did I hur—"

"I am here for your pleasure." Ryan caught Allie's free hand and drew it to her other breast. "Pain arouses me. You can trust me to say enough."

Allie heard the unspoken message. She won't tell me what to do. She'll only tell me to stop.

Allie caught Ryan's other nipple and set up a back-and-forth rhythm, tugging and squeezing, first one then the other. After a few minutes, Ryan's thighs flexed and her hips jutted up with each jerk on her breasts. She panted, her hands lying palm up by her sides, the supplicant before the altar of desire.

"You like this," Allie grunted through the heavy curtain of lust that clouded her vision. Her jeans cut into her swollen sex, riding over her clit, rough and raw and almost hard enough to make her come.

"Yes," Ryan said through gritted teeth. "Christ yes."

"Get up."

Allie barely gave Ryan time to get her balance before she grasped Ryan's breast and sucked the nipple into her mouth. Ryan's flesh was hot, so hot. And sweet. She bit down, unthinking, aching inside. So hungry for her. She pressed her crotch against Ryan's iron-hard thigh. She wanted to get off, needed to. She bit again, mindlessly.

So softly Allie could barely hear, Ryan whispered, "Harder."

Allie shivered and fanned her fingers over Ryan's throat. Blood raced wildly beneath her hand. "Would you like that? For me to suck on your breasts, leave my marks on you?"

Ryan swallowed convulsively, her hands trembling on her thighs. She had not been given permission to touch. "Yes."

"Then why should I?" Allie mused, struggling to appear calm when all she wanted was to rub her hard, wet clit over Ryan's skin and drench her in come. But that would be too easy. For both of them. "I'm not here to pleasure you, am I?"

"No, Mi—"

"You may call me Allie," Allie said, molding her palm to the soft, warm leather between Ryan's legs. She squeezed and massaged the firm cock inside. "Say my name. When you beg me to let you come."

Ryan's legs jerked and she moaned. She panted out, "I...stop, please...I want...oh..."

She's good. I wonder just how much she's playing. Allie jerked her off methodically, relentlessly, until she knew it wasn't an act and that Ryan would come with a few more twists of her wrist. She wanted her to, wanted to see this strong, sexy woman writhe on the floor, coming for her. But she hadn't reached the end of her fantasy just yet.

"Should I stop now?"

"If it pleases you to stop," Ryan gasped. "I want...I..."

"What, Ryan. What do you want?" Allie demanded harshly.

"Let me make you come...Allie."

Allie yanked her hand away and in one motion stripped off her tee. She cupped her own breast and fisted the other hand in Ryan's hair. She jerked Ryan's head down. "Not until I say."

Ryan's mouth was warm, her tongue just rough enough to burn her nipple with rapid swipes in between the tease of teeth. Eyes closed, Allie swayed beneath the onslaught, releasing Ryan's head to fumble with her own jeans. She got them open and the zipper down.

"Stroke my clit," Allie gasped. When she felt Ryan's hand skim down her belly, she grabbed her wrist and forced it down the tight vee of her jeans. "Oh yes...hard, I like it hard."

The force of Ryan's arm pumping and Allie's hips thrusting in response propelled them toward the bed. Allie's knees hit the edge and she fell, Ryan following her down. The fingers on Allie's clit drove into her cunt, impaling her with pleasure. She arched off the bed, screaming as she came.

Before the last electric jolt pulsed from her clit to her core, Allie shoved Ryan off and onto her back. Just as fast, she pushed her jeans off, straddled Ryan's hips, and pinned her to the bed with her hands clamped on her shoulders. "I did not tell you to make me come," she panted, sweat dripping from her face onto Ryan's.

"I...I'm sorry, Allie," Ryan murmured, licking the drops from her lips. Her chest was damp, washed gold in the slanting lamplight, her stomach tight, muscles rippling.

"I don't care if you're sorry." Allie ran her nails down the center of Ryan's stomach, twisting the silver bar in her navel as she passed. Ryan groaned. "You do not make me come without permission."

"Yes, Allie."

Allie tugged loose Ryan's belt, then cinched it around both of Ryan's wrists and looped it over the bed frame, tethering her arms above her head. "You do not come until I say."

"Ye-yes, Allie." Ryan's thighs twitched.

"You ask to come." Allie flicked open the button on Ryan's pants and pushed her hand inside, watching the pulse jump in Ryan's throat. She pulled out Ryan's cock, raised her hips, and took it in to the hilt. She nearly came with the sudden pressure on her clit. Her head snapped back and her breasts heaved. She closed her eyes and rode. "Oh, so good."

"Please," Ryan whispered. "Touch my breasts."

Allie tugged on Ryan's nipples to the tempo of her pistoning hips. Ryan's thighs went rigid and she arched from the bed. "Fuck my cock, Allie. Fuck it."

"Yes, yes," Allie chanted, sliding almost all the way off the thick length before plunging back down, one long stroke after another. "Yes yes yes."

Ryan thrust to meet her. Faster, harder, deeper—"I'm going to come!"

Allie's eyes snapped open. "You are not!"

"Please, please," Ryan gasped, head thrashing as she struggled to free her wrists. "Allie, please…oh please…I need to co—"

"Ryan," Allie shouted, pulling Ryan's head back by her hair. "You will not come before I do."

Ryan's eyes were glazed, her mouth soft and vulnerable. "Yes, Allie."

Allie's cunt spasmed and clamped down on the cock. Her clit turned to stone. "Ohh, here I come." She brushed her breasts over Ryan's face and shuddered, bearing down, forcing the cock into the base of Ryan's clit. "Come with me."

"Thank you, Allie," Ryan gasped, her mouth against Allie's breast.

Allie came twice as Ryan plunged into her, coming long and hard with broken shouts of pent-up pleasure. When Allie's muscles were too weak to hold her up any longer, she fell onto her side. Ryan's cock slipped out. "Unh, miss you already." She released Ryan's wrists, then dragged her hand down Ryan's hip and grasped the shaft, tugging it until Ryan twitched and groaned. "Nice."

"Thank you."

Allie opened one eye. "How did you know I'd want it?"

Ryan grinned. "Didn't. Just wanted to be prepared."

"Good idea." Allie sighed contentedly and skimmed her fingers over Ryan's mouth. "Mine for the night, you said?"

"As long as you desire. Mistress."

"I can see you still need instruction." Allie kissed her. "This time, try to do as you're told."

Ryan laughed. "Yes, Allie."

BONUS NIGHT

W e're causing a stir," Allie murmured as she and Ryan waited for the elevator in the lobby of the Four Seasons Hotel. A woman in a floor-length gown and dripping with diamonds stared at them with an expression of distaste. Allie supposed it wasn't every day that the guests of the five-star hotel saw two women dressed in leather from head to foot. Allie ran her gaze over Ryan's long, rangy body. As always, she was dressed totally in black: tight T-shirt, studded belt, motorcycle pants and boots, and—Allie knew from personal experience—a thick black cock strapped around her lean hips. Allie smiled and jutted her hips so that her already short black leather skirt rode dangerously close to her crotch. "You are just too hot to go unnoticed."

"I think it's more likely to be you, babe." Grinning, Ryan traced an index finger down the center of Allie's chest, dipping inside the deeply scooped Lycra top to skim over her breasts. A gasp of outrage was audible behind them, and Ryan laughed.

"I love you when you misbehave, but I'm not so sure about the rest of this," Allie said as the elevator opened and they stepped into the empty car. Not surprisingly, the woman waiting with them did not get on. "What if the client isn't happy about me coming along?"

Ryan leaned her shoulder against the wall. "Trust me, I know her."

"She might just see another top as competition."

"She's hinted at things. She'll like it."

"Well, we know she likes you," Allie said, "since she calls you every time she's in town."

"Jealous?" Ryan teased.

"If I got jealous every time you went out on a call, I wouldn't have time for anything else." Allie leaned close and cupped Ryan's crotch. "Considering how popular you are."

Ryan murmured in approval but the tiniest bit of unease flickered in her eyes. "It's just work. You know that, right?"

"I've known since the first night we met that women pay to top you, baby," Allie said, "since that's how we met." She laughed. "I still can't believe Cindy and Jeri hired you to be my slave for the night. I'll never be able to repay them for that little present."

"Neither will I." Ryan nuzzled Allie's neck, sucking hard enough on the soft skin at the base of her throat to elicit a groan.

"I don't remember hearing you ask if you could do that," Allie said in a dangerously soft tone of voice, pressing her palm flat against Ryan's chest and pushing her back against the wall. "Have you already forgotten that tonight you'll still be a slave?" She edged her thigh between Ryan's and quickly drove her knee into Ryan's cock. "Hers and mine."

Ryan stiffened from the unexpected pain and the pleasure that followed immediately from the pressure on her clit. "I'm sorry."

"Not as sorry as you'll be if you forget your manners, especially in front of another mistress."

"She's not my mistress," Ryan whispered.

"For however long she pays you to be, she is," Allie said sternly. Then she kissed Ryan softly and stroked the thick lock of dark hair that fell over her forehead away from her face. "You have my permission to please her in any way she requires."

"Yes, Allie."

The elevator opened into a quiet hallway, dimly lit with sconces at intervals along the corridor. They made their way to the corner suite, where Ryan knocked. A moment later, the door opened and a woman with collar-length, honey blond hair regarded them silently. Allie judged her to be somewhere in her late forties or early fifties. She was Ryan's height and several inches taller than Allie, statuesque in a classic way. Her full breasts were evident beneath a black silk shirt, the top three buttons of which were open to reveal creamy cleavage. Her waist, circled by a thin black belt, was not narrow, but appeared solid beneath tailored charcoal trousers. Her hands, one of which rested loosely on the doorknob, were large and elegant.

"Ryan," she said by way of greeting before her gaze shifted to Allie and traveled slowly over her body. "I didn't realize we were having company."

"If it pleases you," Ryan said softly, "Allie will see that you are well served."

"Really," the blonde said with interest. She turned her cool blue eyes to Allie. "Is she yours, then?"

"Yes," Allie said.

"May I ask why you're willing to share?"

"I've never seen her work. I'd enjoy that."

The blonde nodded thoughtfully, then held the door open wide. "I'm Deirdre. Please come in."

Deirdre led the way through the suite, to where an iced bottle of champagne stood in a gold-plated cooler beside a king-sized bed. A platter of cheese, fruit, and crackers had been placed on a nearby table, next to which was an oversized silk-upholstered chair. She indicated the food with a sweep of her arm. "Please, help yourself."

Ryan stood next to the chair while Allie poured a glass of champagne and handed it to Deirdre. Then she poured one of her own and lifted a plump ripe strawberry to her lips. She bit into the strawberry, then sipped the champagne, noting the hungry look in Deirdre's eyes as she stared at Ryan.

"Ryan, you haven't properly greeted Deirdre, have you," Allie said softly.

Wordlessly, Ryan knelt before Deirdre. "Good evening, Mistress."

Deirdre stroked Ryan's head absently, sifting dark strands of hair through her fingers as if Ryan were a favorite pet, her eyes on Allie. "Will you allow me to command her?"

Allie savored the last of the fruit, licking the juice from her lips. "Of course."

"Please make yourself comfortable," Deirdre said to Allie, nodding nearly imperceptibly toward the chair. "More champagne?"

"Thank you," Allie said as she stepped around Ryan's still form and settled into the large chair. She extended one arm along the broad armrest and held out her champagne glass for Deirdre to fill. As she sipped, she watched Ryan while Deirdre idly caressed Ryan's face and neck, judging by the rapid rise and fall of Ryan's shoulders that she was already excited. Allie knew from experience that just the thought of being dominated was enough to arouse her lover.

"She's a lovely animal, isn't she," Deirdre murmured, tilting Ryan's face up and rubbing her thumb over Ryan's mouth. "And so talented."

"Yes," Allie agreed, imagining Ryan's lips and the magic they were capable of. She saw Deirdre take a step closer, thread her fingers through Ryan's hair, and rub her crotch over Ryan's face. She knew Deirdre would feel the heat of Ryan's breath on her clit even through her trousers, and her own clit twitched as she watched. She hadn't known what to expect when Ryan had suggested that she come along, explaining that Deirdre had intimated more than once that she enjoyed watching a good scene. Allie was discovering the same was true for herself. "She has a marvelous tongue."

"Let's put it to work." Deirdre smiled lazily at Allie, then leaned down and kissed Ryan. "Help your mistress with her clothes, Ryan." When Ryan reached for Deirdre's belt, Deirdre stepped back. "Allie's."

Ryan couldn't quite hide her look of surprise as she turned toward Allie, but Allie carefully kept her expression neutral, even though her pulse jumped. She sipped her champagne as Ryan moved to kneel between her legs and slid both hands along her thighs beneath her skirt, guiding the leather up her hips. Allie had worn nothing under it and she was wet. She knew Ryan could smell her excitement and wondered if Deirdre could see the glistening evidence of her passion. Ryan caressed Allie's hips but made no further move until Allie cradled the back of Ryan's head and drew her gently forward.

"Slowly, Ryan," Deirdre said as she stepped to the side of the chair. "Let me see you lick her."

Allie caught her breath at the first touch of Ryan's warm tongue separating her swollen lips. She released Ryan's head as Deirdre's hand gently brushed hers aside. When Ryan delicately ringed the hard prominence of her clitoris, she shuddered. When the tip of Ryan's tongue teased at the hood covering her most sensitive spot, she drained her champagne glass and set it down with a trembling hand. Ryan knew her body so well that she could keep Allie on the edge of orgasm for hours, but her stomach was already fluttering and she was afraid she would come too quickly.

"Don't suck her yet," Deirdre whispered, as if hearing Allie's fears. She looked at Allie, her own lids heavy, her voice husky. "She makes you want to come right away, doesn't she?"

"Yes," Allie admitted thickly. Lids nearly closed, she rested her head back against the chair, a trembling smile on her face. Ryan's head moved in time to the steady thrusting of Allie's hips. "Especially when she flicks her…oh!" Her eyes opened wide. "She's making me come!"

"Ryan!" Deirdre said sharply, tugging Ryan's face away from Allie's sex. Allie cried out, her hand flying to her clit. Even though a stroke would push her over, she did nothing but press her thumb to the base of the rigid core, forestalling her orgasm. Her chest heaved, nipples straining against the tight Lycra shirt.

"Did I tell you to make her come?" Deirdre demanded.

"No, Mistress," Ryan gasped, her eyes dark with desire.

"Take out your cock," Deirdre ordered, walking around behind Ryan. "Quickly."

Ryan yanked open her heavy belt buckle and tugged at her fly. Then she dug inside and pulled out the long, thick length of her cock. When she started to rise, obviously expecting to enter Allie, Deirdre pushed her back down with a firm hand on her shoulder. Then Deidre knelt beside her, angling her body so she could see Allie's face. She wrapped her fingers around Ryan's cock, making an appreciative sound deep in her throat. Ryan groaned when Deirdre worked her hand quickly up and down the shaft.

Looking at Allie, Deirdre said, "Are you ready to come now?"

"God yes."

"Suck your mistress, Ryan," Deirdre ordered softly, her arm vibrating rapidly between Ryan's rigid thighs. "She wants to come in your mouth."

Ryan leaned forward, her eyes on Allie's, and closed her lips around Allie's pulsing sex.

Deirdre smiled at Allie. "I'm going to jerk her off when you come. Tell me when you're coming."

"Soon," Allie gasped.

"Is she making your clit hard?"

Allie nodded, her head twisting from side to side. "Her mouth is so damn hot."

Ryan was panting, her clenched fists pressed to Allie's thighs. Her hips jerked unevenly as Deirdre pounded the cock into her tortured clit.

"Lick me, baby," Allie sobbed. "I'm so close."

Deirdre ran her tongue over the rim of Ryan's ear. "Your mistress needs to come, Ryan. Suck her now, harder."

"Oh, I'm coming!" Allie cried, grasping Ryan's head.

Deirdre pumped the cock furiously and Ryan stiffened, moaning into Allie's cunt while Allie rode her mouth. Tears leaking from her eyes, her gaze riveted to Allie's face, Ryan came against the base of the cock while Allie's clit exploded between her lips.

Allie wasn't aware of Deirdre moving until Deirdre yanked Ryan's head from between Allie's legs.

"Get your cock into her," Deirdre ordered.

Ryan, still shaking from her own climax, struggled to guide the fat head of her cock between Allie's drenched lips. The added pressure against her overly sensitive clit as she pushed inside made her stomach tighten reflexively. "I'll come again," she gasped. "Please…may I come?"

"Wait, baby," Allie said gently, bending her knees around Ryan's leather-clad thighs and setting the rhythm by pushing herself up and down Ryan's cock. "Fuck me nice and slow. You can come when I come."

"Allie…" Ryan's face was contorted, her face and hair dripping sweat. She braced both arms on the chair. "I don't think I—"

"Listen to your mistress," Deirdre commanded, her voice strained. She hurriedly kicked off her shoes and pushed down her pants and underwear. She stepped close to Ryan, one hand opening herself, exposing her fully aroused clit. "Bring me off while you fuck her."

Allie stared at Ryan's face pressed between Deirdre's trembling thighs. "Suck her clit, baby."

Deirdre cupped the back of Ryan's head and, groaning quietly, smiled shakily at Allie. "I'm going to come on her face. Soon. Are you…oh fuck…she's so good." Deirdre's eyes closed for a second but she forced them open. Her breath came in short pants. "Is she making you come?"

"Uh-huh." Allie arched, slid her fingers to her clit, and masturbated, the cock buried to the hilt inside her. "Coming now…so hard." She screamed, her shoulders jerking up from the chair.

Ryan thrust blindly, driven to climax by her lover's cry.

Deirdre laughed harshly, shooting off in Ryan's mouth.

When Allie opened her eyes, Ryan was slumped between her legs, her head resting on Allie's stomach. Allie caressed her damp cheek. "Okay, baby?"

"Mmm," Ryan murmured, eyes closed. "Wasted."

Allie sighed and turned her head, searching for Deirdre. She was leaning against the bed, dressed once more, lighting a cigarette. "I think we might need to pay you."

"Oh, I don't think so." Deirdre drew in the smoke and exhaled with a satisfied smile. "Ryan alone is priceless. Tonight? This was bonus night."

HELPLESSLY HERS

My girlfriend gets off making me come in public. The more likely we are to be seen, the better. She likes looking some guy in the eyes—guys are the only ones who ever watch…women, if they even figure out what's going on, quickly look away—but the guys, at first they can't believe it. And then they really can't believe it. She loves staring them down while she works over my clit, her arm sliding smoothly up and down, up and down, in my lap. They almost always watch her even when my eyes start to roll back in my head and my ass lifts off the seat and my clit explodes in her hand. They don't care about me, not when they're imagining her hand on their cocks. The ones who don't shoot off in their pants probably go somewhere to jerk off right away, but I can never tell because I'm usually deaf and blind for a few minutes after she makes me ejaculate.

She always gets me hard, it doesn't matter if I'm nervous or embarrassed or worried. I can't stop from wanting to come when she starts in on me. She knows just how to make me hard really fast, sliding her fingers up and down my clit and squeezing just enough to pull the hood back and forth over the head. As soon as I'm completely erect, she starts the teasing. Tapping with her fingertip, rubbing little light circles, pinching when I don't expect it. By then I'm so wound up I don't care who might be watching. All I care about is that she keeps going, doing me until I come.

She's careful to do it where nobody can get at us—in the car, under the table at a restaurant, in the theater. Once she did me on a park bench underneath a newspaper I was pretending to read. She made me sit there, still as a statue with that fucking newspaper clutched in my hands while she curled against me, her hand under the newspaper, inside my running shorts, rubbing my clit. She whispered to me like we were having a serious conversation but she was really telling me what she was going to do next.

"You're nice and hard now, baby, just about ready to cream for me. I'm going to rub that spot you like, just underneath…uh-uh…don't move now. There you go. That's the special spot, isn't it? Gonna make it feel soo good. Careful, baby. Quiet. Is all that hot wet stuff for me? Here, let me rub it on your clit, get it all slippery so you slide through my fingers so nice. Feels sweet when I squeeze your big fat clit, doesn't it, baby. Oh, what's this? Is that your head poking out, looking to get some attention already? You're awfully impatient, aren't you? You want me to rub it faster, baby? You do, don't you, baby. Right on that spot. You want me to work it, rub it, make it pop. Don't you. Don't you, baby."

I knew I wasn't supposed to, but I came right then. She wasn't happy with me.

She has rules—very strict rules. I can't talk while she's doing me except to answer her questions. I can't move, I can't make any sounds, I can't ask her to speed up or slow down or to squeeze me harder. I can't come unless I ask permission and she says yes. If I break her rules, she stops. Even if I'm good and do everything I'm supposed to do while she masturbates me, if she feels like stopping before I come, she does. She doesn't care how big my clit is or how much it hurts or how bad I need to come, or how hard I beg. I'm hers to play with, and it's all about what gets her hot.

Sometimes she plays with my clit in the dark for the entire length of a movie without letting me come. Then she tells me to go in the restroom and get off before we can leave. So I end up leaning against the wall in a narrow stall or slumped on the seat, my teeth clenched tight, working my clit like a maniac while chattering women troop in and out, talking about the movie or their dates, peeing and flushing and fixing their makeup. It takes a long time and when I finally come, I have to bite my own hand to keep from crying it feels so good just to finally get some relief. When I practically stagger out of the bathroom, my hair dripping with sweat and my hands shaking, she looks at me and laughs.

"Did you come nice for me, baby," she asks, sometimes loud enough for people to hear. But I don't care who hears because my clit usually stays hard after being teased for so long and I want her to do me again right away and if I say anything other than yes she won't touch me again all night. She'll just make me sit in a chair by the bed and watch her masturbate, over and over, with a vibrator or a cock or both while my clit swells and I beg her to make me come and she says no.

But if I'm good, if I'm good like I was tonight, once we get home she makes me tell her all about my restroom jerk-off session while I'm fucking her. About how swollen my clit was and how bad I needed to come and how fucking pissed off I was that she got me so hot I practically humiliated myself in public. And how I couldn't wait for her to do it to me again. Anywhere. Any way she wanted.

"Did you have to squeeze it really hard to get off, baby," she gasped, rubbing just the tip of her clit with one finger while I stroked inside her with four. The walls of her cunt tightened rhythmically around my fingers and I knew she'd come if she just pressed her clit a little harder, circled a little faster. But she didn't. She loved to tease, to make her clit burn. I know. She did it to me all the time. "Were you too hard to come?"

"You already know I was," I grunted, working up a sweat thrusting in and out of her. "How hard my clit was. How fucking stiff. You made it that way."

"Mmm, yeah," she said, half dreamy, half hungry. Her index finger flicked at the ruby red head. "Like a little torpedo between your legs. Just ready to blast off." Her eyes widened, as if she felt something really really good, and she started to pant. "Tell me what you did to it."

She was already close, but she needed more. Every time I stroked I curled my fingers so I pushed on that spot inside that kept her clit stiff. I got up on one knee for a better angle, and so I could see her face or look down and see her mauling her clit. "You know how hard it is for me to come when I get like that, don't you?" I rubbed my thumb over the underside of her clit while she twirled the tip and the smallest moue of surprise escaped her. "I have to work it and work it to get off, and it hurts. It hurts and I have to come so bad and I can't."

"How?" Her eyes were rolling, her belly trembling. "How?"

"I get the head between my fingers and squeeze it until all the blood is pushed out," I growled. I leaned over and bit her nipple and her shoulders jerked off the bed. When I released her and checked what she was doing, she had a white-knuckle grip on her clit, squeezing it dry.

"Feel good?" I whispered.

"Yes. No. No. Oh God, I want to come. I want to come." She whipped her head from side to side. "Tell me not to come, baby. Tell me not to come."

"Let go of it," I ordered. I knew she was seconds away but she loves the torture, and she taught me how to give it as well as take it. I grabbed her wrist and yanked. "Now. Hands off."

Her control is amazing and even though I knew she could feel herself starting to come, she pulled her hand away. Her clit pulsed up and down and her whole cunt opened and closed around my fingers, but she didn't finish.

"God!" She half sat up and grabbed the arm I was fucking her with in both hands and shoved my hand deeper. "Oh fuck me, baby. I need it right now."

"I needed it too and you made me masturbate in the fucking restroom." I twisted my hand so my thumb hit her clit with every thrust. Her fingers inched down toward her clit. "I almost couldn't do it. I kept milking it and milking it and I'd almost start to come and someone would laugh or pull on the door and I'd lose it."

She had her clit between her fingers now, me rubbing it underneath while she stripped the shaft. Her muscles clamped down on my fingers and didn't let loose.

"My clit hurt so bad," I said.

"Yes," she whimpered, pulling on her nipple with her free hand.

"I finally had to use two hands." I pressed the flat of my hand against the base of her belly and pushed in, making her clit stand up. Immediately, her fingers moved faster.

"Oh." Her eyes went out of focus for a second, then she fixed on my face. "Did you pretend I was…sucking you?"

"My clit was so filled with blood I could hardly stand to touch it, so I pretended my fingers were your lips, and I could feel you sucking me, baby." My clit was about to beat itself off between my legs without me even jerking it, but I forced myself to focus on her. She didn't have long. "I held it between two fingers and skimmed the hood back so I could work on the head with my other hand."

She whimpered again and I knew she'd switched to rolling her clit like a worry bead between her thumb and fingers. I'd watched her masturbate to orgasm enough times to know just what she did to get herself over. She just needed a push.

"I felt your mouth close on me and your tongue whipping me up so hard."

"I'm gonna come soon." Her hips jerked and the muscles in her neck stood out like cords. "You want it? You want it, baby? You want my come?"

"I shot my load all over my hands and pretended it was in your mouth," I grunted, fucking her harder.

"Oh you bastard, you bitch, you...you're making me come." She raised her shoulders, she has incredible abs, and stared wide-eyed at my hand pumping in and out of her. "Oh no," she wailed, pummeling her clit, "I'm losing it, baby. I'm losing it. Oh baby it's so fucking good." She jumped and jerked and came on my hand and I kept going inside her until she pulled off and collapsed on the pillows.

"Come here," she said lazily, her eyes sleepy and satisfied. I crawled up next to her and turned sideways in her arms so my head was on her shoulder, my breasts against her breasts. She reached between my legs and laughed. "You're all hard again." She squeezed my clit and I whined like a girl. Which I so was right then. She started masturbating me for the fourth or fifth time that day and all I could think about was coming, like it had been months instead of hours. "What should I do with it?"

"Suck it?" I asked pitiably.

"Is that what you want?" she murmured, her tongue skating around my ear, her fingers jerking me faster.

I nodded vigorously. "Please." She was close to making me come already, and I wouldn't be able to stop it. I was powerless to keep from coming when she fondled my clit that fast, no matter how hard I tried.

"You want me to put your wet, hard clit between my lips and suck on it and make you come?"

"Yes, please." The muscles in my stomach tensed and I couldn't get my breath. "Ohh, I think you're making me come right now."

"I don't think you should, do you?" she whispered, her fingers right on the spot. "Not when I want you to come in my mouth."

"You are, you are, you're making me...I'm going to..."

"Get up here," she snapped, letting me go with a twist that brought tears to my eyes and pushed my orgasm back inside.

I threw my leg over her chest and crouched above her face, my arms braced on the wall. I watched her pull me open with her thumbs and latch on to my clit, sucking me deep. She slid me in and out, licking and sucking, and up I went again.

Very slowly, afraid she still might leave me out on the edge, I warned, "I am going to come so hard all over your face."

She laughed around my clit and the vibration and the rapid sweep of her tongue set me off. I came and came and came, helpless to stop. Helplessly, hopelessly, totally hers.

SURPRISE PACKAGE

Happy birthday to me!
    Briefs. Boxers. Thongs. Jock straps. Silk. Pro stretch. Cotton. Button fly. Y fly. Pouch front. Mesh. Drawstring. Satin stretch. Trunk. Micro rib.

Who knew there would be so many colors and styles and fabric? My five-minute stop in the men's department had morphed into the better part of my lunch hour, and I still hadn't made a decision. I staggered from one rack to the next—fingering, fondling, everything but smelling—my mind filled with possibilities, all of them delicious. I caressed material, eyed flies and pouches, and visualized bulges and butts until my mouth was dry and my pussy was wet.

I imagined the curve of a thick cock tenting out the front of those black silk boxers, me on my knees, my lips wrapped ever so delicately around the fat head, sucking until I'd made a perfect wet *O. Oh, oh, oh...oh baby, come in my mouth.*

I admired the way the white cotton briefs bunched the payload into a tight fistful of promise I could jack off in my palm. I could almost feel the quivering abdomen beneath the wide elastic waistband, the trembling thighs encircled by the snug leg openings, the strangled grunts of pleasure, the hiss of breath before the big bang. Go ahead, baby, come in my hand.

Then there were the jock straps. Could anything be sexier than a slash of white cutting across a firm tanned thigh, unless it's the hard-on swinging in that arrowhead sheath? Let me ride, baby, ride till I burst.

Too bad I was likely to combust before I could make a purchase. My eyes blurred and my stomach did the little jiggly thing it does when

I need to come. All the thinking about what I was thinking about was making my clit dance. I glanced at my watch. I was going to have to find a restroom so I could masturbate or I'd never be able to go back to work. No way could I sit for another four hours in court like this. Not and concentrate. Not without squirming.

"May I help you with something?"

I hated to disappoint Mr. Tall Blond and Handsome, but what was to help? I mean, I knew how everything worked. It's not like they were complicated enough to require instructions. You put them on, you pull them up, you settle the various and sundry equipment into the little extra spaces so cunningly built into the crotch, and Presto! Ready for action.

There was one thing, though. It might be my present, but I didn't want to be entirely selfish about the whole deal. I kept my gaze carefully above shoulder level, not wanting any reason to speculate about just what version he was wearing under his casual gray trousers.

"Which ones make you feel the sexiest?"

He blinked, but his smile never faltered. "Well," he said with perfect salesperson cordiality, "I prefer boxers."

"Without getting X-rated, any particular reason why?"

"Freedom of movement and, ah, multiple avenues of easy access."

Oops. There I was on my knees again, only this time I saw myself peeling up the bottom edge of the leg opening so I could get my hand around a thick, stiff shaft. And of course, my mouth followed. I could feel it, hot and hard against the back of my throat.

"Gotcha." Back to the black silk boxers then. Or maybe the blue.

Yes. I smiled and reached for the royal blue. The blue was the exact color of her eyes.

Court ran late and I never did get a chance to get off a quickie do-it-yourselfer. By the time I got home, barely five minutes before Jordan, and spread out my little birthday surprise on her pillow, I was ready to come just from the feel of the silk sliding between my fingers. Just another few minutes, I whispered to my screaming clit. I ran for the shower. Since she worked at home in the converted garage, her schedule never varied. Even when I'm hurrying, it takes me fifteen minutes, so I knew she'd be waiting.

When I came out, she was lounging on the side of the bed, shirtless, shoeless, wearing threadbare jeans, a big grin, and—as I ascertained in one quick glance—a nice fat hard-on. I glanced at the pillow and saw that it was bare. Thank God she knows her woman. "Hi, baby."

"Hey," she said, casually brushing one hand across the bulge in her crotch, "I thought you were the one supposed to be getting presents, seeing it's your birthday."

I smiled. "I'm going to. Starting right now."

She was leaning back just a little, an arm out to either side, her palms flat on the mattress. The position lifted her small, tight-nippled breasts into perfect kissing position, and seeing as how they were there, I dropped the towel I'd loosely tied around my chest and, naked, straddled her legs, my crotch a few millimeters above hers. Then I had only to dip my head to clamp my teeth around the taut pink nub. I worked it with my lips and my tongue and my teeth until she was moaning and making quick jerking motions with her hips. Every time she did, her cock bumped my clit. I was dripping onto an ever-widening wet spot on the front of her jeans. I was already so ready, if I rubbed my clit over that denim-covered cock, I'd come until tomorrow. Oh, Jesus, how I needed to. But it wasn't denim I wanted to soak with my juices when I came screaming all over her. I let her tortured nipple pop from my lips and knelt on the floor between her hard, quivering thighs.

"Whatcha got for me in here, baby," I crooned, tugging down the top of her jeans with one hand and exposing the royal blue waistband where it cut across her belly. I slipped my fingertips underneath the edge of her boxers and swept back and forth over her belly, stroking silk above and below. She tensed and hissed, Oh yeah. I popped open the first few buttons on her fly and the ridge of her silk-covered cock sprang out. Her clit had to be as stiff as mine under that load. I laid my cheek on her boxers, right over her cock. "Where's my present, huh?"

"Keep digging, sexy," Jordan murmured, twisting a fist in my hair and bumping the corner of my mouth with her hard-on. "There's more than one in the package."

She wanted me to suck her. She likes to come like that, with me jerking her cock and her clit together while I blow her. But making her wait always makes me come harder, and I wanted to come so so hard. I flicked open two more buttons so I could lick the length of her cock. I took my time, working the slippery material back and forth with my lips over the hard ridge and fat head, sliding the wet fabric up and down like a blue silk foreskin. I licked and sucked and bit until the blue was black with my saliva, her hand all the time clenching and unclenching against the back of my neck, her belly heaving.

"Suck it, honey, Jesus, suck it," Jordan groaned, pushing my head toward her cock. "Get me off, please get me off."

I teased the waistband down until just the head was bare, the rest of her cock still pinned to her stomach by the top of the boxers. Mouth open, eyes glazed, she stared at me as I fisted the shaft through her shorts and delicately tongued the tip. The sound she made, something between a whimper and a plea, shot to my cunt and it convulsed like it does right before I come. Shuddering, I clamped my free hand hard between my legs and squeezed until the orgasm backed off a breath.

"Get your jeans off," I ordered around a mouthful of her dick, "and get up on the bed. Hurry."

I gave her one last tug and leaned back enough for her to push her pants off and shove her body back up the bed. She knew better than to touch her boxers, and now her cock, freed from the tight jeans, sprang up beneath the bright silk. I clawed my way up on top of her and spun around until my cunt was over her face.

"Lick me," I ordered as I chewed on the soaked boxers stretched across her crotch. Her mouth closed around me and I screamed into her cunt, "Suck it, goddamn it, suck it there, there, oh yeah fuck…"

My insides clenched, spurting juice in her face, and I shoved both hands up the leg holes of her shorts. Dimly I remembered Mr. TB and H saying, "easy access." The harness straps framing her cunt were slick with her come. I fingered her open and mashed on the base of her clit so the tip would protrude, bare nerves crushed under the base of her cock. She pleaded some more, and I smiled and dug her cock out through the opening in her shorts. It stood straight up, with the blue silk gathered in folds around the base. Another series of quick clenches in my cunt and I couldn't hold back anymore.

"I'm gonna come all over your cock, baby," I gasped, swiveling around until I crouched over her hips. "Hold it for me."

Groaning, her face glistening with my come, she fisted it, her fingers white against the royal blue ocean. Her eyes closed and she hissed in a breath.

"Nuh-uh, no jerking off," I snapped as I saw her wrist vibrate.

"I gotta get off," Jordan pleaded, hips twisting. "Ten seconds. Just ten—"

"Not yet. Now hold still!" I lowered myself, an inch at a time, onto the length of her cock, my cunt more than wet enough to take her in. When I hit bottom she slid her hand off, but not before she twisted my clit a time or two. "Bitch." She laughed.

I was flying, and I knew she was too. I reached behind me and squeezed a handful of silk and skin and leather and cock and jerked her hard and fast until her eyes went blank and I knew she was on the edge and then I stopped. "I'll tell you when you can come, and not before I... uh..." I was suddenly dizzy with how full she made me. "Oh fuck, I'm gonna come now. Fuck yeah, here I come."

I grabbed a fistful of her boxers on either side of her cock, twisting the waistband around my fingers like a horse's reins, and I rode her like she was my stallion. Head back, staring into her dazed face, I whipped my hips and pounded her cock, in and out, in and out. Her fingers dug into my ass, the muscles in her arms tight as ropes.

When I knew I was there and there was no stopping it, I slid all the way up her cock until the just the head was in, and then I yanked on her boxers so hard her hips jumped off the bed. Her cock slammed into my cunt and I came and came and came all over her cock and what was left of the royal blue silk.

"Ohhh, man," she yelled, her legs jerking straight out, her belly heaving as she shot her load inside her shorts.

"Uh-huh," I sighed, collapsing on top of her, sweaty and sticky and totally, wonderfully fucked. "Blue's such a great color on you."

"I think I heard them rip," Jordan muttered, her voice slurring as she dragged a hand lazily over my ass.

"S'okay. There's about a dozen other ones I wanna try."

Briefs, thongs, jock straps, button fly, Y fly...oh yeah.

PLEASURE POINTS

Y ou have a great clit."

"Huh?"

"Seriously." I tilted my head as it rested against your thigh so I could see all the sweeping undulations of tender skin that cradled the upthrust prominence like protective hands. Even unerect, the pale pink, butter-soft tip peeked out beneath the thicker, dark rose hood. "It's beautiful—especially when you're turned on. I love the way it gets so shiny, the head poking out at me when it's hard." I ran my fingertip along the side, pressed deep enough to feel the core, grinning to myself when you gasped.

"Jesus," you whispered when I thumbed the tip gently and your clit twitched.

Mmm, here it comes. Oh yeah, get hard for me, baby.

"And," I continued matter-of-factly, enjoying the power, "I like feeling it swell right before you come." I moved to that spot just underneath that always makes you wet and rubbed—slow and steady. Small circles, not too hard yet. "You get so big then, so stiff righ—"

"You're gonna make me come...if you...keep doing that." Breathless, legs twitching, one hand twisted in the sheets.

"Sorry. I'm just playing around." I eased up on the pressure, slowed my strokes even more. Flick. Flick.

"Oh come on." That tilt of hips I loved, the silent plea for just a little more, just a little harder.

"I'll be good." I really wanted to reach down and stroke my own pulsating clit, but it would be too distracting, and I needed all my concentration to tease you to orgasm. I knew all the signals—I should, we've been lovers for years—but I still needed to listen to the currents of your blood, sense the call of your flesh. Despite how well I knew your body, it still fascinated me. There was both comfort and exhilaration in knowing just how to create desire—how to control the pace, direct the passion, determine the depth and moment of your release. There were times your body demanded to be satisfied immediately—screamed to come—and then I gave you what you needed, just exactly the way you needed it. But there were other times, like now, when I led and you followed, willingly—or not. Dancing to my tune, coming to my song.

"I think you're bigger than me," I mused, switching to long strokes of the shaft between my thumb and finger, squeezing lightly when I got to the tiny ridge just in front of the head. You whimpered. I smiled. My clit beat a frantic rhythm between my thighs, and I clenched my muscles deep inside, holding back the thunder of blood that would soon drive me insane. I started to jerk you off a little faster. "But that's okay—it's a win-win for me. I get your big clit to play wi—"

"You've gotta make me come," you pleaded. "Please, I really need to."

I knew you did. Your clit was stone between my fingers, your legs and ass clenched tight. My fingers were drenched in come, and the beat of your heart pulsed through your clit like hammer blows. I wanted you to come as badly as you did. I couldn't breathe for the beauty of it.

"Ohpleaseplease…right…there…ohyeahbabythat's…just… right…ohright…there I'm gonnacome…oh yeah oh yeah…"

Your clit is gorgeous when it shoots off—dark red, full and hard, jumping against my fingers. If I could, I'd make it do it all day. But now the pressure in my belly was so huge I thought I might scream, and as much as I wanted to keep going, I needed you. I slid up beside you and even though you were still coming, you reached for me.

"You've got a great clit, too," you whispered, your voice raspy, your sweat-dampened face against my neck, your clever fingers already working me to the boiling point.

"Mmm, you make me so crazy," I moaned. Eyes closed, I rubbed my hand over your stomach, found the barbell in your belly button, and tugged on it in time to your fingers jerking my clit. I pulled harder; so did you. "Gonna come."

"Uh-huh."

I twitched at the jewelry, you stroked my clit; I twisted it, you pressed; I rolled it, you squeezed. My fingers flew, so did yours. And then my clit exploded, and I came and came.

"Oh God," I sighed at last, still feebly flicking the piercing in your navel. "You are so good at that."

"You know," you muttered, sleepy and satisfied, softly rubbing my clit, "you work my piercing the way you want me to get you off."

"Yeah?"

"Mm-hmm. Makes me hard when you do that."

I laughed. "Honey, everything does."

"I wonder what would happen if it wasn't in my navel."

I was suddenly wide awake. "Huh?"

"What if it was in my clit?"

❖

"You sure about this?" I asked three nights later as we made our way through the crowds on South Street. There were head shops, piercing parlors, and tattoo places on every block.

"Yeah," you said, blushing cutely. "I've been sorta thinking about it for a long time."

"Well, I know we fooled around talking about it. But this is…a big deal."

"I thought you said it would be sexy." You stopped at the corner of Third and looked into my face. "Don't you want me to?"

"It's not that." I looked away, then sighed and met your worried gaze. "I really want you to. But not for me, okay?"

You grinned, your blue eyes clearing. "Okay. I won't let you play with it, then."

I grabbed your hand and pulled you close to the side of a steak joint, angling my body to shield you from passersby, and then gripped your crotch. I squeezed. "Sure about that?"

"Come on," you protested a little desperately. "I have to get naked in a few minutes. Don't make me wet now."

There was something about knowing that my touch made you weak that drove me a little nuts, but I eased up. I knew you were nervous. Hell, I was almost nauseous worrying this was going to hurt you. "Okay. But if you want to quit—any time—you just say, and we're done. We'll walk out, no problem, okay?"

"I really want to," you said firmly.

I grinned. "Me, too."

I followed you down the street toward Body Alchemy. It looked typically grungy from the outside—flat-black-painted door, windows frosted so we couldn't see in from the street. When you made up your mind, though, you didn't hesitate. You shouldered through, and I was right on your heels. One long, narrow room, a glass-enclosed counter along one side, a curtained doorway at the end. Behind the counter a youngish guy in a black T-shirt and jeans, piercings in every visible orifice and then some. Both earlobes sported fat glass plugs a half inch in diameter. His nose was pierced, his forehead, his lower lip. I didn't want to, but I imagined what his dick looked like. *Don't go there. Jesus.*

He studied us back, neutrally. I wondered what he thought of two butch dykes in jeans, T-shirts, and boots. He looked from me to you, then settled on you.

"How you doin'?"

"Great," you said, leaning down to look at the jewelry under the surprisingly spotless glass.

"Need something pierced?"

"Uh-huh," you replied absently, staring at the fat silver rings. Fourteen-gauge looked huge to me right about now. You looked up. "My clitoris."

His expression never changed.

"You'll want Venus, then—she's the best at that kind of thing."

"Venus," I repeated quietly.

"Yep." He turned to me. "Very experienced. She did my co—"

"Thanks!" I interrupted brightly. I saw you smirk and wanted to slug you. "Is she free?"

At that moment a Tristan Taormino look-alike came through the door in a crotch-high leather skirt, high-heeled boots laced to the knee, and a red tube top that almost covered her nipples. Red lipstick, short red-lacquered nails, and big dark eyes. My taste runs to boy-bodies and short-cropped hair, but she made my heart beat a little faster.

"Oh, hey, Venus," the studded guy behind the counter called. "Got a customer here for you."

She looked our way and smiled. "Hi."

Fabulous voice.

"Both of you?"

"Just me," you said.

"Great." She pointed to the curtain at the end of the room. "You ready now?"

I piped up. "I'm coming, too. I'm her lover." Okay, maybe I was just a little more forceful than necessary, but no way was she getting her hands on your clit without me in the room.

"Oh, cool," she replied brightly. "Come on back."

The hallway beyond the curtain was narrow and lined with eight-by-ten framed photos of tattooed and pierced body parts. Not people— parts. One penis had half a dozen rings through the undersurface of the shaft and a barbell through the head. Ouch.

"Here we go."

The room was maybe ten by twelve, with a tiny sink in one corner, a padded table in the middle, and a moveable floor lamp in one corner. A box of latex gloves sat beside a series of squat, square stainless-steel trays on the counter by the sink. The room smelled of disinfectant and spices.

"So," she said briskly, indicating the table. "Sit up here a minute and let's figure out what's going to work for you. What kind of piercing do you want?"

"Genital," you said immediately.

"Labia or clitoral?"

"My clit."

I leaned against the counter and stuck my hands in my pockets. It's weird, but they were shaking.

Venus nodded thoughtfully. "You're over eighteen, right?"

We both laughed.

"Had to ask that. And I won't pierce you if you're high."

"Nope. I'm clean and sober."

"Cool." She shifted a little in the smallish space so she could address us both. "What kind of clitoral piercing are you interested in? For show or for sensation?"

"Sensation," we both said together.

"Then you want either a vertical hood, where the jewelry goes under the hood so the ball on the end will rest on the head," she gave us a look to see if we understood, and we both nodded, "or you want a triangle piercing...under the clitoral shaft. The triangle will heighten sexual arousal the most."

"That one," you said without a second's hesitation.

We'd looked at pics on the Internet, read the pros and cons, but I didn't know you'd absolutely decided.

"That's the most serious one we do," Venus advised. "It will hurt a little more and take longer to heal."

"I understand," you said.

"It might make your clit get bigger from the constant stimulation and the healing process—sometimes a lot bigger."

You grinned and damn if my clit didn't get hard.

"No problem."

Venus nodded. "There are two places I can put it—the standard triangle piercing goes low, where the labia join the hood. Or I can do a deep hood, up high under the base of the shaft. The ring will circle the shaft then."

"Like a little cock ring?" Your voice rose with interest. My clit twitched.

"Uh-huh. If you're built for it." She reached down, opened a drawer in the table, and pulled out a clean white sheet. "Take everything off from the waist down and let's see. You can cover up with the sheet."

While you stripped, she turned on the little spotlight, washed her hands, and pulled on gloves. Then she motioned me over to the table opposite her and gently reached between your legs, parted your labia with the fingers of one hand, and felt your clit. I saw your legs tense, and when she touched your clit, I got a jolt. I love your clit. Even seeing a stranger touch it turns me on. I kept my face completely still.

"Nice," she commented in a surprisingly clinical tone. "You've got a prominent shaft and the hood," she did something with her thumb, and I heard your breath catch, "slides back easily." She straightened. "I can do the deep hood if you want. But that ring is going to keep you erect all the time."

She is anyhow, I thought.

You looked at me, and I rested my fingers on your arm. I knew what you wanted; I always do when it comes to this. "Go for it. If you don't like it, we'll take it out."

"Okay," you said to Venus. "Let's go the whole way."

"I'll put in a fourteen-gauge to start. If you want bigger later, we can change it." She met my gaze. "I have to be sure not to hit the shaft where the nerves run. I need her to be erect so I can tell what's what—it's safer that way. I can do it, or one of you can."

"I'll do it." I didn't even raise my voice this time. I wasn't going to let her or anybody else work you up. Besides, I wanted to be a part of it. I was dying to touch you. "Okay, baby?"

"Yes," you said, your voice husky and low.

Venus turned away and did something in the background with things that clattered quietly. I leaned over, looked into your eyes, and slipped two fingers on either side of your clit. It was instantly hard. I watched your pupils flicker and dance as I carefully rolled the firm core of you between my fingers, pulling slightly at the end of each stroke. I got wet when I felt your warm come glaze my fingertips.

"Don't make me come," you whispered breathlessly.

"I won't," I murmured, but I wanted you just as stiff and swollen as I could get you. I wanted Venus to feel exactly where your clit was.

"I'm getting close." There was a note of desperation in your voice and perversely, I wanted to push you closer. You were mine, after all, and in a second I was going to have to hand you over to a strange woman. Your hips lifted and I felt your clit pulse, then go rigid.

"That's it," I said hoarsely, looking up to see Venus across from me. There was a small tray beside her with things on it. I didn't look too closely.

"Good." She smiled at you, then me. "Some people orgasm while I'm doing this. It's from the stimulation of the nerves. Don't be embarrassed or anything, okay?"

As she talked, she swabbed something on your thighs, then reached down with one hand. She grasped your clit, then squeezed at the base. The head popped out, and you made a small choked sound.

"You'll probably feel like you need to come as soon as I pierce you. It actually helps ease the discomfort if the clitoris can decompress, so don't fight it."

She reached for something else on the tray, and I looked into your face. A second later, your eyes got wide and you muttered, "Oh, fuck, baby. Oh, I think—Oh!"

You pressed your face to my side. Venus took my hand and placed it gently on your clit.

"Touch her right there. Easy."

I stroked you the way I always did when you were just about to come and you did, sweetly, in slow steady waves, crying out softly with each pulsation. I watched your clit coming. God, it was beautiful. I was always ready to stroke you off, but now…how was I going to keep my hands off you?

When you got your breath back, you pushed up on your elbows and checked yourself out. Grinning, you looked at me. "What do you think?"

"You've got a great clit, baby." I stroked your leg but stayed clear of your piercing. "I don't know how I'm going to stand not being able to play with it for a while, though."

You eyed my crotch. "Good thing we've got a spare."

SNOW DANCING

As I stood in the middle of my driveway and slowly turned three hundred and sixty degrees, I understood what inspired the title: *Pure as the Driven Snow*.

There was no question that everywhere I looked the view was painfully beautiful and hauntingly chaste. A pristine, sparkling blanket covered everything: overhead, tree branches bowed beneath the feathery weight; the road narrowed to nothing more than a path between encroaching drifts; and all around me, swirling white nymphs floated on the air. Not a single footprint or errant noise suggested that I was anyone other than the last survivor in a world where sound and fury had succumbed to the inexorable march of millions, trillions of falling flakes.

I have always loved to shovel snow. It's always so very quiet, and the steady scrape of metal on stone is like another heartbeat keeping me company as I work. I'm an orderly shoveler. I outline boxes, starting first along the edges of the drive and then connecting the trenches at intervals with perfectly perpendicular ones, exactly the width of my shovel. Once the area is mapped, I clear the box closest to the house, then make another and move forward. If I'm feeling particularly adventurous, I might on occasion make a diagonal through the box. I'm careful about how I pile the snow, being certain to leave enough room on the top for later accumulations. Bend, extend, lift, and throw. A rhythmic cadence, an endpoint in sight, a job accomplished. When I reach the end of the driveway and look behind me, noting the perfectly squared edges and the even mounds of snow lining both sides, I have a sense of satisfaction and even pride. My secret pleasure.

Unfortunately, today promised to be an instance of delayed gratification. There were fourteen inches of powdery white stuff covering my eighty-foot driveway. There was going to be a lot of bending, extending, lifting, and throwing going on before I reached the street. To make the situation even more interesting, it was still snowing. Steadily. I could barely see to the end of the driveway. With one last reverent glance and a whispered apology, I broke the surface of tranquility with my shovel.

Time to begin my assault on nature.

Thirty minutes later, it was clear to me that nature was winning. I wasn't even a third of the way done, and when I looked behind me, the area that I'd already shoveled was blanketed again in a substantial coat of snow. I was reminded of the story I'd heard: that it takes so long to paint the Golden Gate Bridge, that once the crew reaches the end of the bridge, it's time to go back to the opposite end and start over.

Bend, extend, lift, and…

"Need some help?"

I could just barely see the figure at the end of my driveway, looking pretty much the way I did, I figured. That is to say, shapeless. Large, snow-covered, and shapeless.

"That's okay. Thanks. I've got it."

The form trundled forward through the mists of snow, slowly emerging as a recognizable human figure ten feet away. Blue woolen watch cap pulled low over straight dark brows, a few strands of dark hair escaping from the back and curling on the jacket collar, slightly above average height, blue nylon jacket, blue jeans, blue gloves. A study in blue with eyes I was willing to bet were the same color, but I couldn't tell through the curtain of falling flakes.

"My driveway is about a third the length of yours. I'm done with it, and I don't mind lending a hand."

Lovely voice, melodious and deep. Second alto or countertenor, depending on the gender. Which for the life of me, I could not discern.

I lifted a hand to shield my eyes, blinking as the crystals caked on my lashes. We were standing in the middle of a blizzard. "Yes. Thank you."

With a brisk nod, my new accomplice in this losing battle strode purposefully back to the opposite end of the driveway. As I watched, he—or she—made a neat square ten by ten feet wide and began to shovel it clear. Oddly comforted, I rededicated myself to the task. When I reached the midpoint of the driveway, I finally looked up again in time to see her toss her parka onto the top of a towering snow bank. And there was no question about the *her* part—the swell of breasts beneath the tight blue, silk thermal top put all doubt to rest.

"You'll freeze," I called.

"No," her voice carried back to me. "I'm naturally hot-blooded. This feels great."

From where I was standing, it certainly looked great. Her jeans molded to her firm ass and solid thighs as if the material had grown there. She moved—bend, extend, lift, and throw—with an economy of motion and a precise rhythm that was mesmerizing. I was slowly becoming a snow statue as I stood unmoving, watching her work. I could almost imagine the muscles in her strong shoulders bunching as she thrust the blade into the snow, could almost feel her powerful thighs flexing, then lifting, as she threw the load clear. Oddly, I wasn't cold. If anything, I was pleasantly warm, and the heat escalated the longer I watched. Taking care to follow a path already shoveled so as not to pack down the snow beneath my boots, making it more difficult to remove later, I made my way to her.

"We've been out here quite a while. Can I offer you something hot? Coffee, cocoa, soup?"

She leaned on her shovel, her arm bent at the elbow and her legs casually crossed. She did have blue eyes. Blue blue, sky blue eyes. And they were appraising me in a way I hadn't seen for quite some time, but still recognized. I met her gaze so that she would know that I knew she was looking, and she smiled.

"Cocoa and soup?"

I laughed and extended my hand to introduce myself. "Fin Brewster."

"Jules Howard," she replied. "I'm new to the neighborhood."

"Ah, you arrived just in time for our annual snowfall." I turned and started back toward the house with Jules beside me.

"This is all there is, huh?"

I'd left the garage door open, and led her through to the small mud room that adjoined my kitchen. "You can take your boots off and leave them out here. Your jacket and things as well." I was busy shedding my own outerwear as I spoke. "Actually, we probably get two or three substantial snows, and it's always an event."

"It is pretty," she remarked.

As we shuffled about in the small space, we bumped shoulders and thighs several times. When I nearly knocked her over as she stood on one foot to pull off her boot, I grabbed her around the waist to steady her, laughing.

"Sorry. You first."

Unexpectedly, her weight settled into my arms, her back to my chest, and I found myself holding her in a loose embrace as she lifted first one foot, then the other to untie her laces. Her hips rolled gently in the curve of my pelvis as she bent forward to pull off her boots. My arms were wrapped around her middle, fingers splayed on her stomach. When the muscles contracted beneath the single thin layer of silky material, I had the sudden nearly overpowering urge to slide my hands up and cup her breasts. I stood completely still, barely breathing.

"I'm warm deep inside, but everything else is cold," she whispered. "The heat from your hands feels so good."

When she straightened I didn't let go, but merely leaned my shoulders against the wall, braced my legs, and took her weight once more against the front of my body. My mouth was very close to the back of her neck. A few snowflakes still lingered, the edges blurring and melting before my eyes. I have no idea what I was thinking, but I touched the tip of my tongue to a single shimmering droplet that clung to her skin, and when I did, she sighed. A long, shuddering sigh of pleasure.

"It's warmer in the kitchen," I said, my mouth against the shell of her ear.

"You're just what I need."

She reached between us and placed her palms flat against my thighs. I looked past her shoulder to a small mirror on the opposite wall and saw us reflected there. Her eyes were closed, her head tipped back slightly, her neck exposed above the crescent of navy blue. In the mirror, I watched my fingers curve around the column of her neck and dance along the taut muscles until I cupped her chin. When I pressed ever so slightly, she turned her face until I could brush my lips over the corner of her mouth. Her skin was soft and cool.

"You're going to get chilled," I murmured, skimming my lips along the angle of her jaw until my mouth was against her ear. "The snow is melting, and your jeans are soaked."

"You're right," she said, her voice husky and low.

She moved one hand from my thigh, and I heard the unmistakable sound of a zipper sliding open. "I should take these off."

"I'll do it." Watching her face in the mirror, I smoothed my hands down her abdomen to the waistband of her jeans, slid my fingers underneath, and pushed the material downward. She never opened her eyes, smiling gently as she shifted her hips from side to side to help me. The undulating pressure of her body rolling between my thighs made my stomach clench, and my hands trembled on her bare flesh.

She was shaking too and from the heat of her body reaching me even through my T-shirt and jeans, I knew it wasn't from the cold. With one arm around her hips, clasping her to me, I found the bottom of her shirt with my free hand and slipped underneath. I heard her murmur what sounded like a *yes*. She stretched against me, letting her head rest in the angle between my neck and shoulder, her hands braced against my thighs again, as I cupped her above and below. Her nipple hardened in my palm even as the silky evidence of her passion slicked my skin through the whisper of cotton between her thighs. I squeezed gently, then rolled my hand over her flesh, massaging her until her cool pale skin glowed red with the burn of desire.

"Jules," I whispered.

"Mmm?"

"It's supposed to snow again tomorrow."

"Oh," she sighed, covering my fingers with hers and guiding me inside her panties, drawing my fingertips up and down over the spot where she needed me. "Did I mention…oh, do me harder…yes yes just like that…"

She was hot and slippery, her clit so hard I could barely stay on it. I rubbed and stroked and felt her knees buckle. "Mention what?"

"How much I love…"

She whimpered and I pushed inside, the heel of my hand crushing her clit. She slapped a hand over mine and ground against my palm.

"Tell me what you love," I urged, my throat tight, my heart hammering so loudly I feared I would not hear. She was close, her eyes tightly closed, her mouth a silent *oh*. I didn't expect an answer.

She pumped hard on my fingers and laughed. "How much I love…
to shovel. Oh God…please, don't stop…"

"I won't," I murmured, watching her face in the mirror as she
climaxed, the planes and angles blurring like a snowflake melting in
my hand.

SWEET NO MORE

H aving second thoughts?"

"No," I told Phil, my best friend from work, for the tenth time.

"Okay, then." He said something I couldn't hear to the bouncer on the door and then motioned me inside. We paid our cover at a window in a closet-sized vestibule, and Phil pushed aside the black vinyl curtain blocking the entrance to the club. "Have fun."

The minute we walked into the Ramrod, Phil and his boyfriend melted into the crowd, and I was on my own. I couldn't complain. They said they'd bring me, they never said they'd babysit. I didn't really think places like this existed anymore, post-AIDS—a warehouse-sized room illuminated by black lights, rough brick walls, exposed pipes in the ceiling, pounding bass beat, and wall-to-wall bodies—mostly naked and at first glance, mostly men. Bare chests, pierced nipples, chaps over naked skin, straining cocks beneath codpieces and jocks. I felt overdressed in my leather vest and pants, even though I had nothing on underneath either one. The place smelled like stale beer, acrid poppers, and the musky odor of sex. Lots of sex.

It was exactly the kind of place I fantasized about while I jerked off, picturing what I thought might happen so many times it was getting tough to come that way anymore. I needed the real thing—or maybe I needed something I hadn't yet imagined. Trying to look like I belonged, I wended my way toward the bar. I shoehorned into a place at the bar and worked not to stare at the guy standing next to me while another guy knelt in the cramped space and sucked on his cock with gusto.

"Beer," I shouted when the bartender glanced in my direction.

When the guy next to me grunted, I automatically looked over just in time to see him yank his cock out of the other guy's mouth and pump it frantically, his face a twisted mask of concentration. Then he smiled at me half-apologetically and came all over the guy's chest.

"Nice shooting," I observed and reached for my beer. I drank half of it off to steady my nerves.

"Thanks," he gasped after he caught his breath and wiped his hand clean in the other guy's hair. "You alone?"

I kept my gaze on his face but I could hear the guy on the floor whining as he jacked off. From the sounds of things, he was about to unload a gallon so I inched away to keep the stuff off my boots. "Came with friends, but I lost them already."

"I brought a friend too." He looked me over. "You a novice?"

"No," I lied. "Why?"

"Because she's not."

My clit shot out an inch and turned to marble. "Sounds just right."

He didn't look convinced. "What are you looking for?"

"I'm not here to look." Praying he couldn't see my hands tremble, I unbuttoned my vest and uncovered my tits. They were small and round with neat dark areolae, which made the silver rings through the center of each nipple all the more obvious. I gripped the rings and pulled, tenting my nipples until they turned white. "I've done sweet. Now I want something else."

"Like what?"

I twisted both rings until my nipples wouldn't stretch anymore without tearing. The pleasure and the pain fused into a fierce ache in my clit and my knees nearly buckled. He watched my face and I knew he knew I was struggling not to moan. "I guess that will be up to her."

"I'm Jerry." He stuffed his limp cock back into his pants and sidled away from the guy slumped on the floor. I hadn't noticed him shoot, but the puddle between his legs and the come splattered on the bottom of Jerry's pants lit up like neon under the lights. "Follow me."

It was the best offer I'd had so far, so I did. I didn't bother to close my vest. I was just another body. Besides, my nipples were engorged after the twisting and so sensitive if they rubbed against the leather vest now, I'd have to go somewhere and jerk off. I wanted to anyway. My clit was pounding like I'd been working it for an hour.

We went through the bar and down a hallway and into another room. The only music now was the grunts and cries and moans of people fucking and coming. Jerry paused for a second, then said, "Over here."

He led me toward the far side where a leather sling hung from the ceiling by chains. A young blond guy with smooth pale skin reclined in the sling with his head thrown back and his legs bent up to his body while a dark-haired guy whose face I couldn't see stood between his legs, a fist up the blond's ass and the other hand jerking the blond's jutting cock. The guy doing the fucking was slender with finely muscled shoulders and a hairless back that tapered into a narrow waist, and he wore nothing but chaps that left his high, round ass exposed. His sweaty skin glowed beneath the lights as he rotated his forearm in the blond's ass and worked his cock like a piston.

The blond raised his head and stared at the hand jerking his cock, his face dazed and his stomach heaving to the beat of the fist in his guts. "I'm gonna blow," he yelled. "I'm going to blow my fucking load."

The guy fisting him never stopped pumping the iron-hard dick as come arced into the air, the first shot hitting the blond in the face, the next couple spurts landing on his chest, and the last few squirts finally dribbling into little puddles on his belly. A third guy leaned over and licked up the blond guy's come, then took two steps back and shot his own load in the blond's face.

"Jesus," I whispered, my clit twitching like crazy. I needed to jerk off now more than ever and wondered if I could just go lean against the wall like a few guys I could see and get a quick shot off.

"That's his lover," Jerry whispered, pointing to the guy who'd just blasted off in the blond's face.

"Who's their friend?" I asked, tipping my chin toward the dark-haired guy who eased his hand out of the blond's ass, stripped off a glove, and tossed it on the floor.

"That's who I want you to meet."

Before I could reply, the fister turned to face us and I was looking at a woman so hot I forgot all about my stiff clit and needing to jerk off. Her eyes were dark like her hair and her expression remote, as if she hadn't just fucked some guy for an audience. She had smallish breasts about like mine and stomach muscles that were etched and pumped from the workout she'd just had. Her mons was trimmed, not shaved, and framed by her chaps, which was all she was wearing. From what I could see of her cunt, it was swollen and shining with come. If she hadn't gotten off during the fisting, she must really need it bad now.

"Ask her if I could please suck her off," I said desperately to Jerry, having no idea what the correct protocol was, but I didn't care. "Ask her, please. Anything she wants if I can just suck her clit."

I stood still while Jerry made his way to her and said something. Then she stared at me for a long moment before walking over. I didn't say anything as she held open the edges of my vest and stared at my breasts. She flicked one nipple ring with a long finger.

"Are these for show?"

"No," I croaked.

She unzipped my leathers and slid her hand down my pants. I sucked in a breath as she explored my clit with one finger. After a minute of that I started to sway, but I was afraid to touch her to steady myself.

"What do you want?" she asked, dragging her fingertip up one side of my clit and down the other, over the head and back again.

"I want to suck you off."

She pulled her hand out of my pants and I fought not to whimper. "What about that pretty little hard-on you've got in your pants?"

"I'd like to come for you," I whispered. "I'd like to come for you harder than I've ever come for anyone."

"Any way I want it?"

"Yes."

She gripped my wrist and dragged me through the crowd, past the sling where she'd fucked the guy, to the corner where a padded pole a foot thick ran from the floor to the ceiling. She stripped off my vest and dropped it on the floor, slammed my back up against the pole, and jerked my arms around behind it. I felt her buckle leather shackles on my wrists before she came back to face me. She yanked my pants down to my ankles and kicked my feet as far apart as they would go.

"Is there anything you want me to know?" she said, rubbing her palms in rough circles over my breasts, bringing my nipples screaming back to life again.

"I don't fuck men."

"What else?"

"I'm not sucking anybody's cock."

"That's it?"

"That's it."

She grabbed my face and shoved her tongue into my mouth. I couldn't breathe so I bit her, just hard enough to make her ease back. Then I sucked her tongue until she couldn't breathe.

She pulled out and licked my lips like she wanted to eat them off my face, flicking her tongue into my mouth too fast for me to catch it again, although I snapped my teeth and tried. She laughed.

"You think I'd waste these sweet lips on a cock?" She bit my lower lip and twisted my nipple rings. I whimpered. "I'm saving your mouth to come in myself."

Breathing fast, she rubbed her cunt on my leg. She was hot and slippery and her clit was a hard knot in the center. "I'm going to drown you in juice."

She kept at it, rubbing and sliding, until she shivered once, hard, and jerked away without coming. My cunt was spilling and I was drenched to my knees with her come and mine. She forked her fingers, clamped my clit in the vee, and squeezed.

"Fuck," I whispered, sagging against the pole.

"You've got a nice fat one, don't you?" she murmured, jacking me slowly. Too slowly to make me come but enough to make me need to so fucking bad tears leaked out of my eyes. She pinched the head with her nails and I did cry. "Poor baby. Let me make that better."

"Please," I begged, all pride washed away in the sea of blood pooled in my cunt. I wondered if I was supposed to resist but I didn't care now. I just wanted to come.

She pulled something off the waistband of her chaps at the same time as she spread my cunt open with one hand. I couldn't see much, but when I looked down, my clit was standing up between her fingers. Even in the dim light I could tell it was wet and the dark color it got when I was about to come. If she jacked me now, I'd shoot.

She did and my legs started shaking and my clit got extra hurting-hard the way it did when I was ten seconds from coming.

"I'm coming," I said because I thought I should tell her, but she must have known because she stopped cold. "Uh uh God...I'm about to come...please."

"Breathe, baby," she whispered, and before I knew what she was doing, she replaced her fingers on my clit with a two-inch spring-loaded clamp. It closed onto the shaft of my clit with a snap and the rows of blunt teeth dug in and banished the blossoming orgasm into oblivion.

I screamed.

"Shh, shh, shh," she crooned, her mouth on my neck oddly gentle as she licked the sweat and tears that ran down from my face. She rubbed my lower belly, pressing into me in deep circles that somehow made the profound ache inside almost bearable. "Does it hurt, baby?"

"Yes," I whimpered. My cunt throbbed like someone had kicked me and needles of pain speared through my clit.

"You've got a beautiful clit," she whispered, jiggling the clamp with one finger. "Look how big you are now."

I bent my head and tried to see, but the tears clouded my vision. My clit pulsed between the jaws to the beat of my heart and I felt something else, something even more powerful than the pain. "I need to come."

She flipped the clamp back and forth. The pressure surged in my clit and my cunt opened and closed like a fist.

"Oh fuck that's so fucking good."

She gripped the clamp and twisted.

"I want to come so bad."

"And I want you harder. Harder than you've ever been for anybody." She pulled my nipple ring and jacked my clit with the clamp. The teeth dug into the hood and pulled it back and forth over the head with every tug—pleasure, pain, pleasure, pain, pleasure, pain. "Now you might be hard enough to shoot a nice load for me."

"I don't think I can," I moaned. The clit torture made me harder than I'd ever been but it wasn't hitting me right to get me off. "I really really need to come."

"Watch me do you, baby."

I tightened my stomach and bowed forward, shaking sweat from my face so it wouldn't run into my eyes. My clit was stretched out, impossibly swollen, the head bulging beyond the clamp. Seeing her fingers, slick with my come, tugging the clamp was too much. "Oh God you don't know how bad I need to come. I think my clit's gonna burst."

"Now it might," she said, and pulled off the clamp.

Blood rushed in, my clit doubled in size. The nerves in the head short-circuited from the sudden stimulation. Pain and pleasure blasted up my spine in equal measure. I thrashed and tried to get loose. I had to hold it, rub it, do something, anything, to stop the agony.

"What's the matter," she whispered, fingering my nipple rings rapidly again.

"I gotta come," I howled. There were more people around us now, most just staring, a couple jerking off. I didn't care about them. I didn't care about anything except coming.

"Let me help you." She fingered the head and, oh God, it hurt. It was so good and it hurt and I wanted to come so much and it hurt and I couldn't and I was fucking dying.

"Oh Jesus, don't touch it!" I moaned. "It's too hard now. It hurts. Oh Jesus. Fuck." I was blubbering, tossing my head around. I thought I might throw up.

She seized my face again and forced me to look into her eyes. "Shut up and breathe." She kissed me, so gently I felt like she was rocking me in her arms. "I'm gonna make you come, baby, so sweet."

She kept kissing me, her tongue delving deeper and deeper until I was sucking it again. Then I felt her fingers glide over my clit and my body jerked. She rubbed it and it felt so good and I moaned. She backed out of my mouth and straddled my leg, her wet cunt hot enough to burn my skin. She whimpered and I realized how long she'd been holding back.

Some guy close to us groaned and I could hear the frenzied slap of his hand on his cock and she growled, "Shoot on the floor, cocksucker, not on her," and he did.

"Get ready, baby." Then she lowered her head and took my nipple in her mouth, chewing on my nipple and tonguing the ring while she switched her grip on my clit and started to jack me. With so much stimulation happening everywhere at once—her cunt, her fingers, her mouth—the pain in my tortured clit didn't prevent the orgasm from building this time. My clit couldn't get any harder, but it started to throb inside, and the pressure spread into my belly, and I knew nothing was going to stop me.

"I'm gonna come," and my cunt started to spasm.

She shoved her fingers into me and raised her head to stare at my face. "Give it to me." Her palm thudded against my unyielding clit as she fucked me, and I unloaded into her hand and over her arm, crying and yelling *oh fucking God it's so good*...

She didn't quit until there wasn't a drop left in me and I was twisting to get away from her fingers, my clit so fucked out I wasn't sure I'd ever need to come again. She reached behind me and released my hands and I fell to my knees, trying to drag air into my lungs. She didn't care if I could breathe or not. She grabbed my head and tilted my face up and jammed her clit into my mouth.

"Now suck me off," she ordered through gritted teeth, her clit like rock and already jumping. She bucked her hips and pumped her clit in and out of the circle of my lips, jerking herself off in my mouth and muttering, "uh uh uh."

She was starting to come, so I sucked her just hard enough to keep her clit in my mouth. I wanted it to last for her.

"Here it comes, baby," she gasped, her fingers trembling in my hair. "Get ready to swallow. Sweet baby, you're making me come."

I clutched her ass and yanked her hard against my face, sucking her clit in to the root and clamping my teeth around it. She cried out and ejaculated on my face and down my neck and I felt her legs go. I wrapped my arms tightly around her thighs to hold her up because I knew she would hate to go down in front of everybody. When she stopped coming I licked up the juice that clung to her cunt and tongued her clit until she murmured a protest and pulled away.

Somehow I got my legs under me and heaved myself to my feet, hauling my pants up with me. My clit was still so tender I couldn't zip up. She backed me into the pole again and leaned an arm on either side of my head so she could lick her come off my face. Her whole body trembled and I risked putting my arms around her.

"That was sweet, baby," she whispered so no one else could hear.

I kissed her and she let me, and as I played my tongue inside her hot mouth, I realized that I had been wrong about what I had been looking for. What she had given me was sweeter than sweet.

SECRETS OF THE HEART

I must have looked suspicious because the sales clerk moved to the end of the counter nearest me, leaned his elbows on the smudged glass surface, and fixed me with a baleful stare. I suppose the fact that I'd been standing in front of the card rack for twenty minutes, unmoving, struck him as odd. If he'd known me, he wouldn't have found it strange. He might even have appreciated how impossible it was for me to choose a Valentine's Day card for this particular woman.

From the instant I'd scanned the messages scattered over the ubiquitous pink and red cards, I'd known it was hopeless.

Be Mine. Forever Yours. Your Forever Love.

Perfect sentiments, and everything I wanted to say. Except she didn't know, and I didn't dare tell her.

"Help you with something?" he grunted.

When I didn't answer, he probably thought I was crazy or just plain rude. He had no way of knowing that I wasn't seeing any of the cards and that his voice barely registered as background noise. I was replaying the conversation I'd had over breakfast that morning with the woman who had put me in such a quandary.

❖

"So," Sheri said as she stuck her head in the refrigerator and rummaged around on her shelf for something I wouldn't even recognize as food, "got a date tonight?"

"Uh-uh," I replied around a mouthful of last night's pepperoni pizza. We'd agreed when we moved in together that we'd keep our food separate because she pronounced my eating habits "disgusting," and I contended that cold pizza and beer was an All-American meal. On the other hand, yogurt and granola and things that resembled the stuff that came out of a lawnmower bag struck me as being unnatural.

She turned around and leaned her back against the closed enamel door, spoon in one hand, a carton of purplish gooey stuff in the other, wearing only a lacy white bra and very, very tiny bikini panties. In between those minuscule scraps of material masquerading as garments was an acre or so of alabaster skin that stretched and dipped over one of the nicest landscapes I'd ever seen. The rosy areola blushed beneath the snowy white silk as if embarrassed by my scrutiny, and I hastily looked out the window. I fixed on the latticework of telephone wires superimposed on the zigzag line of the fire escape that hung by a few loose bolts from the adjoining apartment building. If I squinted, the view resembled a Mondrian, which was far safer for my blood pressure than the image of a Judy Francisconi calendar model that I saw every time I looked at Sheri. Being a MFA grad student tended to make me think like that. Sheri, on the other hand, was studying modern dance. Her body was her instrument, and she thought nothing of displaying it. We were roommates. I was gay. She wasn't.

In all fairness, it wasn't that she didn't think of me as a sexual being when she walked around the apartment in less than a chin-to-ankle cloak, which is probably the only kind of garment that wouldn't have made my heart sing and my lower regions beat out a frantic rhythm in accompaniment. She was just comfortable in her skin and had no idea that I dreamed about using her body as my canvas to paint upon. I had decided months ago on gold body paint. Just a subtle rendering, to accent the already perfect picture—a circle around her right nipple, connected by a diagonal slash across her high arched ribs to a ring that rimmed her shallow belly button. I could feel her skin beneath my fingertips as I spread the wet glitter along the path my tongue longed to follow, ending in a dusting of promises in the blond curls between her thighs. My gold-tipped fingers would guide her legs apart, and then I would lower my head to—

"Davy? Da-vi-da. Hel-lo-o."

I jumped and flushed. Or, flushed more, to be strictly accurate.

Sheri stopped with her spoon halfway to her mouth and looked at me with an odd expression. "What's the matter with you? You look sick."

Lovesick, maybe.

"Nothing," I croaked. Then I coughed, trying to cover how tight my throat had become as I'd made my imaginary journey down her body. My hands trembled, and I shoved them between my blue jean–clad thighs.

"So?" she asked.

I shook my head, totally befuddled. Had we been talking about something? My nipples were stiff beneath my T-shirt, tingling and tight, unashamedly clamoring for attention. The rest of me was on point too—hard and wet, the desire to taste her skin so intense it sucked all the blood and good sense from my brain. Jesus, it was getting so I couldn't be around her for more than five minutes without going crazy. "So, what?" I finally managed.

She cocked a hip, which tightened that little patch of silk flush across her mound, hinting at the prominence of her clitoris where the tantalizing rise gave way to the valley beyond. I brushed the back of my hand over my mouth, afraid I might be drooling.

"Do. You. Have. A. Date. Tonight?"

"It's Tuesday," I said stupidly.

"It's Valentine's Day, so that doesn't count."

Valentine's Day. But I want you to be my Valentine.

"Oh. No. I forgot."

I supposed I should ask her the same thing, but I just didn't want to know. It was getting harder and harder to watch her go out on dates and then spend the night pretending I wasn't thinking about what she was doing, or about what someone might be doing to her. I'd envision her in her sexy short skirts and tight little tops, having dinner with some guy, or dancing with him, or—uh-uh, no. I couldn't go there. In fact, I'd started spending more and more Friday and Saturday nights away from the apartment just so I wouldn't see her going out. I was getting to be a regular at the all-night movie theater around the corner on Chestnut.

"Does that mean no date?" she probed.

I nodded.

She gave me a quick little smile and dropped her spoon into the sink. Then she leaned over, opened the cabinet beneath it, and discarded her yogurt container. When she straightened up, my eyes were still leveled at the place where her breasts had been seconds before, riveted on the nipples just peeking out over the scalloped lace edges. I tore my eyes up her body to her face, and she grinned.

"Me neither," Sheri said. "Wanna have dinner with me?"

"Sure. You want to try that sushi place we read about in the *Weekender*?"

Her smile got kind of funny, as if I'd missed something.

"No, I thought we'd eat here. You buy some wine, and I'll make dinner."

"Like cook?"

She walked past me and ran her fingers through my hair. "Yes, dummy. Like cook."

❖

Be Mine. Forever Yours. Your Forever Love.

I stared at the cards. It was impossible. She'd think I was crazy. I turned around and walked out of the drugstore empty-handed.

I did better with the wine. Sheri pronounced it, "Yum. Good."

"That looks good too."

I stood behind her as she stirred colorful things that didn't really look like food together in a big pan on top of the stove, her wineglass on the counter beside her. She'd pulled her thick blond hair up off her neck and held it in place with a tortoiseshell comb. A few wisps had escaped, and they trailed down over her throat. The steam, spicy and rich, rose from whatever it was she was cooking and mingled with something sweeter, something her. I leaned in closer to breathe her scent, and my crotch brushed over her ass. The touch charged through me, setting every nerve ending ablaze. For a second I was so stunned, I didn't move. Then, before I could jump away, she gave a little roll of her hips and pushed back into me. That's when I knew I'd lost my mind. Because she couldn't be doing that. Could she?

"Davy?"

"Huh?"

"Reach up to that cabinet right over my head and get me the cumin, will you?"

"Sure."

To accomplish the task, I had to lean against her and stretch over her shoulder. I had a choice of steadying myself on the burner or her waist, which was bare for a good eight inches between the bottom of her tight black cropped T-shirt and the top of her hip-huggers. I hesitated for a few seconds, figuring the end result would be pretty much the same. Whether I stuck my hand in the fire or rested my palm against her skin, I was going to go up in flames.

"Something wrong?"

I swear she did that thing with her hips again, and I had to lock my knees to stay standing. What the hell, if I was going to burn, it might as well be worth it. I curved my hand around her waist and reached up over her head. "Not a thing."

I was right. Her skin was hot. Hot and smooth and so fucking soft. The tips of my nipples ached as my chest brushed over her back. My crotch was so tight up against her now that my fly nestled in the little cleft between her cheeks. My clit was so hard it felt like it was going to come bursting right out through the faded denim.

"Don't move," Sheri said in a tight little whisper as she did something in front of her to make the steam disappear. Then she leaned back against me, turned her head, and licked my neck.

I forgot about the cumin and wrapped both arms around her waist. If I turned my palms up I'd be holding her breasts, and there wouldn't be any way I could pretend that was an accident. I was shaking all over; I couldn't move a muscle.

She pivoted in my arms and slid hers around my neck. Her face was very close, and she had that little smile again, the one that said I was still missing the punchline.

"What?" I whispered.

"How long have we been roommates?" She kissed the tip of my chin.

"Ten months."

I edged my hand under the back of her shirt and stroked my fingers up and down her spine. She threaded her fingers into my hair and rubbed against the front of my body like a cat.

"You haven't been around much on the weekends the last couple months," she commented. She kissed the corner of my mouth, then very daintily bit the center of my lower lip.

I was still reeling from the heat of her mouth when she yanked my

T-shirt from my jeans and pushed it out of the way so she could slide her bare belly over mine. She did that a few times while she kissed me for real, her tongue slicking in and out of my mouth like steam running down the windowpane, hot on cold, and wet. My thighs started shaking the way they do when I have to come really bad, and I knew I wasn't going to be able to hold us both up much longer. I walked her a couple steps to the right until her butt bumped up against the counter. I grabbed onto it, bracing my arms on either side of her hips.

"What are you doing, Sheri, huh?" I muttered while I grazed my teeth down her neck.

She arched her back and gave me her throat, and while I sucked, she gasped, "When's the last time...you saw me go...out on a date?"

"Don't know."

I bunched her tee in my fist and dragged it up to get at her breasts, licking at her nipples while I shifted just enough to get her thigh between my legs. She grabbed my ass and squeezed while she pushed her breast into my mouth. My teeth were going to leave marks.

"That's because...it's been months, you dummy."

She took one hand off my butt and scrabbled around on the kitchen counter while I lost myself in the wild race of her heart and the piercing pleasure of her leg squeezing my clit while I rode her. She pulled my head up with a hand in my hair and waved a little white square in front of my face.

"Here," she said breathlessly, her eyes huge, her lips swollen and the color of Valentines. "This is for you."

She started opening my fly while I struggled with the little envelope. My hands were shaking so badly it took forever, but I finally fished out the simple red heart with the white letters that said, *Be My Valentine.* Underneath the words, she'd written *I Love You, Sheri.*

So easy, after all. I said yes, and then I kissed her and kept kissing her while I undressed her. She tried to do the same with me, but I brushed her hands away. I had not yet given her her Valentine. I knelt between her legs and followed with my mouth the secret path I had painted on her body so many times in my mind, tracing my tongue over her softness, her sweetness, her sharp tangy places, until she started making little whimpering noises, and I knew it was time to tell her all the things I'd been wanting to say to her for forever. I pressed my fingers to her thighs, teasing her clitoris with my tongue until she got impossibly hard and her fingers clenched fitfully in my hair.

"You're making me come," she whispered, a note of awe in her voice.

Be Mine.

"Oh. You are. You're making me come right now."

I love you.

"Please there. I'm coming. There, there, oh there…"

Forever Yours.

"There," she sobbed. "Oh now…now…now…"

I closed my eyes and sucked her gently until I felt her swell and burst inside my mouth.

Your Forever Love.

ALL ABOUT US

Although I had a trailer all my own, with words I was secretly very proud of printed on the side—Rafe Bevalaqua, General Contractor—I still liked to eat lunch with the crew. Even on a sweltering July day in the middle of a half-finished subdivision where there wasn't a single tree to offer shade. Even when I had a little air conditioner in my unit where I could have taken a break in comfort. I liked eating with the guys, and that included the girls, because even though I was the boss, I needed them as much as they needed me. Besides, it wasn't all that long ago that when I was one of them, a union carpenter with big dreams. Now I had my own company, which was a good thing, because I also had a wife and two kids.

Being a parent and the major breadwinner changes how you look at everything. Most of my day—hell, most of my life—was spent working so I could be sure they had what they needed. Not that Donna didn't work just as hard with a two- and a four-year-old at home and a part-time job proofreading for a lesbian publishing company. But where my biggest worry used to be what restaurant I'd take Donna to for a romantic evening, now I worried about college funds and health insurance. That's the other thing that had changed. Since the kids, there wasn't a whole lot of time for us.

We were both dog-tired at the end of the day, and we didn't have the money or energy to do a lot of things we used to do when we first got together. We didn't go out clubbing or even out to dinner much anymore. Once in a while we caught a movie when my sister or Donna's mother could babysit, but we didn't party with our friends until all hours and we didn't stay up until dawn fucking like we used to. We were lucky if we could steal a couple of minutes on Sunday afternoon for few quick kisses and a fast come with a vibrator.

I missed coming home at the end of the day and finding Donna stretched out on a lounge chair in the backyard with a drink in her hand and a smile that said *I've been waiting all afternoon for you to take care of me*, and I'd go down on my knees right there and pull her skimpy panties aside and she'd already be wet and I'd lick her until she came with her fingers twisted in my hair and her pussy riding my face. I missed waking up on Saturday morning to her jerking me off nice and slow and easy while I just lay there, letting her do me like only she knows how. I missed strapping on a big dick and sliding inside her with long deep strokes, watching her face turn all dreamy and her eyes fill with tears because it felt so good and she was going to come so hard for me.

I loved my wife and I loved my kids. I loved my life. But sometimes I missed us like we used to be.

"Hey, Rafe," Joe the electrician called. "You gonna eat what's in that lunchbox? Cause if you're just gonna stand there with it, I'm good for seconds."

I stared at the black aluminum lunch pail in my right hand and realized I'd been standing outside my trailer daydreaming and blowing a good part of my lunch hour. Plus, I'd worked myself up pretty good just thinking about sex with Donna. My clit ached and my boxers were wet. "Yeah yeah. Forget it, you mooch."

I pulled myself up onto a half-finished concrete wall next to Joe and a couple of other guys, ignoring the way my clit jumped as it was squashed against the seam of my khaki work pants. I flipped the top on the big box and pulled out my thermos, listening to the guys complain about the weather and the Yankees and the high cost of gas. When I reached in for my sandwich my fingers closed round something that definitely didn't feel like lunch, and I yanked my hand out so fast I almost dropped everything onto the hardpacked dirt at my feet. Fortunately, none of the guys noticed my reaction. Turning so no one could see what was inside, I opened my lunch pail again. The first thing I saw was the note in Donna's handwriting.

Rafaela. I'll be there at one. And I'll be hungry.

Underneath the note, neatly arranged next to the sandwich that Donna fixed for me every morning, rested my harness and a fat cock.

"What time is it?" I croaked.

"Five to one," Joe said. "Why? You got a plane to catch?"

I slammed the lid and jumped down. "I forgot. I got a...phone conference. I'll be busy for a while."

Then I ran for the trailer.

Once inside, I twisted the knob on the window air conditioner to high and hopped around the room on one leg and then the other trying to get my boots off. I finally took a breath, sat down on the small sofa pushed against one wall, unlaced my boots, and shucked my pants and underwear, all the time keeping one eye on my watch. Two minutes to go. I got myself geared up, redressed, and zipped just as a knock sounded on the metal door. The sound went straight to my clit, which was already pounding against the underside of my dick.

I opened the door and grinned at my wife. She was wearing very skimpy baby-blue shorts that matched her eyes and a halter top that tied behind her neck. Her blond hair was loose and just touched her tanned shoulders.

"Hey, baby," I said, feeling as nervous as a first date.

Donna stared at my crotch for a beat or two and then climbed the metal steps and brushed past me, bumping her pelvis to the bulge between my legs as she went by. "Hi, honey."

Knees shaking, I closed and locked the door. I leaned against it to re-gather my cool. "So where are the kids?"

"At my mother's." Donna dropped a shopping bag next to my desk and looked out the little window that didn't have an air conditioner in it. "Good. No one can see in."

"I got your note." My hands were sweating I wanted to touch her so bad, but this was her show. She knew what she wanted and whatever it was, I was going to give it to her.

"I noticed." She slid her hand between my legs and cupped the cock in my pants, jacking it slowly while she kissed me. Her tongue filled my mouth, thrusting slowly in and out to the rhythm of her hand working me. I untied her skimpy top, let it fall, and stroked the soft surface of her breasts with my fingertips. When I skimmed her nipples, already puckered and hard, she moaned and jacked me faster.

"You don't want to do that so hard, baby," I warned breathlessly. "Not unless you want me to come in my pants right now."

She eased up on me a little and ran her tongue around the rim of my ear. Her breath was hot and her voice husky. "Play with my nipples. That makes me so wet."

I knew exactly what it did to her. I could make her come if I tugged and twisted them hard enough and fast enough and long enough, but I knew that's not what she wanted. So I took her up to the edge a couple of times while she whimpered and clutched my shoulders and rubbed her pussy over the lump in my khakis. I backed off just before she was ready to shoot over the top and palmed her ass so I could buck my hips and bang her clit with the dick in my pants. She sagged against me.

"How you doing?" I asked, watching her struggle to focus on my face.

"I want to come," she whispered.

"Is your clit all swollen, baby?"

She sucked on my neck and rubbed herself all over the front of me. "You know it is."

"Do you want to come on my cock? Is that what you're doing here?" I walked her toward the little couch, my cock jammed into her pussy, while she nodded and made incoherent sounds. Then I sat down, spread my arms along the back of the couch, and opened my legs so the cock formed a tent in my khakis. "Show me."

Instantly, she was on her knees, fumbling with my fly. I bit back a groan when she pushed her hand inside my pants. She was so anxious to get at my rod she almost got me off from the pressure on my clit when she twisted the cock around to set it free.

"Jesus, take it easy, baby," I gasped. Any chance I had at being cool was gone.

She laughed and went down on my cock. She's a genius at timing the pumping action of her fist with the slow glide of her mouth down the shaft, so I can watch her suck me off and feel it in my clit just like it was a cock. The first time she did it to me I was going seventy on the interstate and she pulled my dick out and leaned over and blew me in about two minutes. I wasn't going to last two minutes now. I cupped the back of her head to slow her down.

"Not so fast. I want to come inside you."

"Do you? Sure about that?" She smiled up at me while she kept jacking and licking the head of my cock. Her eyes said she knew just how bad I wanted to come in her face. She kept at it until my legs went stiff and my belly got hard and I was one stroke away from going off. And then she stopped.

I groaned but I kept my hands clenched on the back of the couch, staring in a daze as she stood and slid her hand into her shorts. Her fingers twitched between her legs.

"I'm so wet."

She pushed her hand deeper.

"Mmm. Feels so good."

Her fingers danced faster and she threw her head back, eyes closed. I knew what she looked like when she came and she was almost there. I leaned forward and yanked her shorts down. Then I swatted her hand away.

"Get down here and fuck yourself on my cock."

She kicked off her shorts, straddled me on the couch, and sank onto my cock in one movement. Her head snapped back and she gave a high thin cry. She pushed up, almost all the way off, and sank down again to the hilt. She rode it that way, slow and deep, while I pulled on her nipples. I could see her clit each time she slid up the shaft. It was deep red, glistening, standing up between her parted lips.

"Feel good, baby?"

"The best," she gasped.

"Gonna come all over me soon?"

She nodded wordlessly, her body trembling. I knew what she needed, but I waited for her to ask. She managed another couple of strokes before she wrapped her fingers tight around my forearms and gasped, "Rub my clit."

I knew just how she liked it too. Back when we had all the time in the world, I used to watch her masturbate so I'd know just where to tease her clit to make her come. Now I pressed my thumb into the base of her clit until the head was bare and standing up, then I circled it with my fingers, dipping low to carry her cream up and over the top. She got super hard almost at once and I knew nothing was going to stop her now. Her nails dug into my arms and her hips flailed away at the cock while she half whispered, half cried, *I'm coming I'm coming I'm coming coming coming...*

I caught her when she fell into my arms, her legs still splayed on either side of my thighs, my cock still deep inside her. She always comes more than once this way, and while she circled her pelvis working up to another come, I could finally let go. I was almost sick, I needed to get off so bad. I slid the fingers I'd used to work her clit lower between our bodies, beneath the leather harness and onto the hot stone that was lodged between my thighs. I got the slippery shaft between my fingers and squeezed.

"Oh yeah. Oh baby, yeah."

Through half-closed lids I saw Donna raise her head to watch my face. "Are you going to come inside me now?"

I nodded, jerking my clit as best I could while she kept riding my cock. I couldn't breathe enough to talk.

"Ooh, I'm going to come again," Donna gasped, looking surprised. She pushed up so she was nearly sitting, her hands braced on my shoulders. I shoved my hand lower and pounded my clit while she pounded herself off on my cock.

I felt it coming from a long way off, that jangling of nerves that spreads from my clit straight into my pelvis and deep down the inside of my thighs. I waited till the last second, timing my come to hers, and then I let go of my clit and grabbed her hips and jammed her cunt down on my cock.

She was already crooning her come song when I yelled, "Here I come right inside you, baby."

I shot for so long, my hips jerking so crazily, that Donna got one more tiny come out of it before she pushed herself off and collapsed next to me on the couch.

"Oh my God, I haven't come like that in so long," Donna said.

I stared at my crotch where the dick bobbed in time to my pulsing cunt. My pants were soaked with come. My arms and legs felt boneless.

"I'm wasted and I can't go back to work looking like this."

"Aww, we really made a mess, didn't we," Donna said, sounding not the least bit concerned. She kissed my neck, then took a tiny nip. I didn't even have the strength to move away. "I brought you clean pants, sweetheart."

I turned my head in her direction, my vision still hazy. "Yeah? You think of everything."

She fisted my cock and gave it a little shake. "Guess so."

I grabbed her hand, too sensitive for any more stimulation. "I'm done, baby. I can't get it up again. I'm sorry."

She sucked on my lower lip until I groaned, then kissed the sore spot. "You were very patient. Did you come nice?"

"Gangbusters."

"You held out a long time so I could come again." She kissed me, gently this time. "Thank you."

"Hey, you made it happen," I whispered. "So I wanted it to be great for you. I wanted it to be all about you."

Donna shook her head. "Every once in a while, honey, we need it to be all about us."

Like always, she was right. Which is exactly why I married her.

SLICKER THAN SLIK

I promise it won't hurt, baby," Tina said as she leaned in the doorway of the bathroom, her hips cocked and a razor dangling seductively between her fingers. It helped that she didn't have any clothes on, but not all that much. If I could have kept my attention on her tits, round and firm and just right for squeezing, or her sleek belly and high tight ass, I would have been fine. But the little steel blades of the razor glinted and I couldn't take my eyes off it.

"I'll suck you off when we're done," she coaxed.

"You better do more than that," I muttered. I did not shave my cunt. That was a girl thing. Trim, maybe, sure. Tina liked it when I trimmed. She said it was easier to find my clit, and believe me, anything that got her hot mouth cinched around my stiff clit worked for me. She gives the best head of any femme I've ever met.

"And after that, I've got a surprise for you." Tina showed me a tiny bit of tongue.

"If it involves you strapping it on and fucking me, forget it." But I was grinning, too. She'd been wanting to flip me forever, and to tell you the truth, the idea had its appeal. Whenever I let her top me she got this intense look on her face, like every move was the most important thing she'd ever done. When she pushed her fingers inside me, her eyes got big like she'd just discovered the secret to the universe. And when she made me come, as much of her hand crammed into me as she could get and her thumb beating my hard-on and me yelling my head off, she'd laugh out loud as if she'd just been given the best present of her life. So let's just say I could be persuaded. Pretty easily. But she didn't need to know that.

"What sort of surprise?" I was still playing unconvinced.

"As soon as we finish, I'll show you," Tina said. "I've got this incredibly cool outfit for you to wear to the party."

"Explain why that requires shaving." I crossed my arms and pretended to resist. The fact is, anything she wants from me, she gets. And not just because of the sex, but that's another story.

"You'll see. Come on, Dannie, you promised I could dress you up for my birthday."

Yeah, sure I promised, when she had her little finger tickling the inside of my asshole and her tongue making fast figure eights around the head of my clit. I'd needed to come so bad I'd have agreed to march down Market Street in a frilly apron and nothing else at that point. I sighed.

"Okay, but be careful. No nicks. And, Jesus, watch my clit."

She perched me on the edge of the tub and lathered me up with warm water and shaving cream, and she was careful. The biggest problem was that she couldn't shave me without touching me—stretching my lips out to get in the crevices, pressing down on my shaft to get that little cleft right at the base, and generally tugging and pushing and pulling all the parts that are hotwired right to my clit. By the time she was done washing the soap off and patting me dry, my cunt was smooth and my clit stood straight up like a fat, red thumb.

"Suck it, baby," I whispered, looking down as she knelt on the floor between my spread legs, her face just inches from my crotch.

She smiled sweetly, pursed her lips, and sucked my clit all the way in to the root. My legs shot out straight when the tip of her tongue poked underneath the hood. I mumbled a lot of "lick, suck, oh Jesus that's good, and please, baby, do me there" while trying not to come. Watching her suck on my clit like it was a Tootsie Pop usually makes me shoot off right away, and I was already making those girlie sounds I can't help making when I'm about to come. She was stretching it out like plump taffy, her red lips sliding around the purple head, tugging at the crown with her teeth, and I felt the tight coiling in my cunt break loose and whisper down along my thighs. My clit went rock hard like it does just before it hops and pops.

"Ooh, I'm gonna shoot," I whined.

My clit flew out of her mouth a second before I went off. She sat back on her heels and gazed up at me with her big brown eyes.

"Not yet." She knows me well and made a quick grab for my

hands before I could get my fingers on my clit. A couple of good jerks and I would have come in her face.

"God damn it, Tina, I need to get off." I was growling, but I kinda liked it when she made me wait. Sometimes my stomach hurt the next morning from being clenched so tight for so long until she finally let me come.

"Let's go in the bedroom first." She kissed the tip of my clit and I let out a pathetic whimper. "It's time for your outfit. Come on."

Like I could walk. But I got up on shaky legs, my clit a hot coal in the center of my cunt, and trailed after her into the bedroom like an eager puppy. What can I say. I had a wicked hard-on and she was my salvation.

I didn't see any clothes in the bedroom, and what I did see made me almost forget about my clit. The bed was covered with some kind of plastic sheet. Now I'm up for almost anything, especially on Tina's birthday, but she'd never mentioned water sports before.

"Uh, babe? What's going on?"

"Lie down on your belly," Tina directed. "Are you warm enough?"

"Warm?" I laughed. "I'm about to incinerate. Just do me real fast before we get dressed. It won't take long. I'm ready to pop."

She ran her nails down between my tits, over my belly, and dipped one finger into my cunt. When she rubbed my clit, my legs almost gave out. I grabbed her wrist and tried to shove her hand inside me but she backed away quickly and pointed to the bed.

"Face down."

Intrigued despite being slightly pissed that she wouldn't let me come, I stretched out on the cool smooth surface. I turned my head and watched her set out a strange assortment of objects—a stainless steel bowl, some kind of lotion, and a can of something that I didn't recognize.

"What's all that?"

Tina gave me a look like a little kid at Christmas, excited and pleased with herself. "Your clothes for tonight."

Then she proceeded to open the can and pour a viscous black substance into the stainless steel bowl. She set it aside, picked up the lotion, and sat on the bed beside me. "You'll be wearing a jock strap and a cropped sleeveless T-shirt."

"I don't get it."

She squirted something cool and thick on my back and started to rub it all over me, concentrating on my shoulders and ass. The second she started touching me, my clit was twitching again.

"Latex body paint." She slid her lubed fingers into the crack of my ass, worked them back and forth, did a quick pass over my cunt, and jerked my clit. "Stay hard for me."

"Oh, yeah," I grunted, humping her fingers. "It's a stone."

"The lotion will help the latex come off later," she said like we were having a normal conversation rather than me about to come all over her hand. She let go of my hard-on and I cried. Real tears leaked out of my eyes.

"I wanna come. I wanna come so bad."

"I know you do. Be good."

My ears were buzzing so loud I couldn't tell what she was doing until I felt her smearing something different on my ass with her fingers, drawing patterns of some kind.

"Oh that looks so cool," Tina said. "I'm painting the jock on with the latex. It's so sexy."

"Can I come?" I was pretty much on a one-way track to anything-you-want-just-please-let-me-shoot by then. I didn't care what she was putting on me or if it ever came off. She smoothed two fingers down between my legs, along the far outside edges of my cunt. I wanted her inside, fucking me, and lifted my ass so she could get to me.

"Stay still, Dannie. I want this to dry smooth. It only takes a minute."

"Rub my clit. Make it shoot. Please, Tina baby."

She smeared more latex over my ass, then leaned down and ran her tongue around the inside of my ear. "You can play with it while this dries, but you can't come. I want you to shoot that big load in my mouth."

"Fuck," I muttered, raising up enough to get my fingers around my clit. Nothing feels as good as shooting off in Tina's mouth, and I wasn't gonna settle for creaming in my hand when I could have that. I know how to work a hard-on without losing my load, so I just squeezed and tugged every now and then while this second skin tightened around my ass. I must have been twitching a little too much because every now and then Tina whispered for me to lie still. Just when I didn't think I could take it any longer, she told me to roll over. As soon as I did, she knelt between my legs and latched on to my nipple with her teeth. That just about finished me, and I would have come except she grabbed my hand and yanked it off my clit.

"Fuck!" I yelled this time.

Laughing, Tina worked my tits over for a few minutes, then spread the lube over my breasts and belly and started with the latex again. This time I could watch her and I almost forgot my aching dick. She scooped handfuls of the stuff onto my tits and smoothed it in swirly circles, using one finger to outline the edges, making it look like a T-shirt that just barely covered my nipples. Then she moved down and painted the waistband of the jock just above my pubes. Or where they used to be. I eased up on my elbows so I could see her slicking her way to my crotch. The latex dried smooth and flat, and when she put a second coat on it looked like clothes you could see through, only not quite. She had everything covered but the few inches right around my clit. That was still poking out like a fat red cherry.

"You not gonna cover that, are you?"

Instead of answering, Tina ran the flat of her tongue slowly between my cunt lips, sucking up my come and dragging the slightly rough surface of her tongue over the head of my clit. Stars burst behind my eyes and my legs started doing a jittery dance on the rubber sheet.

"I'm gonna coat right up to it," Tina whispered in between licks. "So when you're at the party no one will see your hard-on." She sucked me hard and fast and I started to come. "But I'll know…"

My clit was jerking against her lips and I was making crazy crying sounds.

"…it's right there."

She sucked me in deep so I could finish shooting in her mouth, and then my arms gave out and I fell back in a daze. About all I could move was my tongue, which was a good thing, because Tina flipped around on the bed and straddled my face.

"Lick me off, baby," she purred, and while I did, she kept running her fingers over the black shiny stuff covering my tits and crotch, polishing it up.

"Slick, so slick," she crooned as I sucked and licked her sweet, hard clit. Right before she whimpered and gushed all over my face, she sighed, "Oh baby, you're slicker than Slik."

POPCORN, SODAS, AND SEX

I scanned the skimpy half-page entertainment section, looking for something to occupy my time until I could outlast the stifling heat and maybe fall asleep—at least long enough to catch a few hours' rest before I had to get up and look interested in the prospect of buying 500 acres of sand and scrub pine out in the middle of nowhere. Being the point "man" for a land development company wasn't all it was cracked up to be. I spent as much time in backwater counties talking to eager farmers as I did wheeling and dealing with real estate entrepreneurs in slick offices in LA or Fort Lauderdale. This was definitely one of those "up-country" excursions.

I scanned the movie listings in the nearest city, which was a forty-minute drive away on twisting roads with which I wasn't particularly familiar. I didn't really want to see the last episode in the Star Wars saga all that badly, especially considering it had been released on DVD a year earlier.

Then I saw something I hadn't seen in years. An honest-to-God drive-in theater listing. I hadn't been to one since I was in college and all I could remember was the cramped front seat of my car, stale popcorn, flat soda, and hot sweaty sex. I smiled. Not bad for a few bucks and a couple of gallons of gas. I looked at the playbill.

Seed of Chucky, Starsky and Hooch, The In-Laws...things weren't looking so good. And then, a glimmer of hope. *Bound*. So what if I'd seen it more than a few times and it was a solid decade old. Some women you never tire of looking at. Jennifer Tilly as sexy Violet was one of them. I grabbed my keys and my county road map and headed out the door. The sun slanted into my eyes, a hazy yellow filtered through the dust kicked up in the unpaved parking lot by the most recent arrival. A dirty black Mercedes coupe was just pulling in next to my rental car. It wasn't the typical vehicle for this part of the country. I squinted as the driver stepped out, and blinked hard when I saw Jennifer Tilly. Shining shoulder-length black hair, lustrous red lips, lush body, and a lazy smile that made my clit quiver as if she'd flicked it with a ruby red nail.

"Hello," Jennifer said.

I stared, looking foolish, I'm sure.

"It's just too hot out on the Interstate, even with the air-conditioning on in the car."

She walked around and opened her trunk and started wrestling with an oversized suitcase. I finally got my brain to connect with the rest of my body and leapt to her side.

"Here, let me get that for you."

"Thanks, I appreciate it."

She smiled at me, her eyes doing a slow crawl down my body and back up to my face. Since I hadn't planned on running into a movie star, I was wearing shapeless navy-blue cotton shorts with no belt, a sleeveless gray T-shirt—clean but faded to the point that the lettering was indecipherable—and boat shoes without socks. Oh so very much not my suave best. She, on the other hand, somehow managed to look wrinkle-free in a sleeveless white linen blouse and charcoal slacks.

When I'd yanked the monster out of the car and onto the ground, trying to look as if lifting the thing hadn't nearly given me a hernia, she held out her hand. "I'm Sheila. Sheila Tyler."

By this time, of course, I'd figured out that she wasn't really Jennifer Tilly. She was better. I shook her hand and told her my name.

"I don't suppose you have any idea what there is to do around here?" Sheila asked, turning in a circle and surveying the landscape. "It's beautiful country, but I hadn't really planned on stopping tonight. I don't even have a book with me." She shook her head as if surprised. "I had this sudden urge to stop driving and I just pulled off the highway and here I am." She blushed. "I'm not usually impulsive."

"Well, the sign says the rooms have cable but mine doesn't. There's no pool, so a swim is out. The air-conditioning is, well…" I shrugged and hefted her suitcase, aware that the weight made the muscles in my arms and shoulders tighten. I caught her glance lingering on my chest and knew that the same jolt that had stiffened my clit had made my nipples tighten into small hard knots. She looked into my eyes.

"So how were you planning to spend the evening?"

"I was just about to go to the drive-in movies."

She threw her head back and laughed, a dark-chocolate smooth and rich laugh. "You're kidding."

I laughed too. "Nope."

"You'll roast."

"I'll open the windows." We headed toward the motel office. "Besides, the sun's almost down, and it will cool off a little bit after dark." Somehow I managed to open the door for her and not knock her over with her suitcase. "You're welcome to join me."

She stopped just inside the door and studied me with a tiny smile. "I'd have to change."

"I can wait."

"What are we seeing?"

"*Seed of Chucky.*" Her eyes widened and I grinned. "How about *Bound*? Ever seen it?"

"As a matter of fact, no," she said contemplatively. "But I'd like to."

I nodded toward the reception desk where a thin, balding man appeared to be dozing behind the counter. "I'll get some sodas from the machine outside while you get settled. Coke okay?"

"Perfect."

I leaned against the fender of my rental car, wishing it was a '57 Bel Air convertible, and drained one can of soda while I waited for Sheila to change. She came out wearing khaki shorts and a tank top and looking as fresh as if she'd never been kissed. Maybe she hadn't. Not by someone like me.

"Is everything all right?" she asked, regarding me curiously.

I jumped and spun around the car to open her door. "Everything is just fine."

She slid in and didn't ask me anything else, and I was glad. How could I tell her that the hot summer night and the fresh, simple way she looked and the buzz of anticipation in my belly made me feel as if I was sixteen again and about to go on the date I'd always wanted, but never had.

While I fiddled with the radio, she navigated, searching out the small blue road signs that marked the county roads. We missed a few turns and had to backtrack a time or two, but it really didn't matter if we were late or not. The journey was proving to be every bit as enjoyable as the destination hoped to be. We didn't talk about our jobs or where we lived or where we were going. We talked about the last books we'd read and the music we liked and laughed when I had to stop for a flock of chickens in the middle of the road that appeared wholly unconcerned by our presence. Sheila leaned out the window and made shooing motions while I inched the car forward, praying that I wouldn't feel a bump at any moment.

Finally we saw the giant movie screen looking obscenely out of place amongst the rolling hills and valleys, and I turned onto the macadam road that sprouted clumps of scraggly grass through cracks in its uneven surface. I hitched up one hip to pull my wallet from my back pocket but Sheila stopped me with her hand on my arm.

"You buy the popcorn, I'll get the tickets."

Her fingers were cool and firm. She leaned across me to extend a $20 bill out the window and her breasts pressed against my bare upper arm. I jammed my foot down hard on the brake to keep my hips from jumping, but it didn't do anything to stop the wetness I felt pooling between my thighs. I stared straight ahead and hoped to God she didn't recognize the sex seeping from my pores.

When she settled back into the passenger seat, I inched the car forward over the rough ground. A half dozen cars were scattered over a lot the size of a fairground.

"Where to?" I asked in a strangely gravelly voice. I tried to swallow around the desire in my throat and started to cough.

"Here," Sheila said, offering the can of soda she had been sipping from on the drive. "Let's park in the back. The angle is always better that way."

I nodded and drank, aware that as my lips touched the can they were exactly where hers had been only moments before. I wondered if that counted as some sort of phantom kiss. I jockeyed us into a space that actually had a speaker attached. At least half of the places within sight had only wires dangling from bent poles.

"This place is in pretty rough shape," I commented.

"It's good we came when we did, then," Sheila said pensively. She reached down beside her seat and worked the controls for a few seconds before turning to me. "Can you pull the car forward a little bit so that we can see the screen from the backseat? I can never get comfortable with my legs under the dashboard." Then, without waiting for me to answer, she opened the door, hopped out, and just as swiftly got back in the rear. She rolled down the windows on both sides, then leaned over my seat, one hand on my shoulder, her breath warm in my ear. "Go ahead. I'll tell you when it's just right."

I turned the key in the ignition so hard I was surprised it didn't snap off. With one quick glance at her out of the corner of my eye, I drove us forward until she said, "There. Stop."

"Is that good then?" I asked inanely. All I could think about was her hand on my shoulder. Her fingertips rested just beyond the edge of my T-shirt collar, against my neck. I wanted to rip my shirt off and scream, "Oh please touch me." My nipples ached from the constant contraction, and I knew that only her fingers rolling and tugging them could soothe the hurt.

She brushed her hand lower over my chest, then drew away. "After you go get us some popcorn and come back here with me, everything will be perfect."

I was out of the car so fast it must have looked like the seat was on fire. As I hurried off toward the low, square building that housed the concession stand and the restrooms, I heard her laughing. On the enormous screen behind me, the credits started to roll.

Ten minutes later I was back, my arms filled with popcorn and fresh sodas. The cardboard containers of Coke were sweating and the insides of my arms were wet from condensation. I stopped next to the car and leaned down to look in the open window. Somehow she'd managed to push the front seats forward and she was stretched out with her legs propped on the console between them, her head tipped back. She turned lazily when she saw me and smiled.

"Oh good. I missed you."

My knees got wobbly but I managed to stay standing. She held out her arms and I passed the drinks and popcorn in to her. Then I followed. The movie was already in progress, but I wasn't watching the screen. I angled in the seat so I could see her profile while I pretended to watch Jennifer Tilly. I couldn't remember now why I'd thought Jennifer was so hot. My whole body was wet and it had nothing to do with the heat.

I couldn't get comfortable. My stomach hurt from tamping down the arousal that sluiced through my cunt like a raging river cutting canyons in age-old rock. I shifted, trying to find a place where my muscles didn't cramp and my clit didn't ache.

"Stretch your legs out next to mine," Sheila said, leaning forward to set her drink and popcorn in the front seat. When I eased my legs onto the console next to hers, she settled back, one thigh half on top of mine, and put her hand in the bag of popcorn I held in my lap. "Do you think she's sexy?"

"Who?"

Laughing, Sheila gave me a look. "Are you watching this?"

"Seen it." My insides tightened into a hard knot. What the hell. "You're much sexier."

Her breath caught and she took my soda from where I held it balanced on my knee. She sipped through my straw. "Are you flirting?"

"Do you want me to be?"

"Have you ever made love at the drive-in?"

I groaned and my thighs jumped with a life of their own. She must have felt it. "Not exactly."

"Meaning?"

Her voice had gotten low and soft.

"Meaning I rolled around a little in the backseat when I was a teenager, but I'd hardly call it making love."

"Mmm," she said musingly, dipping into my popcorn again. "There's something to be said for taking your time with the good parts."

"Sheila," I started to say, not sure what I was going to say next. *I'm so hot I could burst into flames, I'm aching to touch you, Do you even want me to touch you*…but the words died in my throat when she dropped a handful of popcorn in my lap.

"Oh, sorry," she murmured, delicately reaching between my legs to collect the fluffy white blobs. The backs of her fingers brushed my crotch.

My hips jolted so hard, my body levitated and my breath whooshed out like I'd been punched.

"Sorry."

She didn't sound sorry. More amused. And when I looked down, her hand was still there, her fingertips resting gently on the seam of my shorts right over my clit. She pushed in, slow and steady, and I crushed the paper bag of popcorn in my fist. A mushroom cloud of kernels erupted all over us both.

"Uh," I muttered.

"Don't worry. I was done." Sheila leaned over me, her hand squeezing down on my crotch, and kissed me lightly on the mouth. "With that."

Then she took the soda from my other hand, poured the contents out the window, and dropped the container on the floor. While I looked on in a haze of confused lust, she calmly braced her arm on the seat next to my head and levered herself over me until she straddled my waist, a knee on either side of my hips. My body finally caught up, and I tugged her blouse from her shorts as gently as I could.

She made a little humming noise when I slid my palms up to her breasts. Her bra was tissue-paper thin, her nipples small and hard. Before I could, she reached one hand down the front of her blouse and unhooked the clasp between the cups. Her full firm breasts came spilling out and I squeezed, not so gently now.

"Oh yes," she sighed, moving her hands from the seat to grasp fistfuls of my hair. "Play with them. Just like that."

While she kissed me thoroughly, her tongue starting at my lips and exploring every dip and hollow deeper inside, I circled her nipples with my fingers, closed down around them, and thumbed the tips. She drew back and caught her lip in her teeth, watching my hands move under her blouse while she rocked in my lap.

"Take your blouse off," I whispered hoarsely. There was no one nearby, and the movie flickering on the edges of my vision afforded me enough light to see her. And I wanted to see all of her. I kept up the nipple play while she bared her upper body. The instant her breasts appeared I covered one nipple with my mouth. I licked and strummed it with my tongue and she crooned with pleasure. I was so lost in the sound and the sweet taste of her I didn't realize she'd put her hand down the front of my shorts until I felt a vise-like grip on my clit. I groaned with the sudden stab of pleasure and almost came. "Easy."

"You know," Sheila panted unevenly, "I always wanted to do this."

"What," I asked, kissing my way back and forth from one nipple to the other.

"Make love in a car at the drive-in."

"Why didn't y—" I choked when she twisted and tugged on my clit and my vision went red. "You're going to get me off doing that."

"Keep pulling my nipples," Sheila ordered, jerking me off more gently. "I want to come with you sucking them." She slid one finger down between my lips and dragged hot, slick come back up over the head of my clit. "Lick me while I make you come. I want to feel you come in my hand."

I sucked and bit and squeezed and she rubbed and pinched and stroked.

"Oh yes I'm coming soon," she whispered, her mouth against my ear. "You're making my clit tingle so...nice. Oh. Are you...coming? Come soon. Come...oh."

She writhed on my lap, rubbing herself against her own arm where it disappeared down my pants. I didn't care about coming—I just wanted to watch the pleasure shimmer across her face. Her breasts got hot and heavy in my hands. She shook and shuddered and moaned and while she came I unzipped her shorts.

"Oh nice," she finally sighed, sagging against me.

"Yeah," I said and skimmed my fingers over her hard clit. She twitched and gasped. "You're not done."

She laughed. "Not hardly." She sucked on the skin just above my collarbone. "You didn't come."

"I got distracted." She still had her hand in my pants and slid half off me so that her head was on my shoulder and her body curled along mine. Her fingers skittered over the stiff length of me and I groaned. Now I felt how close she'd gotten me with all the clit play.

"Who's not done, huh?" she teased.

"Ten seconds," I said through gritted teeth. I was lying. It took three seconds and two long strokes down my cleft and back up again to send me shooting off like a cannon. I must have done something to her clit while I was bucking and shooting because I heard her cry out in surprise and then she was pushing my fingers inside her and coming all over them.

"What a great movie," she murmured some time later.

"Uh-huh." My hand was still inside her and my arm was cramped from the angle but I didn't care if it fell off from lack of blood flow. Not as long as I could feel her pulsing and quivering all around me the way she was still doing.

"You know when I first saw you outside the motel," Sheila said lazily, "I thought you looked just like Gina Gershon."

"I thought you'd never seen this movie before," I said with a laugh.

"Mmm, well, not at the drive-in." She kissed me and ran her finger lightly back and forth over my clit, making me shiver. "And you may not have noticed, but Gina's got nothing on you."

I pressed my palm down on my shorts over her hand. "You'll get me wired up again."

"Well, I like reruns." She tightened inside around my fingers. "And there's still plenty of popcorn."

INTERVIEW WITH A PORN STAR

How can you fuck strangers for a living while people stand around and watch?"

That's the question everyone wants to ask me, although most people try to sound more polite. Sometimes. I hate doing interviews because no one ever believes my answer. It's too simple, I guess. The truth is, acting in erotic videos is the perfect job for me because I never have to fake coming, and you can always tell when a girl is faking it. Of course, when I say that, they either look really, really skeptical or say, "But how can you come when it's all so fake?"

Sigh. Like girls can't get off just like guys for no other reason than it feels good?

Then I have to explain that there is nothing fake about having a girl lick your pussy or stroke your clit. And that I really get off on people watching her do it. Having sex in front of other people makes me come like nothing else. Oh, I get off plenty of other ways and it's always good, but I never come as hard as I do when I know someone else is looking. So the minute I walk onto the set, even if the director and the cameraman and the sound techs aren't standing around the bed yet, my pussy gets wet. Put me with another actor in a roomful of people watching us fuck or go down on each other and my biggest challenge is not coming before I get through the scene. I still have to concentrate on holding off until the director wants a come shot, but I've been working on that ever since the day I completely embarrassed myself at my first film audition.

I didn't know what to expect, so I was psyched when it turned out the director was a hot woman. That was the first plus for me. The second, even better bonus, was that she was looking for an actor to make it with other girls. I have nothing against guys, but girls really do it for me. There's nothing quite like a pouty mouth slick with lipstick cinched around my clit, unless it's a small, hard fist pounding inside my cunt. Besides, girls look so sexy when they come. It doesn't matter if I'm fucking them or sucking on their hot, hard clits or watching them do themselves, I love the way their mouths open with surprise and their eyelids flutter and their bellies quiver just before they cry and throw their heads back and gush all over.

Oh yeah, I like to watch almost as much as I like to be watched. Almost.

So I told the director I was good with the girl action and we got through the age thing and the health thing and all the other routine stuff pretty fast. Then she put the paperwork aside and stood up.

"Do you mind if I take some stills for the Web site? I like to feature our new actors before the film release."

"Sure. That's fine."

"Right this way." She led me into an adjoining room that was set up like a photography studio. Except this had a big bed right in the middle of the room. We were the only ones there.

"Go ahead and take your clothes off. Then stretch out on your back on the bed."

While I got comfortable against a pile of big fluffy pillows, she fiddled with the equipment.

"Let's run through the basics," she said as she walked to the foot of the bed with her camera. "Are you comfortable masturbating in front of other people?"

I almost laughed. I first discovered I really liked people to watch me come when my housemate walked in on me one afternoon while I was masturbating to a porn video. She wasn't supposed to be home for another two hours and when the front door opened and she strolled in, I was like thirty seconds from coming. My clit had done that thing where it plumps up right before I pop and little electric shocks were running through it into my stomach and down the insides of my legs. The girls on the screen were sucking each other's pussies and the way their mouths sounded on each other's cunts, wet and slippery and yummy, had me rubbing my clit as hard and fast as I could. I turned my head when I heard the door and saw her and my orgasm stalled just before I hit the top, but my cunt was so swollen and achy I couldn't let go. She looked at the TV and then at me, her gaze zeroing in on my skirt hiked up to my waist and my hands working between my legs.

"You're home early." I gave her a lazy smile and slow-stroked my clit, my fingers coated in juice.

"Sorry," she said, but she didn't look sorry. Her eyes were huge and I could see her breathing fast from across the room, her nipples hard little balls under her tight tee.

"It's okay," I murmured breathlessly. "But do you mind if I finish? I really need to come."

"No, I don't mind," she said so quietly I almost didn't hear her. "Could I...could I watch?"

The look on her face, so hungry and helpless, made my hips jump and oh, God I was on the edge again, every bit of blood and bone and muscle coiled so tight it felt like my clit would shatter. And it was so good, I knew I'd come really hard, even harder than when I was about to come from watching the movie.

"Sit next to me." I circled my clit as softly as I could so I wouldn't come right then, but I really really wanted to.

She just about ran across the room, but she didn't sit on the sofa like I expected. She knelt on the floor between my knees, put her hands on the inside of my thighs, and leaned over until her face was a few inches from cunt.

"You like it?" I asked, flicking at my clit with a fingernail.

"Oh yes."

I spread myself open with the hand that wasn't teasing my clit so she could see everything. "Tell me."

"You're all red and puffy," she whispered. She looked up at me briefly, her face filled with wonder. "Have you been doing this long?"

I nodded, my stomach clenched so hard I could barely talk. Having her see how excited my pussy was made it open and close like a fist. God, I wanted to just let go all over her. "Almost an hour."

"Oh," she breathed, refocusing on my pussy. "You must have to come awfully bad now."

"Uh-huh," I whimpered, rolling my clit between my fingers. Across the room one of the girls on the screen was wailing and thrashing and rubbing her pussy all over the other girl's face. Usually that's when I come, watching her face twist and listening to her cry and mauling my clit until I force my cunt to spasm and flood. But not today. Today I'd found something so much better. "Can you see my clit?"

"Yes, it's beautiful. Big and shiny." Her eyes were hazy and unfocused, like she was stoned but I knew she wasn't. She was high on the smell of my cunt and the squelch of my fingers sliding through it and the sight of my stiff, wet clit. "Does your pussy feel good when you rub it like that?"

"Mmm, makes me wanna come. Can you tell how hard my clit is?"

"Oh, yeah. It's sticking way out and the more you tease it the darker it gets."

I moaned and circled the head of my clit. Watching her lick her lips and blink rapidly while she followed my fingers was making my pussy spasm and I knew I didn't have much time left. "I'm going to come soon."

"Can I play with myself?"

"Do you want to come up here and watch the movie?" I held my breath, almost afraid of what she might say.

"Oh, no." She shook her head vehemently. "No. I want to watch your come spurt out on your fingers when you go off."

My legs jerked and I couldn't hold back a tiny come. I moaned and clamped my fingers tightly around my clit, preventing the rest of the explosion. "Go ahead. Play with your clit."

She yanked her zipper down and shoved her hand into her jeans. Even though her body convulsed, she never looked away from my fingers. I was still squeezing as hard as I could, afraid if I stroked even once I would come all over the place.

"Hurry," I whispered, "if you want to come with me."

The cords in her neck stood out as she shook her head again. "Watching you come will make me come." She looked up at me, her eyes glazed. "Your pussy is so beautiful, so open and wet."

My clit couldn't get any harder and I rubbed it faster, big sweeping circles reaching as far down as my opening and then back up over the top, sliding the hood down and over the head with each swipe. "Watch my clit," I gasped. "I'm going to come."

She whined and pumped her arm faster, mumbling, "Please come, please come, please come."

"Here I come," I cried, pushing down hard as my cunt pulsed like a small heart. "Gonna...come...all...over...you."

And I did. She put her face closer, but didn't touch me, and my hips jumped and I gushed over her lips and her chin and her neck while her eyes rolled back in her head and she came with her hand digging in her jeans. Then she sweetly licked me clean while I watched the girls on the screen and came again.

After that, we got off together a couple of times a week. She especially liked to crouch between my legs in the shower and hold me open with both hands while I hit my clit with a stream of water from the shower massage. The whole time I was making myself come, leaning against the wall on trembling legs, she described the way my pussy jumped under her fingers and how my clit stood out from my body and how the rivulets of come ran down my legs and mixed with the water in pearly strands. She could predict the exact second when I got ready to come from the size of my clit and the color of my pussy.

"Oh yeah, you're gonna come. It's gonna be a huge one. Right. Now."

And the minute she said it, I'd let loose all over. Then she'd suck on my clit while it was still hard, before I was even totally done coming, and bring herself off in her hand. And while she was moaning and coming and mouthing my clit, I'd come again too.

It got so all she had to say was, "Let me see your pretty pussy," and I'd be ready to come. So, no, I didn't have any trouble working myself off in front of other people. I loved it.

"I'm comfortable with public masturbation," I told the director, hoping to sound professional.

"Good. Let's take a look at you."

I spread my legs and as soon as she looked down, I felt my pussy swell. I'd shaved so everything would show for the camera, and I couldn't hide a thing.

"Hold yourself open for me," she said, adjusting a portable light so that it bathed my lower body in hot, bright light. "Use both hands."

I felt a trickle of come slip down between my cheeks. I hope she didn't see my fingers tremble as I pulled my outer lips apart. I knew from masturbating with a mirror how my cunt looked when I was excited—how my lips got thick and red and wet and my clit got long and fat. She must have been able to tell how turned on I was because she glanced up at my face and smiled.

"Looks like you're doing okay."

"Yes, fine," I said casually while my clit twitched and got stiffer by the second.

Click.

I imagined the way my pussy would look in the photograph, open and glistening with come.

Click.

My big pink clit, stiff and exposed, shamelessly aroused.

Click.

I started panting.

"Your cunt's a great rose color. That will look terrific on film."

Every click of the camera was a caress. My stomach started to hurt. I wanted to come.

"Can you touch your clit a little like you were going to masturbate? I want a shot of your finger on that gorgeous clit."

"Okay," I whispered, almost choking on the word.

Click.

I pressed two fingers on the base of my clit. It jumped right up and my belly rolled.

"Work it up just a little more. It looks fabulous when it's erect."

Click.

"Now pull the hood back and get it wet."

I painted my clit with come and that made me so horny all I wanted was for this to end so I could go somewhere and finish myself off.

Click.

"Oh, that's a nice look. Jiggle it a little so it plumps up."

I did and it was too good and I should have stopped but I couldn't and I came. I tried to hide it, but it hit me so fast my whole body jerked off the bed. "Ooh! God!"

"Do you always come that quickly?" she said, clicking away while my pussy pumped.

I shook my head no, whimpering pathetically, still pulling at my clit and coming.

"Hmm." She lowered her camera. "Just really worked up over the audition?"

"I think," I gasped. "I think it's...oh God, this is embarrassing..."

"Hardly. You're perfect, but I still need to know what set you off so I can time the come shots in the scenes. Unless you can hide it a whole lot better than this."

"I can't...not usually," I confessed, thoroughly humiliated. "I come hard."

"Then I need to know your trigger."

"It's you looking at me. At my pussy."

"You get off on having people admire that beautiful cunt of yours?"

"Yes."

She laughed. "Oh baby, you're going to love this job."

She had no idea, and neither did I. I'm easy to pick out in the films—I'm the girl smiling right at the camera and coming, so nice.

CLINICAL TRIALS

PHASE ONE: CALIBRATIONS

Hunger is a powerful motivator. It's amazing the things you'll do that you never would have conceived of if you didn't need money to eat. Or in my case, to eat, pay the rent, and put gas in the car. Not to mention next semester's tuition, textbooks, and the occasional new pair of shoes. All right, it's not quite that bad, but almost. I'm the typical struggling graduate student, and fortunately, in a large university there are always studies being done that pay volunteers to participate. Although I've often thought that if you're being *paid,* you probably aren't a volunteer, but something else. In terms of my newest assignment, that "something else" turned out to be pretty hard to describe.

It started yesterday when I saw an ad in the campus newspaper that said: **Study subjects needed for psychosexual imprinting analysis. Must be 18 or older. Please contact Van Adams at extension 6361 for details.**

So I called, got the secretary in the experimental psych department, and scheduled an appointment for this morning at 10:15. When I arrived a little bit before the appointed time, the same secretary directed me to an office down the hall. The fluorescent lights in the cinderblock-walled, tile-floored hallway seemed overly harsh as my footsteps echoed in the hollow silence. The third door on the left was unmarked, but I knocked as I had been instructed.

"Come in," a disembodied voice called.

The room was spare, and in the few seconds I had to scan it before my attention was drawn to the woman behind the functional metal desk, I didn't notice that any attempts had been made to personalize the space. University-issue bookshelves against one wall, filled with haphazardly stacked texts, file folders, and piles of papers; no rug on the floor; two worn, armless, upholstered chairs facing a desk that sat in front of what I presumed were windows behind closed horizontal blinds. The woman who glanced up with a remote smile appeared to fit the room. Late twenties, smooth pale skin, glossy dark hair pulled back from her makeup-free face, and big, dark, intelligent eyes. She wore a fitted linen blouse in a neutral shade, and although I couldn't see below the desk, I was willing to bet there were tailored trousers in a darker shade and expensive low-heeled shoes to match. Nice package in a professional, no-nonsense kind of way.

"Hello," she said in a silky, rich voice while standing to extend a hand. "I'm Dr. Vanessa Adams."

"Robbie Burns." I shook her hand, wondering how I appeared to Dr. Adams in my threadbare jeans, striped polo shirt, and sneakers. At least I'd had a haircut recently, so my collar-length chestnut waves looked fashionably shaggy as opposed to just plain old messy. At least my eyes, an unusual gray-green, were distinctive. And why that should matter, I hadn't a clue.

"You're here about 769, correct?" At my confused expression, she smiled absently. "Sorry. The multivariant sexual stimulus reaction study."

I held up the page from the campus rag where I had circled the small notice in red. "Would that be this?"

"That would be the one."

I thought I saw another trace of a smile, but I couldn't be certain. She settled down behind her desk and gestured me to one of the chairs that had probably once graced a student lounge but now should have adorned a trash pile somewhere. I sat and waited while she opened a folder and took out a number of forms. The first one she turned in my direction and pushed across the desk. "This is a nondisclosure statement. I'd like you to read it, ask any questions you might have, and sign it before I begin the intake interview."

"There's an interview?"

"Yes," she replied evenly. "There are certain screening criteria which are necessary for inclusion as well as exclusion from the study. The questions I will be asking are both personal and confidential—for you *and* for the study." She paused, studying *me*. "And before we go any further, I need to see proof of age, please."

I grinned and reached into my back pocket for my wallet. After opening it to the clear window that displayed my license, I passed it across the desk for her perusal. "Twenty-five."

"Thank you."

She passed the wallet back, and I replaced it automatically as I scanned the page before me. It was a standard nondisclosure form essentially saying that I couldn't tell anyone the details of the study, the questions I had been asked prior to engaging in the study, or the activities I might be involved in as a study participant. I signed it and handed it back. Dr. Adams took it, tucked it neatly away, and pulled out another page filled with blanks and boxes. Eventually we finished with my name and birth date and other vital statistics. The initial round of questions covered standard medical, family, and social history–type things. She dispensed with them quickly and moved on to the good stuff.

"The remaining questions will be personal ones relating to your sexual preferences, activity, and function. Is that acceptable?"

"Fire away."

"Are you single?"

"Yes."

"Heterosexual, homosexual, bisexual, or transgendered?"

"Lesbian." This was getting interesting. She didn't look up as she checked off boxes in various columns.

"Would you say that you have any kind of sexual dysfunction?"

I hesitated. "Does *not enough* count as a dysfunction?" I thought, but I couldn't be certain, that the corner of her mouth twitched.

She looked up and met my eyes, her face completely composed. "We're more interested in such things as anorgasmia, premature orgasm, or anything which you would define as a physical or psychological problem associated with sexual activity."

Anorgasmia. Thank God for those two years of Latin in high school. But didn't the absence of orgasm follow from my question regarding not enough? *Oh. Anorgasmia as in "the inability to have" orgasms.*

"No. Given the opportunity, I don't have any problem coming, and I generally have pretty good control." *Of course it's been so long, who can remember.*

"Good."

She made another little check mark.

"Do you masturbate?"

I bit the inside of my cheek to prevent one of those stupid responses such as "Is the pope Catholic?" and replied, "Yes."

"Frequency?"

"Yes. I mean…ah…three, maybe four times a week."

"You would be required to refrain from orgasm either with a partner or via masturbation for the duration of the study. Is that acceptable?"

"How long will the study last?" They were going to have to pay me a lot of money for this.

"I can't say how long your participation would be. It will really depend upon your response to the various stages. A week, possibly several."

"How will you know if I'm compliant?"

She still didn't smile, but her dark eyes twinkled. I was certain of it. "It's the honor system."

I grinned. "Agreed."

"Are you able to masturbate to orgasm while being observed?"

Her head was bent over the forms again, her pen raised above another little box. The study was getting more and more interesting by the second, and I was still only in the interview stage.

"Yes. Who's going to be observing?"

She raised her head. "I am."

I have no idea what showed in my face when my clit twitched. Hers revealed nothing.

"If you feel uncomfortable and prefer not to participate in the study," she said gently, "just say so, and we'll terminate."

"I'm okay so far." I took a breath and forced myself to relax. "Is there going to be group activity?"

"Only in the advanced stages of the study, and you may never get to that point." She leaned back in her chair and her voice took on a professorial tone. "The study is designed in levels, or tiers, and these strata are individualized depending upon the study subject's reactions to the test stimuli. Your responses to the early stages will determine the direction and nature of subsequent interactions. Although each set of study criteria is standard, not every subject will participate in the same sequence."

Somewhere out of that doctor-speak I think I got that what was going to happen would depend a lot upon how I performed in whatever it was we were going to be doing. I was curious, more than curious. Intrigued and not a little turned on. I'd always considered myself a sexual adventurer—at least I'd never said no without trying something. *Okay then. Masters and Johnson, here I come.*

"That sounds fine."

Another sheet of paper appeared. More blanks, columns, and boxes.

"Do you object to viewing sexually explicit images?"

"No."

"Do you find sexually explicit images arousing?"

"Sometimes."

"Do you use sexually explicit images as a tool during masturbation?"

Fortunately, I don't blush easily, and we were far beyond that point already anyway. "Sometimes."

"Literature, photographs, or videos?"

"All of the above."

Check. Check. Rustle. Rustle. I was getting wet. The interview couldn't have been more clinical. The subject, however, was getting to me. Talking about sex in any form, in any fashion, under almost any circumstance, turns me on.

"Have you ever used sexually explicit images during mutual masturbation with a partner?"

"How many people are going to read the interview form?"

Dark eyes met mine. "One. Me."

"Yes, I have."

Dr. Adams put down her pen and placed both hands on the desk, her fingers lightly clasped. She regarded me with a slight tilt of her head and a contemplative expression. "If at any time, for any reason, you want to withdraw from the study, you simply need to tell me. I will be administering all of the tests and collecting all of the data."

Well, that got me nice and hard. Administer away. The sooner the better. I nodded.

"I'd like to start tomorrow. Can you be here at eight a.m.?"

"Yes."

"It's important that you be well rested and in as relaxed a state as possible. I know that may be difficult, but I assure you, there is nothing painful associated with any part of the study."

"I promise to go to bed early." I grinned.

"And please remember the stipulation regarding abstinence."

How did she know that the first thing I wanted to do as soon as I was alone was jerk off?

"Got it." After all, she wouldn't know. If I did it. Or if I just happened to be thinking about her when I did.

❖

At five minutes to eight the next morning, I knocked on the door with the small plastic nameplate that read *V. Adams, PhD*. She answered immediately. Today, she wore a moss green shell, hemp-colored linen trousers, and low-heeled brown boots. Her lustrous hair was still severely tamed and tied back with a scarf.

"Good morning, Ms. Burns."

I laughed. "Could you call me Robbie? There's no way I'm going to be able to get excited if you keep calling me Ms. Burns."

"Get excited?" she asked as we started to walk down the hallway in the direction she indicated with a raised hand.

"Well, the only reason I can figure for the questions you asked yesterday and the stipulation that I not jerk…ah, have an orgasm any time except during the course of the study is that I'm going to need to do it here."

"Let's save this conversation for later," she replied evenly. She removed several keys from her pocket and opened an unmarked door at the end of a hallway. Inside was one large room that held a leather recliner in the center surrounded by electronic equipment on rolling carts, a bank of video monitors, and a small glassed-in booth in one corner. From what I could make out, the interior of the booth was wall-to-wall equipment. I also saw a microphone and headset resting on the counter.

Dr. Adams checked the thermostat just inside the door and turned it up. The room was already quite warm. Not overly so, but, I realized, warm enough that someone without much in the way of clothing would be comfortable. Holy shit.

"Today," she said as she gestured to the recliner, "we are just going to establish baseline values." She leaned down, opened a drawer in the bottom of the oversized chair, and withdrew two white sheets, one of which she spread out over the recliner. Turning to me, she held out the other. "Please undress completely and sit here. I have a few notes to make before we begin."

"I guess you'll tell me what I need to do when the time comes, huh?"

"Don't worry. You'll be given specific step-by-step instructions."

Under other circumstances, that sounded like it could be fun. The psychologist went into the tiny booth and must have adjusted the lights, because the overheads in the main room dimmed and the booth went completely dark. I knew she was in there, but I couldn't see her. It's not like I didn't know what was coming. Ha ha. I took off my clothes and got as comfortable as possible, which wasn't very. Hell, my clit was the only thing that *wasn't* twitching.

It couldn't have been more than five minutes before Dr. Adams came out of the booth.

"Ready?" Her voice was soft and warm. Or maybe it was just the room.

"All set." I think I sounded pretty confident. Usually, I *am* pretty confident about most everything, particularly sex. At the moment, I was terrified I might have performance anxiety and blow the very handsome stipend she'd mentioned the day before. Besides that, I wanted to appear studly in front of her. Since she hadn't given me the slightest reason to think she had any interest in me whatsoever other than as a study subject, I couldn't say why.

"Good. I'm going to be connecting you to various monitoring devices," she said as she rolled the carts containing the electronic equipment closer to me.

Most of what she attached I recognized—EEG pads on my forehead, EKG leads on my chest, arms, and legs, and a blood pressure cuff around my left biceps. When she motioned me to lean forward so she could run a thin flexible strap around my chest just below my breasts, I asked, "What's that for?"

"Respiratory rate and excursion."

She was so matter-of-fact about everything that I relaxed without even realizing it. Until she reached for the little alligator clamp with the thin red and blue wires trailing from the tiny jaws. We're talking minuscule, maybe a half an inch long—too small to be a nipple clamp. I had an uneasy feeling about where that was going to go.

"Uh…"

"This morning," she said conversationally as she stood beside me with the tiny clamp dangling from her fingers, "we're going to take baseline measurements during unstimulated masturbation."

"Isn't that an oxymoron?" I couldn't take my eyes off the little tiny teeth along the edges of the little tiny clamp. "Where are you putting *that*?"

"First question first."

I swear to God I heard a hint of laughter in her voice.

"*Unstimulated* in the sense that we won't be using any visual aids. I'd simply like you to masturbate to orgasm unassisted by anything other than…well, whatever you ordinarily use in terms of mental encouragement."

"So fantasizing is okay?" I was struggling not to inch my way over to the far side of the chair. Escape was impossible at this point, unless I wanted to hotfoot it buck naked through the psychology building with electrodes hanging off my body.

"Absolutely. This," she said, indicating the device in her hand, "is a tonometer, designed to measure turgidity in the clitoris." She must have seen my pupils dilate. "I promise, you won't even know it's there."

"Where *exactly* are you attaching it?" There was no way she was closing those little tiny serrated jaws over the head of my clit. No fucking way. Not for a *million* bucks.

"Just distal to the junction of the corpora with the clitoral body."

"Translation?" I asked through gritted teeth.

"On the shaft at the base."

"Okay. Go ahead." As I was fairly sizable, I figured that thing couldn't hurt *too* much.

"I'd let you do it," she said evenly as she drew the sheet up to my waist and leaned over, "but it needs to be precisely positioned to pick up small variations in pressure."

I tried not to tense my thighs and told myself that this was just like a visit to the gynecologist's office as she spread me open slightly with the fingers of one hand and exposed my clitoris. Oh yeah, right. I never get a hard-on in the gynecologist's office. To my acute embarrassment, the second she touched me, I got stiff. Great. Then I felt the slightest bit of pressure in my clit, which only excited it more, and she was straightening up again and adjusting the sheet. I stole a look at her face, but she had that same dispassionate expression she always wore. I was just another lab rat.

"Comfortable?"

"Oh yeah. Perfectly." I was afraid to move in case something fell off. "There's a problem, though."

One of her perfectly sculpted brows rose infinitesimally. "Oh?"

"How am I supposed to masturbate with that little thing on my clitoris?"

"It may fall off, depending upon how vigorous you need to be. But all data is information. Try not to pay any attention to it."

Right. It should be a piece of cake to jerk off while attached to a bunch of machines with a beautiful woman watching and a little probe attached to my clit. No wonder they paid a lot of money for this.

"It would probably be helpful if you closed your eyes while I check the calibrations." Then she turned and walked away.

I leaned my head back and did as she said. Behind my closed lids, I could tell that the room got a little bit darker. I can't say that I was relaxed, but part of me was enjoying this. I'd liked her touching me, even in such a distant and clinical way. Her fingertips were soft and smooth and gentle as she'd attached the electrodes, and she'd handled my clitoris like she knew what she was doing. I pictured her eyes and the honeyed timbre of her voice, and my clit twitched.

"What are you thinking of?" her voice asked from a speaker somewhere nearby. The acoustics were good, and she sounded as if she were sitting right beside me.

Something told me that the only way this would work was if I was honest. "You."

"What about me?"

"That I liked it when you touched me."

"Would you touch yourself now, please."

"Is there a time limit?" I slid my hand under the sheet and rested my fingers on the inside of my right thigh.

"Not at all. Take as long as you need."

I kept my eyes closed as I tentatively ran my index finger between my labia and up to the undersurface of my clitoris. It was nice. It's pretty much impossible to touch an area with that many nerve endings and not feel something. Plus, my clitoris was intimately associated with my hand, and I had pretty strong conditioned responses to fondling it. Namely, I got wet after a few seconds, and if I fooled with it for much longer than that, I wouldn't be able to stop until I came. Out of habit, I carried those first droplets of thick moisture on the tip of my finger up to the head of my clitoris and circled it. I got a little harder. Intending to squeeze the head, I inadvertently brushed the alligator clamp with my thumb and caught my breath.

"Sorry."

"No problem. You're doing fine." There was a beat of silence where all I could hear was my own rapid breathing. Then she murmured, "I'd like you to tell me on a scale of one to ten how you would rate your current level of excitement. Ten being imminent orgasm."

God, she had a great voice. And a fabulous face. And she was watching me jerk off. The sudden realization that I was going to come in front of her, *for* her, hit me in the stomach like a sledgehammer. I soaked my hand.

"Robbie?" Her voice caressed me. "On a scale of one to ten?"

"Six." Christ, how did I know? I was hard as stone and wet and every time I ran my trembling fingers over my clitoris, my hips gave a little jump. Somewhere in my increasingly addled brain I wondered what that little device clamped around my clit was measuring now. Because I certainly felt like I was going to explode. I just needed something to get me past the last bit of nerves. "Can I use two hands?"

"Of course. Do whatever makes you feel good."

I slid my other hand between my legs and toyed with the swollen labia, manipulating my clitoris faster between thumb and index finger. I was starting to get that going-to-need-to-come-soon feeling. I picked up speed with my hand and moaned quietly.

"One to ten, Robbie."

"Eight," I gasped. I curled two fingers inside and rubbed my clit harder. "Oh fuck." I hadn't meant to say anything, but I couldn't help it. I pushed my hand deeper, working the head of my clit frantically with my fingers. My stomach gave a warning clench. "Jesus. *Nine.*"

"I know you're close," the soothing voice, so much like a touch, whispered from somewhere nearby, "but if you can, talk to me as you approach orgasm. Tell me what you feel."

I whimpered, I think. I turned my head and opened my eyes, trying to see her through the glass. I imagined her watching me, then I imagined her touching me, and the fingers stroking me rapidly to orgasm became hers. "I'm so hard now, need to come so much. Almost there…close…oh yeah. Just touch me right there…a little faster, baby. Just a little harder." I arched my back as the tendrils of orgasm fluttered and curled along my spine. Blinking, I tried to focus on where I knew she must be, but my vision was tunneling as every cell in my body ignited. "Oh God. Ten. Oh yeah, please, *ten.*" I surged upright in the chair as my stomach convulsed, my hand moving so rapidly as I forced out the orgasm that the clamp flew off my pulsating clitoris. "Jesus," I groaned, "I'm coming."

Somewhere in the middle of it all, the top of my head blew off. God only knows what the EEG must've shown. I fell back, boneless, my breasts heaving under the chest band, my heart hammering. It took me a minute, maybe more, to get my breath back. When I was finally able to open my eyes, she was standing beside me. Her face, that beautiful elegant face, was still and serene. But her eyes were liquid and hot.

I smiled, a lazy sated smile. "I screwed up."

"How?" Her question was curious, her voice throaty and low. She didn't move a muscle, but I felt her fingers on my skin.

"You can't use those readings for baseline values." I was still trembling and my voice was shaky. I sucked in air and tried to calm down. "That wasn't my normal self-induced orgasm." I shivered as an aftershock gripped me. "Oh man, not at all."

"Oh?"

I nodded, still unable to lift my head, watching her face. She was smiling now, too. "I shouldn't have thought about *you* while I was doing that. It turned the ten there at the end into a hundred."

Something close to pleasure flickered across her face and then disappeared behind her composed, clinical expression. But she couldn't hide the satisfaction in her voice.

"Well, I shouldn't worry too much about that. That's what bell curves are for."

And I couldn't wait to plot the next data point.

PHASE TWO: VIDEO

"Do you think we could switch our sessions to the evening? When I come this hard, I'm not much good for anything for a while, and I have classes in the morning."

Two days later, the words still reverberated in Van Adams's mind, as did the memory of how Robbie had looked when she said this. She'd still had that soft, dreamy look in her eyes that she got immediately after she orgasmed. Over the previous three weeks, they'd had multiple sessions in the lab to establish baseline control values for the psychosexual imprinting study that Van was conducting in the experimental psychology department. By the time Robbie had made the request to change the meeting times, Van had come to recognize how Robbie looked throughout the various stages of arousal, at the moment of climax, and during the postorgasmic recovery stage. She knew how Robbie moved as she climbed through the levels of excitement to orgasm, the restless twitching of her limbs and progressively more frantic thrusting of her hips keeping time to the rapid movement of her hand beneath the crisp white sheet. She knew the way Robbie sounded, from the first slight hitch in her breathing to the soft moans and muttered pleas as she masturbated to orgasm.

Of course, Van's only interest during phase one of the study was in Robbie's physiological responses during the phases of sexual arousal and release as indicated by heart rate, blood pressure, brain wave pattern, respiratory rate, and pressure gradients in the erectile tissue in the clitoris. These readouts were carefully tabulated and charted, means and standard deviation calculated, and time-response graphs constructed. The fact that as Robbie approached orgasm she always turned her head to stare into the glass observation booth where Van sat watching, or murmured soft endearments while holding Van's eyes in the midst of her climax, or smiled up at Van as if they shared a secret while she relaxed in the aftermath of her release, had no bearing on the study and was therefore of no consequence. Besides, Van knew she was invisible inside the isolated chamber where she dispassionately observed, methodically recorded, and neutrally hypothesized.

I know she can't see me. Then why does it feel as if she is looking at me, for me? Why do I feel as if she's reaching out to me as she's coming? She's very beautiful when she orgasms—so expressive and free, unlike anyone else—

Van pulled herself up short, appalled by the way her concentration had wandered. Subjective observations such as these were of no clinical value. She was only interested in reproducible data. That's what the monitors and recording devices were for. After all, sexual arousal and orgasm were merely physiologic responses that could be explained and measured like any other natural phenomenon. Of course, there was a mind-body relationship, which was why the effect of various stimuli on response rates and magnitude were of scientific and behavioral interest. That was part of the purpose of the study. How a particular individual might appear during those brief moments of neuronal discharge and vasospasm had no bearing whatsoever on her work. And therefore did not warrant her consideration.

The alarm on her wristwatch sounded. 6:25 p.m. Robbie would arrive any minute. She was always on time. Of course, this was their first evening session, and perhaps she had been held up by something. A last-minute phone call, an engrossing dinner conversation, an afternoon interlude with a lover.

What are you thinking? She said she was single. Plus, she knows she can't engage in sexual activity outside the study because it might lead to orgasm. And she's not allowed to orgasm with anyone except me. Van gasped at the misstatement. *Except during the study. I meant she's not allowed to orgasm except during the study.*

Van slipped her fingers over the inside of her wrist and felt for her radial pulse. Sixty-eight beats per minute. Elevated. And she felt a little flushed.

Oh dear. I need to get to the gym more. I'm clearly out of shape. No wonder my stress-reduction biofeedback patterns are erratic.

She jumped as a knock sounded at the door, and her heart rate, low under any circumstances as a result of her daily two-hour workouts on the cardio circuits at the gym, skyrocketed to an unprecedented eighty beats per minute. She half stood as she called, "Come in."

The door swung open and Robbie Burns stepped in. Blond, blue-eyed, rangy and lean in low-cut Levi's and a navy blue rugby shirt, she looked confident and relaxed. Grinning, she said, "Hey. Reporting for duty."

"I didn't know you considered it work," Van riposted before she could stop herself. It wasn't her habit to engage in casual conversation with the study subjects. There was just something about Robbie that disrupted her usual modus operandi.

"Well," Robbie remarked, her grin spreading, "usually I don't consider coming a chore."

Van frowned. "You haven't given any indication that your performance during the study periods is significantly altered from your usual—"

Robbie laughed. "Hey, relax, Doc. I was just kidding. After the first time, when I was a little embarrassed just at the beginning, I've been *performing* pretty much the way I always do."

"I'm sorry. I didn't mean to put it that way."

Robbie tilted her head, observing Van curiously. "Is something wrong?"

"No, of course not." Van colored slightly, then looked down and hastily gathered her papers. "Shall we get started?"

"Sure. Can't wait."

As they walked down the hallway together toward the lab, their shoulders inadvertently touched. Van stepped hastily away, aware of a faint tingling in her arm. *Curious. She must have unusually strong galvanic skin conductivity.*

Robbie gave Van another inquiring look, but said nothing. Once inside the lab, Robbie automatically moved to the large reclining chair, stripped down, and settled beneath the white sheet. She watched as Van assembled the various monitors and began attaching electrodes.

"What's on the agenda for tonight?" Robbie asked as Van slid a hand beneath the sheet and applied the sticky pads across her chest, ending just below her breast. Her nipple came to attention as the edge of Van's hand brushed over it several times while arranging the leads.

"We're going to begin phase two with the addition of visual stimuli."

"Yeah?" Robbie tilted her head back to see Van's face. *I don't need anything beyond looking at you.*

Van found herself staring into deep blue eyes, mesmerized by the faint flickering of the dark pupils. She knew that involuntary constriction and dilation of the pupils occurred as an autonomic response to sexual arousal, and the small but powerful minicameras mounted in the ceiling had recorded that very same activity in Robbie's eyes in the seconds before and during orgasm. Van had expected to see that response in Robbie's eyes, but she hadn't expected to be so captivated by it. She'd replayed the tape after their first session a number of times to correlate the pupillary response to other biologic indicators, but she'd had to force herself to focus on the data and not on the mesmerizing expression in Robbie's eyes as she'd come. Even now, when that liquid gaze was merely holding hers, she felt an unusual stirring in her depths. *The thermostat must be set too high. It's very warm in here.*

"Dr. Adams?" Robbie asked softly.

"Yes?"

"Um…" Robbie looked down.

To her horror, Van realized that her hand still rested on Robbie's breast beneath the sheet. She snatched it away. "Just let me get the rest of these attached and we'll get started."

Robbie sat perfectly still while Van attached the EKG, EEG, blood pressure cuff, and thoracic strain gauges. She tensed as Van reached for the last monitoring device.

As Van drew the sheet up along Robbie's thighs toward her waist, she asked, "Is there something wrong?" As she had done during the previous sessions, she reached down to attach the small alligator clamp of the clitoral tonometer and found that her study subject was already in an advanced state of arousal. Robbie's clitoris was nearly fully erect and glistening with the evidence of considerable excitement. "This is a problem."

"Sorry," Robbie said with a small sigh. "I, uh…"

Straightening, Van kept her face expressionless, but her tone was involuntarily strident. "Did you orgasm before coming here?"

"No!"

"Sometime earlier today?"

"I wish," Robbie muttered.

"I'm sorry?" Van's tone was decidedly cool as she wondered exactly who had put her—*her*—study subject in this state.

"No, I didn't," Robbie said adamantly, wondering what the hell had gotten into Dr. Adams.

"I thought it was understood that you were to avoid situations that would lead to sexual arousal, and particularly pre-orgasmic turgidity, for the duration of study."

"Pre-orgasmic turgidity? Oh. You mean a hard-on."

"Regardless of the term," Van said acerbically, "you were to avoid such...circumstances."

"I *have* been—well, except during the night, when I can hardly help it." Robbie's voice rose in defense. "I told you at the interview that I'm used to getting off more than a couple times a week. I can hardly be held accountable if I have a damn wet dream."

Van's eyes narrowed. "That's another issue we are going to have to discuss later. For the moment, however, I'd like an explanation..." She caught herself starting to hyperventilate and ruthlessly lowered both her heart and respiratory rates with a series of biofeedback exercises, then continued, "For my notes. Since your baseline state of arousal is obviously elevated at the moment, I need to account for that in my data."

"You were touching my breast."

"Excuse me?"

"You were touching my breast, and it made me wet."

"That's all it took?" Van's voice was soft, surprised. *You're so hard. So wonderfully wet.* She forgot her biofeedback exercises and her heart rate shot up again. "I barely touched you."

Robbie's eyes found Van's again. A faint flush colored the psychologist's neck and the small triangle of skin left bare by her open collar. "That was enough."

"Is that...customary?" *Do you respond that way when other women touch you? How many women have elicited that response? How many have made you come?*

"No, it's not *customary*," Robbie replied irritably. *Even the sound of your voice is a goddamned turn-on.* She'd been looking forward to the session all day, and not just because she enjoyed the part where she got to get off with a beautiful woman watching. She liked the way Van would sometimes forget herself and look at her with a tender expression, and very rarely, with one of blatant desire. She knew Van was unaware of it, but it pleased her. She'd been primed for pleasure when she walked in that night, and for some reason, Van was in a bitchy mood. But it didn't change the fact that she was beautiful and sexy and she made Robbie hot. And the more Robbie looked at her, even with the heat of anger in her eyes, the hotter she got. Her clit jerked as if to remind her she had things to attend to. "And if you want to get that clamp on me before I'm a lot more than *turgid*, you'd better do it now."

Van held out the small clamp. Throat dry, her fingers trembling slightly, she said, "You'd better do it. I'm afraid if I touch you...it will only skew the data further."

"Oh yeah." Robbie drew a shaky breath and imagined those long, slender fingers closing around her clit. Stroking her. She got harder as her clit throbbed in time to her racing heart. "It'll skew something all right."

Van glanced at the EKG trace and frowned. "You haven't taken anything, have you?"

"What?" Robbie muttered as she held her clit, which jumped and jerked between her fingers, and closed the small clamp around the shaft at the widest part of the base. The pressure felt so good that her eyes closed involuntarily.

"Stimulants of any kind. Amphetamines?"

Robbie's eyes snapped open and she glared at the psychologist. "Fuck, no. Why?"

"Because your heart rate is very erratic and your respiratory rate—"

"I'm *excited*."

"We've established that, but these readings are indicative of a very high level of adrenergic—"

"I need to come," Robbie said softly. "Please...can we just do... whatever."

Van stared and struggled to collect herself. In what she hoped was a clinical tone, she asked, "What level?"

"Seven out of ten." The study required that Robbie rate her approach to orgasm on a scale of one to ten, with ten being imminent orgasm. Anything over five meant she was pretty well along and would be uncomfortable if she didn't eventually come.

"*Seven*," Van said in surprise. "How did that happen? We haven't even gotten baseline readings, and I still have to run the visual stimulation program. In addition—"

"It's you."

"What?" Van's words were barely a whisper.

"I...you...fuck. You make me hot." Robbie shifted restlessly. The insistent tug of blood and heat in her clit was making her a little nuts, and the device ruthlessly squeezing the *turgid* shaft did not help matters.

"Oh dear," Van murmured. "That's going to complicate things."

"*Things* are a lot more than complicated already," Robbie grumbled, stroking her inner thigh beneath the sheet with fingers that trembled. "I'm going to explode here. Can you just go take some readings or something so I can...take care of *things*."

Without a word, Van crossed the room, entered the booth, and dimmed the outer-room lights. As she turned dials and flipped switches, paper began to scroll and tracings flickered on small LCD screens.

"Before we begin," Van said in a detached voice as her eyes moved over the various readouts to ensure that everything was in order, "let me explain today's exercise. I'm going to show you a random video clip of a couple making love, which I would like you to watch through to the end without self-stimulation. If, however, at any time during the viewing of the video you feel the urgent need to masturbate, including to the point of orgasm, you may." She glanced through the glass. Robbie was only a few feet away on the other side and clearly visible in the soft cone of light from the recessed spot just above her chair. Her lids were heavy with arousal and the rapid rise and fall of her small, firm breasts beneath the sheet correlated with the level of stimulation indicated by Van's measurements. "Your present readings are all well above baseline. How do you feel?"

"Like I won't last two minutes," Robbie said with a small grin. "If you're going to show me porn, I'll probably come fast. I'm already so jazzed."

"Don't worry about that—just do your best. We'll work with the results we obtain," Van said dispassionately. "All data is information." She entered a series of numbers into the computer and watched as a randomly selected film segment appeared on her screen. The same segment would be displayed on a larger monitor where Robbie could see it. A young woman reclined on a floral sofa, a shaft of sunlight bathing her naked breasts. Another woman, also naked, rested between her spread thighs, kissing her exposed sex.

Robbie's readouts spiked, and Van felt an unanticipated wave of jealousy, which she immediately suppressed. *It's only a movie. She told you in the intake interview that videos excite her.* Still, she couldn't help but look up from her console and watch Robbie as the video played. Robbie's hands, outside the sheets now and resting on her thighs, moved restlessly in small circles as she watched the screen. Inside the booth, Van heard the rapid ping of the heart rate monitor. She glanced at the respiratory readout—elevated as well. The pressure readings from the clitoral tonometer were nearly at the maximum of any she had previously measured. *She's escalating quickly.*

"What's your level?" she asked through the microphone.

Robbie's eyes flicked from the screen to the booth. "Closing in on nine out of ten."

On the film, the reclining woman moaned and thrashed her head, obviously close to orgasm.

"Jesus," Robbie muttered. "I really want to come."

Van's stomach tightened as she continued to make notations on the graph sheet spread out in front of her. Robbie's voice was thick and heavy, and the sound of her desire was like honey in Van's veins. *Touch yourself. I want to hear you come.* Van bit her lip to hold back the words. In the background, the moans and cries from the video heightened in pitch and increased in volume. A flicker of movement in the other room caught Van's attention, and she saw Robbie's right hand slide beneath the sheet. She knew without looking that all the measurements had peaked. Some had even gone higher than any of her previous recordings. The sound of Robbie's heartbeat raged in the small space. *Do it. God, I know how badly you need to. Do it.*

The clitoral tonometer spiked again, higher this time, at the same time as Van heard Robbie's desperate whisper.

"I'm sorry. I can't wait."

Van watched, the monitors forgotten, as Robbie arched her back and groaned at the first touch of her fingers on her clitoris. On the small screen to Van's right, the woman climaxed with a sharp cry. Van felt a surge of wetness between her thighs. She kept her hands on the counter. Robbie moaned again, and Van's vision blurred.

Five minutes later the film had ended and the monitors screamed around her. Van looked at the readouts, all of them nearly off the chart, and still, Robbie had not achieved orgasm.

"Robbie," Van said quietly. "What is it?"

Robbie slumped in the chair, panting. "I can't do it. Fuck, I just can't get there."

Van's eyes flickered over the measurements. *Oh God, you poor baby.* "Do you want me to run another film?"

"No," Robbie gasped, straining to see into the dark booth. "Could you come out here for a minute? Please."

Concerned at the note of pain in Robbie's voice, Van hurried to her side. She stopped herself just as she extended a hand to touch her sweat-streaked face. "Robbie?"

"It's okay," Robbie murmured, her eyes riveted on Van's face as she began to stroke herself again. Within seconds, her hips lifted, her back arched, and she cried out sharply, shuddering into orgasm. When the tremors slowed, she regarded Van with a lazy grin. "I just needed the right picture."

Van trembled, her hands clenched at her sides, her senses reeling. *You can't know what a beautiful picture* you *make like this.*

"You okay, Doc?" Robbie inquired gently when Van said nothing.

"Just fine," Van finally replied, smiling inwardly. *Picture perfect.*

PHASE THREE: ASSIST MODE

Dr. Vanessa Adams sat in the observation booth next to Dr. Gloria Early, her co-investigator in the sex-stim response study, taking notes on the progress of one of their advanced simulations. She barely registered the beeps, pings, and buzzes of the plethora of electronic equipment that surrounded her. Her attention was riveted on the study subject in the support module in the center of the lab. The recliner that had previously occupied that space had been replaced with a body-conforming platform sporting adjustable side panels that swung over the top once the subject was seated. The panels slotted together to form a partition between the subject's upper and lower body so that she could move comfortably from side to side, but she could not see or touch anything below her waist. A video monitor was suspended from the ceiling and displayed continuous images of erotic encounters. The subject had been provided with a remote control to stop, reverse, fast-forward, or replay any sequence she desired.

"Fifteen minutes of video viewing and the arousal index is still low," Early noted conversationally. "Just below five."

"We know she's a responder," Van replied. "Can you bring up the comparative tracings from the first run?"

Early opened a file and displayed the data on an adjacent screen. Van scanned it quickly.

"Baseline readings are essentially the same, but the escalation curve is much flatter this time. Acclimation effect," she suggested. "The subject appears to have a blunted response to the repetitive viewing of the same or even similar erotic images."

"Hmm. Somewhat analogous to acquired drug tolerance."

"Yes! Exactly." Van made a note. "We should compare the baseline values among subjects to the rapidity with which acclimation occurs—it may be that those with a lower threshold to visual excitement will maintain an accelerated effect, even upon restimulation." Her eyes shone with enthusiasm. "It's possible that we've been looking at the response curve in reverse—it may not be the *stimulus* which is significant, but the receptor sensitivity in the subjects themselves." In the midst of her theorizing, she envisioned Robbie stretching and smiling as she luxuriated in the afterglow of orgasm. Her *baseline arousal state is very high—higher than any of the others—and she has shown no blunting in the response curve with time. In fact, she seems to reach the critical threshold in an accelerating pattern. The last time—*

A series of beeps drew both investigators' attention back to the monitors.

"Ah, good. Level six," Early observed. She flicked the switch on an intercom near her elbow and buzzed the adjoining lab. "Sonja? Come in—she's ready." Then she keyed the mike to the experimental chamber and addressed the subject. "The assisted-mode phase is about to begin. You may continue to watch the video, fantasize, or employ any other maneuver to enhance the experience. You may also give instructions if there's something you need. All set?"

"Yes," the subject responded, her voice already heavy with desire. She indicated no uncertainty or nervousness, but kept her face turned toward the monitor and the continuous loop of sex. Her attention did not deviate even when a door on the opposite side of the room opened and closed quietly.

A short-haired brunette in a forest green blouse and trim, tan slacks moved quickly across the room on a path that kept her out of the line of vision of the study subject. She quickly knelt by the foot of the slightly elevated modular support in the deep vee that had been removed from the far end of the table. The subject's spread legs were comfortably supported on extensions on either side of the access area. Sonja placed her open hand on the subject's left inner thigh. The subject jerked infinitesimally, and her heart rate rose to 120 beats per minute.

From where she sat, Van could see both women. She didn't need to see the readouts on the recorders in the booth to know that the subject was substantially aroused. It was apparent in the combination of dreamy pleasure and anxious anticipation on her face. Van watched as Sonja began to run her fingers up and down the inside of the woman's thighs, stopping each time just as her fingertips brushed the swollen sex.

"Oh," the subject sighed. "That's nice."

"Level seven," Gloria Early commented quietly.

"Yes, expectancy escalating."

Van heard the subject moan, saw her hips clench and twist slightly, and watched on the close-up videocam as Sonja traced her fingertips over the glistening, slick folds. The subject gasped, her legs tensing. Heart rate 140.

"Steady progression," Van murmured, unable to look away from the subject's face. Over the microphone came the sound of increasingly rapid breathing and faint sporadic moans. "Level?"

"Eight."

Sonja leaned closer and blew warm air teasingly across the erect clitoris that she held exposed with her thumb and finger. The subject groaned, staring down the length of her body, unable to see the woman pleasuring her. "Oh God. That feels so good. Are you going to lick me? Oh, I want you to."

"Clitoral spike," Early stated. "Ninety percent of previously recorded maximum."

Van glanced at the close-up image on the monitor by her left hand just in time to see Sonja place a tender kiss on the tip of the reclining woman's clitoris. The soft wail that followed sent a shiver down Van's spine. She could imagine the tense clitoris and the exquisite softness of warm wet lips enclosing it. For an instant, she imagined herself with her lips circling Robbie's erection.

Oh God, no! I can't do this now.

Sonja eased the clitoris between her lips and gently, rhythmically sucked. The clitoral tonometer spiked again to maximum levels and maintained that pressure.

"She's pre-orgasmic," Early said clinically, marking a note on a scrolling piece of paper that showed sharp spikes and a steady line very near the top of the page.

As Van watched, the subject closed her eyes, arched her back, and opened and closed her fists with desperate intensity.

"Please, please. Oh, suck me harder, please. I'm going to come soon. Make me come now…make me come."

Early started a counter on the computer to record the time in hundredths of a second.

Van could almost feel the rigid clitoris swell against her tongue and taste the ripe promise of passion. She fought back a groan when Sonja delicately danced her fingertips over the moist swollen flesh of the woman's sex, dipping her fingers into her and then out as she licked and sucked.

The subject sobbed softly and thrashed her head back and forth. "Oh yes! Oh, I'm going to come…oh, it feels so good! Oh… I'm coming now…" Her pleas ended in a final desperate wail as her heart rate screamed into the 160s and the strain gauge clamped to her exploding clitoris flew off. The stimulation levels peaked and fluxed at max levels as Sonja gently licked and kissed the erratically pulsating clitoris throughout the subject's orgasm, not stopping until the woman in the study module lay quiet and utterly spent.

"Oh, that was so nice," the subject murmured thickly, her breathing finally evening out as her heart rate slowly returned to baseline. Her clitoris remained swollen but without the tonometer, Van could not judge the rate of her recovery.

"We'll have some data skews at the end here," Early remarked with moderate irritation. "We'll have to find a better way to attach the clitoral strain gauge."

Van couldn't take her eyes off the subject's face, having never seen anything as beautiful as a woman in the first seconds after orgasm. As she watched, Sonja placed one more delicate kiss on the tip of the woman's clitoris and then glided away.

"Do you feel that you could achieve orgasm again?" Early asked after keying the microphone. "We'll need to reattach the tonometer to run another sim."

The subject slowly turned her face toward the booth. "Not yet. I...oh God...it was really intense. I don't think I can go again for a while."

"Okay, no problem, then," Early said. "Take your time getting dressed, and we'll go over the details of your next session when you're ready to leave." She reached out and dimmed the lights in the outer room before turning to Van.

"What do you think? Time to run a parallel sequence with another subject?"

Van thought of Sonja or one of the other lab assistants expertly manipulating Robbie to orgasm. Her head ached.

"I might have a slight problem."

❖

"You *can't* just fire me," Robbie protested as soon as she sat down in Van's small, cramped office. She'd been rehearsing her arguments for a week, ever since the morning that Van had contacted her to inform her that she would no longer be needed for the study. She'd been so stunned at the unexpected call and the surprisingly devastating news that she hadn't even asked why.

Van leaned back in her desk chair and placed her reading glasses carefully on a pile of reprints that she had been perusing without actually reading. "It isn't an issue of being fired. Your role in the study is simply over."

"Why? I know that the study is ongoing and that there are other sessions that I haven't participated in yet."

"We don't use each subject for every stage in the study," Van answered patiently with a small shake of her head. She was ridiculously pleased to see Robbie, even though she had been studiously avoiding all thought of her since their abrupt final phone call. At least she'd been *attempting* to avoid thinking of her. Even immersing herself in work didn't completely obliterate the heart-melting innocence of Robbie's smile or the terrible, wonderful memory of her arousal.

"Well, you *have* to let me back into the study. Because something's broken and it needs to get fixed."

Van's brows furrowed as she leaned forward. "What are you talking about?"

"I can't come anymore."

"What?"

Robbie leaned forward as well, and had the desk not been between them, she would have put her hands on Van. Somewhere. Anywhere. She was desperate to touch her. "I. Can't. Come."

"Have you tried?" Van colored. "Well, of course you have, or you wouldn't know that you couldn't." She took a breath, not truly wanting the answer to her next question. "Are you speaking of orgasm during an intimate encounter with a partner?"

"No." Robbie ground her teeth. "I'm talking about me, myself, and I. My *usual* partner. The one who never fails to give me exactly what I need in whatever time frame I happen to be in the mood for. A five-minute quickie for medicinal purposes. An hour of slow satisfaction with my favorite erotica collection."

"Ah," Van began delicately. "Sometimes, we can experience a temporary decline in libido or a transitory inability to achieve…"

"Nope. Not me. *Never.*" Robbie took a breath. "I know exactly what the problem is."

"What?" Van asked anxiously. She couldn't bear the idea that Robbie might have something seriously wrong.

"It's the study."

"The study?" Van paled. "That can't be the problem. The study does nothing more than record your responses to sexual situations or stimulation. It doesn't…"

"I'm imprinted."

"Imprinted," Van echoed as if she'd never heard the word before.

"Uh-huh. Imprinted. On you. I can't come without you."

Van's mouth opened to form a silent "Oh." After a moment, she swallowed painfully. "I don't think we've ever encountered that result before."

"Well," Robbie said matter-of-factly, "you can start writing the case report. Every time I start working myself up, things move along nicely, just like always. I almost get there. Almost. But when I turn my head and open my eyes for that final push, you're not there."

"I'll have to talk to my colleague." Van couldn't think. She was flattered, aghast, concerned, and terribly aroused. All she could see was Robbie turning toward her, searching with her eyes as her body quivered on the brink, and finding her, tumbling into ecstasy. The image was devastating. Devastatingly wonderful. "I'm not entirely certain how to reverse this phenomenon. I suppose we could try aversion therapy or behavioral modifica—"

"I've got a better idea," Robbie interrupted. "Let's go out on a date."

❖

"So what did she say?" Robbie's best friend TJ asked.

"She said," Robbie replied, straightening on the bar stool and assuming a clipped, formal tone, "'I'm afraid that won't be possible due to our previous professional relationship.'" Robbie licked the salt from the back of her hand, downed the shot of Cuervo Gold, and sucked the lime with angry relish. "She's driving me nuts."

"What are you going to do?"

"I'm going to camp out on her goddamn doorste—"

"Uh, Robbie," TJ interrupted. "Didn't you say that she was about five-six with legs for days and a face like a Greek goddess?"

"Yeah. So?"

"Do Greek goddesses wear denim jeans and high-heeled boots?"

Robbie snorted. "Not the last time I looked." With her good humor trying to resurface, she swiveled at the bar and followed her friend's gaze. The blood drained from her head and pooled directly between her thighs. Van threaded her way determinedly through the crowd toward them.

Her hair was down...

It was wavy. Beautifully thick and glossy and Robbie wanted to get her hands into it immediately.

…wearing the aforementioned denim jeans…

They were skintight and faded in just the right places and Robbie wanted to get her out of them immediately.

…and looking at Robbie as if she were the only woman in the room.

Robbie's heart danced in her chest, her stomach flip-flopped, and her clitoris shot straight into high alert.

"Van?" To Robbie's horror, the word came out with a squeak of disbelief. *Oh cool, Burns. Way cool.*

"Hi, Robbie."

From beside them, a voice interjected, "Hi, I'm TJ. I was just leaving. Nice to meet you."

"Nice to meet you, too, TJ," Van said without taking her eyes from Robbie's. "See you again sometime."

"Yeah, right. Right," TJ muttered as she made herself scarce.

Softly Robbie asked, "What are you doing here?"

"Looking for you. I called your apartment and one of your flatmates said you were probably here."

"Yes, but what are you *doing* here?" Robbie's eyebrows drew together into a frown. "This isn't part of the study, is it?"

The corner of Van's mouth lifted. "And what if it is? I thought you wanted back into the study."

"That's because I was desperate."

"Oh, and now you're not?"

As they talked, Van moved closer until her hips lightly pressed between Robbie's thighs. Her right hand rested on Robbie's left leg just below her crotch. The little space between them shimmered with the heat of their bodies.

"No," Robbie murmured, tilting her pelvis forward until her fly snugged against Van's. "*Now* I'm downright dying."

"Well…" Van allowed the weight of her body to rest against Robbie's while bringing her mouth close to Robbie's ear. "There *is* one part of the study we didn't get to."

"Whatever it is," Robbie replied as she circled her arm around Van's waist and pulled her tight into her crotch, "I'm in."

"We'll see." As she'd done that first day, Van whispered, "Follow me."

To Robbie's everlasting gratitude, Van's building was only a short block from the bar, and in five minutes they were climbing the stairs to the second-floor apartment. They'd said almost nothing on the brief, fast walk, but Van had reached down and boldly taken her hand. The shock of Van's skin against her palm had made Robbie gasp in surprise. Van had only looked at her and grinned.

"Come on. The bedroom is back here," Van murmured as she led the way through the apartment.

"Uh, what—"

"Don't worry." Van stopped and turned so abruptly that Robbie walked into her. When she did, Van put her arms around Robbie's neck and her lips on Robbie's mouth.

"Oh," Robbie groaned as she slid her tongue into Van's mouth. It was better than any fantasy, and she'd entertained more than a few lately with herself and Van in the starring roles. She would have been happy to stand rooted to that spot the entire night, stroking the inner surfaces of Van's lips, sucking the tip of her tongue, probing for the spots that made her arch and groan. The pressure in her belly was a constant distraction, but she was in no hurry to relieve it. Eventually, it was Van who drew away, gasping.

"We mustn't take this out of sequence. It will skew the data."

"There's some order to it?" Robbie sucked on Van's lower lip, then bit gently.

"Oh, yes," Van moaned. "A…definite progression. Mmm, you have wonderful lips."

Robbie's head nearly burst. She was so desperate for Van's touch that she wrapped her fingers around Van's forearm to guide her hand between her legs. As if sensing her intent, Van stepped away. Her eyes were glazed, her chest heaving.

"No. Not yet."

"Then when?" Robbie asked urgently. "God, I want you."

Van smiled knowingly. "Really. On a scale of one to ten…"

Robbie growled and took a step closer, reaching for Van's hips. "Seven."

Van backed away. "*Really.* Well. We should move on, then." With that, she turned and hurried into the bedroom. Robbie hesitated only a second and then bounded after her.

"Stand by the side of the bed, please," Van said in as even a tone as she could muster. All she wanted was to feel Robbie's mouth again and hear her deep soft sounds of pleasure. With hands that trembled, she caught the bottom of Robbie's T-shirt and lifted it off over her head. Her gaze fell to Robbie's chest and she moaned. "Beautiful."

"Touch me," Robbie pleaded, all semblance of pride gone. "I can't take any more."

Van nearly broke, but with her last remnant of control, merely reached out and unsnapped Robbie's jeans. As she pushed them down, she allowed herself the pleasure of trailing the backs of her hands over Robbie's thighs. "You forget, I know exactly how much you can take."

"You weren't touching me before." Robbie's nipples were hard, her hips thrusting into empty air as the passion beat through her depths. She managed to step free of her jeans, but her knees were threatening to give out. "Before I was only *imagining* it was you. I'm going to come standing here in a minute."

"On a scale of one to—"

"Oh God," Robbie moaned. "Nine. Please."

"Lie down on the bed," Van whispered, trembling. As Robbie did, Van began to undress. She watched Robbie's eyes, her face, the rise and fall of her breasts, knowing with certainty exactly what she was feeling. She knew every nuance of Robbie's arousal. When she inadvertently brushed her fingers over a bare nipple and it stiffened, Robbie moaned and smoothed the fingers of her right hand along the inside of her right thigh. Van recognized it as a move Robbie made involuntarily when she was highly aroused and needed to touch herself. Van smiled, stepped free of her slacks, and stretched out on the bed beside Robbie. She placed her hand in the center of Robbie's abdomen, circled over the tight muscles slowly, then gently brushed Robbie's hand away from her leg. "I can't let you touch yourself. You're already far too excited."

"You touch me, then," Robbie implored. "I'm dying."

Van caught Robbie's right wrist and guided her hand between her own thighs. Fighting back a moan at the first exquisite touch of Robbie's fingers on her skin, she murmured, "This is what we call…a parallel…simulation." Her hips lifted as Robbie's fingers dipped into the moisture between her thighs. She held Robbie's eyes, which were hazy and huge with arousal as she closed her fingers around Robbie's clitoris. "Follow me."

"Oh, Van, I won't last," Robbie gasped.

"You will." Van sighed and rested her forehead against Robbie's, welcoming the heat that flooded her thighs as she stroked Robbie and Robbie returned her caress. "Remember, I know you. Now, I want you to know me."

A minute passed, an hour, a lifetime as, eyes holding each other fast, they climbed past passion to the crest of wonder where pleasure transcended flesh. Shuddering, smiling tremulously, Van whispered, "Now, Robbie. Now."

As their hands blurred, Robbie pressed close, her vision filled with the image that never failed to carry her away. Van. So easy. So right. Only this time, Van was here with her, coming with her. Her eyes were liquid with pleasure, her face soft with surrender, her skin flushed with the first surge of release.

"Oh, Robbie, Robbie," Van breathed as she finally closed her eyes and slipped into orgasm.

"Ahh, yes," Robbie uttered as her bones melted and her muscles dissolved.

Finally surfacing, Robbie traced her fingers over Van's cheek and laughed quietly when Van caught her fingertip and sucked on it. "How many more stages of this particular experiment are there?"

"Didn't I mention that earlier?" Van sighed and stretched, a grin flickering on lips swollen with kisses. "This was just the pilot study." She snuggled against Robbie's chest, wrapping her arms and legs around her. "And you definitely meet the criteria for inclusion."

Robbie found the sheet with one hand and drew it over them while burying her face in Van's thick, soft hair. Closing her eyes, she murmured, "Well, Professor. Sign me up."

SKIN FLICK SEX

L ights!"
    The room was suddenly plunged into darkness, all except for the stark tableau in the center of a raised platform that held a bed, dresser, lamp, and not much else other than the two naked men crouched in the center of the rumpled pale-blue sheets. Blinding white light from the strategically placed stands around the sides of the stage set highlighted their sweat-sheened bodies in a merciless glare. The smaller of the two hunkered down on his elbows and knees, his face against the bed between his forearms and his ass in the air. A burly black-haired guy with a thin pelt of hairs lightly coating his shoulders and back knelt behind him. His thick thighs were encased in black leather chaps, leaving his ass bare. He gripped his stiff cock in his fist, poised with the head against the smaller guy's asshole.

"Cameras!"

My eyes hadn't adjusted to the darkness, but I could sense movement not far away, a shuffling of feet and an occasional muttered instruction or response.

"Action!"

The dark-haired guy grabbed the hips of the man below him and worked his cock into his ass. Someone grunted. Someone moaned.

I shifted halfway behind a pillar in the cavernous space and hoped I wasn't in the path of anyone who was more used to walking around in the dark than me. I figured I wasn't supposed to be there, but I'd only come inside to tell the crew that I'd parked the catering truck outside the warehouse. I guess the morning shoot was running late. As soon as I'd heard about this production from the driver who'd made the run the day before, I'd volunteered for the lunch run today. I mean, how often was I going to get a chance to check out a porn movie in the making? *Loaded Leather Lads*—all guys, but I figured sex was sex, and I'd gotten off plenty of times watching guys fuck and suck and blow each other. 'Course, usually I was sharing my viewing pleasure with a woman who was doing the same thing to me, but today I was just going to look.

The guy in the leather chaps fucked like a metronome, driving his thick, long cock in and out with the speed and regularity of a piston. The one on his hands and knees muttered *yeah* with every stroke. I flashed on an image of me on all fours while strong fingers dug into the bend of my waist and I strained to keep my ass up in the air. I could feel the slap of leather against the backs of my thighs while I took some stud's dick deep into my cunt. Shifting my hips restlessly, I gripped my crotch and tried to ease the tight denim away for my rapidly swelling clit.

"You're not supposed to be in here," someone whispered in my ear.

I froze, my hand still squeezed between my legs. Her breath was hot against my neck, and she smelled faintly of sweet sweat and something else—something that set my clit thumping harder against the inside of my jeans. Leather.

"Don't talk," she said in a low, throaty growl. "Just watch the show."

The guys had shifted position, and the big one in the leather chaps was lying on his back, his legs spread and his dick standing up. His crotch was toward the camera and I couldn't see his face, but it didn't matter—the waistband of the chaps and the cutaways on each leg framed a triangle around his dick and balls like a shiny black glory hole. The smaller one, blond I noticed now, faced the cameras and me. He straddled the big guy's body, braced his hands on those thick, leather-covered thighs, and lowered himself onto the flagpole. His own cock with its wide, black leather cock ring jerked between his legs. I jerked too and heard quiet laughter.

"You like a bit of cock."

It wasn't a question.

One arm came around my waist and with the other hand she gripped my wrist, pulled my hand behind my back, and crushed my palm into her crotch. Leather, slick and soft. I closed my fingers around the cock sheathed along the inside of her left thigh and she thrust her hips forward, pinning my hand between my ass and her cock. She was hard, would always be hard, would give it to me hard, as deep and as long as I needed it. She bumped her cock into my hand while both arms came around my waist again. One hand traced my forearm down to where my fingers still massaged my crotch, and she pushed my fingertips roughly into my clit. The ache spread into my cunt and I moaned.

"Unzip your pants. And remember to be quiet."

My breath was coming fast and I struggled not to make any more sound. Fortunately, the guys on the stage grunted and fucked so loud I doubted anyone else could hear me. I caressed the cock and imagined straddling her like the blond in front of me, my come sluicing onto her leather pants while I rode her until my cunt burst and I flooded her. I love the slick shine of come on leather. Hand trembling, I opened my jeans. I wanted to slam back on her cock just the way the blond in front of me slammed his ass up and down, up and down, up and down. I watched him and stroked her cock, the smooth leather a second skin skimming up and down the shaft.

When she slid her hand into my jeans and found my clit, my thighs went soft and I shot an arm out against the pillar to hold myself up. She rolled my clit between her fingers, soft and slow, and I bit my lip. I couldn't take my eyes off the cock across the room, flushed red and drooling pre-come as it bounced on his belly. She worked her fingers down either side of my clit and pinched. I whimpered. Hurt so nice.

"Quiet," she whispered.

I wanted to come really bad and I knew I wasn't supposed to. The guy on his back reached around to rub his hand up and down the blond's straining belly, then fisted his cock. The blond worked himself on the cock in his ass in short hard thrusts, all the time digging his fingers into the gleaming leather while the other guy jerked him off. I wanted it to be me, with her cock deep inside me and her jerking off my clit the way she was doing now. She was good, so good. She rubbed the head of my clit with the tip of one finger while she squeezed the core between her thumb and other fingers, pulling and rubbing in time to the guys fucking. I was creaming all over her and in another minute I was going to come in her hand.

Her face was slippery with sweat where she nuzzled against my cheek, and she was panting hard, pressed to my back. I still had a grip on her cock between us and she thrust into my hand making low, grunting sounds in the back of her throat. I wanted more, so I let go of her cock, yanked at her waistband, and got her zipper partway down before she shoved my hand away. She eased back and I rubbed my hand over her thigh. The leather was hot and supple, like I knew her body would be. A second later she slid her warm cock along my palm.

"Jerk me off while I make you come."

I shifted a little to one side with my hand cupped by the outside of my leg so her cock could slide through my closed fist. I tugged it forward, then pushed back, and her fingers convulsed on my clit. Across the room, the blond cradled his balls in one hand while the other guy kept up a steady jerk-off motion. I fell into step, pumping her to the same rhythm. Every time I pushed back, my fist slapped leather, and she said *uh*.

Close by in the dark someone muttered, "Get ready for the come shot."

She lost her rhythm then, her fingers clamped so tight on my clit that tears leaked from the corners of my eyes. My cunt pulsed the crazy way it does just before it explodes. The blond yelled and come jetted from his cock, a milky stream splattering on the leather chaps.

"Oh fuck," she moaned, "here I come."

I let loose in her hand but I managed to keep working her while she shuddered and groaned, her face buried in the curve of my neck, her fingers driving in and out of my cunt. All the while I was coming, I forced my eyes to stay open so I could watch the guys finish. The one underneath yanked his cock out of the other guy's ass, stripped off the condom, and pumped his cock. When he shot, my clit tripped right into another orgasm so hard and so hot I would have gone down if she hadn't been holding me so tight against her. The pleasure jolted through me, and I had to close my eyes.

When I opened them, the room was bright and my back was to the pillar on the side away from the set. I guess everyone else was crowded around the stage, talking and laughing. I shoved my shirt into my jeans and zipped up, took a deep breath, and plastered a smile on my face. Then I swung around the pillar and started toward the group.

A woman in a sleeveless black T-shirt and black leather pants separated from the crowd and met me halfway.

"I'm the production assistant," she said. "Can I help you?"

"I'm the lunch truck driver."

"Good. We worked up an appetite."

I glanced down at her crotch and she brushed her fingers over the hint of a bulge. The leather gleamed wetly when she moved her hand away. My come. Her cock. Leather slicked with sex.

"No problem." I met her eyes and grinned. "I brought enough for seconds."

FIRST SIGHT

Three pairs of eyes probed my naked flesh. Hers were remote—blank discs of impenetrable blue, so impersonal as to leave a chill in their wake. His were clinically appraising—studying me with curious neutrality, making me wonder if my heart still beat.

Only your eyes were alive—slow-dancing over the hills and valleys of my body, dipping into my secret places with unfettered abandon. The satin-covered marble beneath my thighs was slick and unforgiving. If I moved at all, every fragile dream would be exposed.

"Uh...we need a model...for the special class I take at night...to pose," you said, looking past me out the window to the quadrangle far below. "Nude."

I laughed. We'd been roommates for eight months, and you were still shy with me. I suppose it was because when we all showed up for the fall semester and got our room assignments, there'd been whispers about you. Lesbian, they'd said. Carefully polite, but with just that little hint of prurient excitement. Sure, everyone seemed cool about it, but you must have known that everyone was just waiting to see who would be in the bed across from yours, ten feet away, for the next nine months.

I sensed the others stare at me when first your name, then mine, was called. But I was watching you. Your eyes darted to my face and then away, and then cautiously back again. I was still looking at you when you finally searched my eyes for the answer. The uncertainty in your expression made me want to hold you, and I'd never felt that way about anyone before. I wanted to say, "I don't care what they say. I don't care who you love. Just don't look so scared." But I didn't know if the words would hurt more than help, so I said nothing. But I smiled, and that must've been all right, because you smiled back.

"Nude, huh?"

You nodded silently.

"Sure, I'll do it."

"Bend your knee up, please," the faintly accented voice of the instructor requested from just beyond my field of vision. "Very nice. Open just a little…yes, just like that. Perfect."

It was my fourth session, but only the first time I could see you clearly as you worked. I'd been aware of you before, sitting expectantly with charcoal in hand as I removed the white robe and let it drop behind me before settling onto the dais. The room was always very quiet as I bared myself, but the very first time, I imagined I heard a small hitch in your breath. You were careful not to look at me then, at least not until I could not see you.

You were always so careful around me. Careful not to walk in while I was changing. Careful to keep your eyes on the ceiling while we lay naked in our respective beds, talking late into the night or delaying the moment in the morning when we would have to separate. Careful not to ask me about the dates I went on, when I returned to find you still awake, sitting cross-legged on your bed with a book in front of you that I was certain you had not been reading.

I was careful too. Careful not to tell you that I'd rather stay at home with you, laughing about our day, or bitching about our classes, or confessing what we thought about and dreamed about and hoped for in our futures. I was careful around you the way I never was around the other girls, because I understood that you weren't like the other girls. And to treat you as if you were would have been cruel, as if I didn't know you at all. I didn't tell you I was a virgin, and I don't know why. I guess because you weren't like the other girls, and I liked that.

I liked that a lot, and sometimes, sometimes I wished that you would look at me as if I weren't like the other girls, either.

Once I became "the model," a breathing still-life, I couldn't watch you any longer. I was a prisoner, unbound but restrained nonetheless. I could not turn my head to see if the heat I felt building inside was the result of your charcoal tracing the line of my skin on your paper. And always, when I was finally released from my invisible bondage, you had already risen, hurriedly packing your things with a downcast gaze, rushing to leave. I was forced to walk home beside you as if I had not just spent an hour with the promise of your hands upon my body. We never talked about it, and you were so careful not to look at me.

Not so tonight. Tonight your eyes were everywhere.

Tonight, you'd shifted your easel to a new spot. I could look at your face, and you, it seemed, could look directly into my soul. You sat upon a stool, a rectangle of canvas propped upon wide-spread wooden legs the only barrier between us. Your face was unmasked, your emotions as exposed to me as my body was to you. Your hands moved out of sight, sliding over my breasts, down my belly, between my legs, with swift sure strokes. Your eyes, wide and dark and unknowingly hungry, swept over my body in the wake of your touch with far less restraint, grazing my nipples to hardness and teasing my inner thighs to a soft sheen of welcome. To everyone else I was a profile, an abstraction, a study in light and shadow. To you alone, I bled and breathed and quickened.

You did not know what your expression revealed, and I did not disclose what I saw, lest you hide your passion and your desire. Thus we sat, souls on display, pretending we were blind.

"Thank you, that will be all for tonight."

I read the disappointment in your face, felt the loss of our connection immediately. You did not, as you usually do, immediately begin to gather your charcoals and pencils. I rose slowly while the others prepared to leave. Within minutes, we were alone. I held the robe before me but did not yet put it on.

"You're not finished, are you?" I said at last.

You gave a start, as if surprised that I had spoken. Then you blushed.

"No." You indicated the canvas with a sweep of your hand, your voice laden with frustration. "Tonight was the first time I felt like I might capture some part of…you."

"Why tonight?" Although I knew.

You looked up from the image of me and into my eyes. "Because tonight was the first time I let you see me. Before tonight, you've been the only one brave enough to do that."

"All the other nights," I whispered as I moved closer, "you looked at me, but tonight, you touched me."

You nodded and I saw you shiver. Your voice when you spoke was urgent and low. "I could feel you lead my hands over your body, guiding me, teaching me." You held my gaze so desperately, your longing so open and pure, I ached. "I was almost there."

In the distance, I heard a door close as the others left. I let the robe fall, a ribbon of white gathering between us on the dark floor. "I want you to finish."

You stared for an instant, a soft groan escaping from somewhere deep inside, then you turned with outstretched hand toward your charcoal.

"No." I grasped your wrist and brought your hand to the center of my chest. The edges of your palm nestled against the inner curve of my breasts. "This way. I want you to look at me. I want to watch you looking at me."

Your fingers were hot and trembled on my skin. Oh God, you whispered as I shuddered.

I focused on your face as you softly traced my breasts, my heart pounding wildly as the wonder rose in your eyes. You stepped closer until your jeans brushed my thighs and you brought your thumbs to my nipples, fingers splayed to cradle the weight of my breasts. I tilted my head back as pleasure bowed my spine and when you put your mouth on my neck, warm and wet, I made a sound I'd never heard before. A whimper, a plea, a paean of delight. My legs quaked, and I sagged into you, trusting that you would not let me fall.

You pressed your face to my throat, your breathing ragged, while your hands, those sensitive wonderful hands, explored my body with slow reverence. I was your canvas and you painted me with desire.

"Don't be careful anymore," I begged. "Tease my nipples. Touch me. Touch me before I shatter."

You whimpered then, long fingers clamping around the hard points of my breasts. Sharp, pure, delicate pain. My clitoris hardened and ached. I braced my arms on your shoulders and sought your mouth with mine, needing you somewhere far deeper than my skin. Your cheeks were damp, and I kissed away your tears. You drove a thigh between my legs, and I soaked the denim. Seconds, minutes, hours passed as we thrust and moaned and gasped, until I couldn't stand the slightest barrier between us. I curled my fingers in the thick damp hair at the back of your neck and put my mouth against your ear.

"I need you. I need you inside me."

With your mouth fused to mine, you wrapped an arm around my waist and turned me until my hips hit the stool. I sank gratefully upon it and you pushed between my legs, one hand knifing high between my thighs. I arched to take you in, and you hesitated, fingertips dipping into me, but going no further. I framed your face with my palms, my fingers trembling over your cheekbones and your mouth.

"I've been waiting for you," I whispered. "Please."

You kissed my fingers as you parted my swollen flesh, caressing my clitoris with swift, hard strokes, making me come. So close now, I succumbed to the hunger in your eyes as you slid deep inside me. Filled with you, surrounding you, coming for you, I saw what you hadn't wanted me to see all these months.

Desire. Passion. Love.

You touched me, and, finally, I saw.

A FLASH OF GOLD

I feel like I'm in college again." I surveyed the common bathroom and shower facilities and shuddered. Cold tile floors, toilet stalls that undoubtedly didn't lock, and one huge cubicle with showerheads on three walls. At least the pungent bleach smell was oddly comforting.

"Well, you are in a college dorm, after all." Taylor dropped her equipment bag and bent over the sink, one shallow basin in a long row of them set into a stainless steel counter beneath a smudged rectangular mirror.

"I don't know why I let you talk me into coming back every summer."

"Because you love to have five days of uninterrupted cruising." She splashed cold water on her face and neck. We'd been in weapons class all morning in a poorly air-conditioned gymnasium, and we were both dripping with sweat.

"Ha. Five days of martial arts hell is more like it." Her position afforded me a very nice view of her spectacular ass. It always looked good, high and firm and tight, but in her slightly baggy white cotton karate pants, it was downright mouthwatering. I sidled up behind her and wrapped my arms around her waist, leaned over her, and snuggled my breasts to her back and my crotch to her butt. Her hard, tough butch butt. I wiggled a little, enjoying the way it made my clit hum. "The next time we come to one of these training camps, we're staying in a hotel. I can't even find a working outlet for my hair dryer in here."

Taylor spun around in the circle of my arms and grabbed my hips, pulling me between her spread thighs. She nuzzled my neck, licking the salty streaks. "In another few hours, everyone will be too tired to notice what your hair looks like."

When she felt me stiffen, she wisely hastened to add, "And besides, baby, your hair always looks fabulous."

"Easy for you to say." I ran my fingers through her short, thick black hair. "You don't have to do anything to yours."

She laughed and tugged up the blue silk tunic top I had worn for my tai chi swords exhibition. "One of the many advantages of being butch."

"Oh yeah?" I bumped my crotch into hers and she gave an appreciative grunt. My clit had revved up to full force now. "What are the rest?"

"This, for starters," Taylor muttered as she pushed my sports bra aside and latched on to my nipple with her teeth. She tugged and sucked at the same time, and I gushed come all over my thighs.

"Honey," I protested halfheartedly, "someone might come in."

She turned her face, rubbing her cheek over my breast, and grinned up at me. "Since when do you mind anyone watching?"

"That one time out on the balcony, and she was too far away to see all that much anyway." I remembered lying on a lounge chair outside our hotel room while Taylor fingered me to orgasm. Just when I was about to come, I looked across the courtyard into the hungry eyes of a woman who stood statue-still, staring at us. I came so hard that time I almost flew off the chair. I moaned now, a heavy feeling in my stomach, but I kept my tone light. "And truck drivers getting a three-second glimpse while you do me in the front seat of the car don't count."

"But you like thinking they can see me getting you off, don't you?"

"Maybe." I pushed my breast back into her mouth. "And you don't?"

"Mmm." Taylor worked my nipple around and palmed my other breast, squeezing and twisting gently.

"Stop it. You know that makes me need to come." I pulled on her hair. "Come on, honey. Let's go to our room."

Taylor straightened, easing her thigh between my legs. "We have another class in twenty minutes."

I cupped her crotch, dug my thumb and forefinger into soft cotton, and scored a direct hit. Her eyes went wide as I jerked her clit. "Ten minu—"

The door swung open and a woman about our age hurried in. I got a two-second snapshot image—blonde, small and trim, pretty—before she stopped dead and blurted, "Oh. God. So sorry." Then she turned around and rocketed out the door.

Taylor laughed. "Oops."

"Great." I started to move my hand from between Taylor's legs, but she slapped her palm over mine and humped her hips encouragingly.

"Do me like that a couple more times and you'll make me come."

"Really?" I nipped at her chin, then centered myself, relaxed the muscles in my forearm, and used my hips and thighs to pivot my body easily out of her grasp. "Hold that thought."

Taylor groaned and slumped against the counter. "Who ever said butches get to call all the shots."

"I can't imagine," I said sweetly, then caught her hand and tugged her toward the door. "Time for class."

The rest of the afternoon was taken up by nonstop workouts until 6:30 when it was time for dinner in the—surprise!—campus cafeteria. Since summer classes hadn't started yet, the fifty of us martial arts practitioners had the place to ourselves. The scenery was way better than the food.

"I'm going to skip the evening session," I said, pushing away my plastic tray. "My legs are already stiff, and if I don't take it easy, I won't be able to train in the morning. I'm going to take a shower and go to bed."

"Good idea. I'll come with you."

Taylor stood and gallantly collected our trays and utensils and bussed them to the conveyor against the wall. I grabbed our gear bags and followed her upstairs. We stowed our bags in our room—two twin beds, how quaint—and headed down the deserted hall toward the showers. I flicked on the overhead lights just inside the bathroom and, blinking against the fluorescent glare, immediately shut them off. Even my eyes were tired. A few scattered security wall lights provided enough illumination to see by, and I started for the shower enclosure, stripping as I walked and tossing my clothes in a heap just outside the cubicle. Taylor grabbed towels from a stack by the door and followed me. The warm water felt like heaven, and I sighed with gratitude as my tight muscles began to unwind. I'd forgotten how hard it was to train nonstop for hours, especially now that my crazy call schedule made it difficult for me to work out as regularly as I once had.

"Turn around," Taylor said, "and I'll wash your hair."

"I adore you," I muttered, leaning both hands against the wall. I felt Taylor's breasts slide over my back as she lathered shampoo into my hair. Her strong fingers stroked my scalp in deep, wide circles. I moaned and dropped my head back against her shoulder. "Don't stop. Ever."

Taylor laughed and wrapped one arm around my waist, scooping a handful of suds onto my breasts with the other. She massaged my chest with the same firm circles, caressing my breasts, her thumb pausing to flick each nipple as she passed. I heard her breathing pick up.

"I'm too tired, honey."

"No you're not." Taylor bit down on my earlobe, then sucked the hurt away when I protested weakly. My body was so relaxed I was afraid I might dissolve into a puddle on the floor. But when she circled her index finger in my navel, my clit twitched.

"Mmm, I felt that."

"Oh yeah?" Taylor fanned her fingers between my legs. "How about that?"

"Honey, don't tease." I turned my head and bit her neck.

She hissed in a breath and rubbed her crotch over my ass. Then she slid two fingers down my cleft and circled my opening. "I'm not."

"Oh Jesus, Taylor." My cunt rolled and my thighs went soft. "Then fuck me if you're going to."

Taylor growled and pushed me up against the wall, her arm between me and the cold tiles, her fingers buried in me, her crotch humping my ass. "I'm. Gonna. Make. You. Come."

Every word was bitten off, her hand and hips thrusting in time to the harsh syllables. The water streamed over our heads and I drifted on a mist of steam, a storm gathering in the pit of my stomach. I was just starting that smooth glide to a deep come when I heard a thin cry float above Taylor's labored grunts. "What was—?"

"It's nothing," she gasped. "Oh shit, baby. I'm gonna come all over your ass."

Her hips jerked and her fingers hit that sweet spot high up inside me and I came in her hand, my eyes half closed and blurred with water. I thought I saw a flash of gold at the edge of the steam clouds, but I was too far gone to be sure.

Taylor collapsed against me, panting, and it's a good thing she did because I needed her weight to hold me up.

"God, honey," I moaned.

"Yeah."

She kissed the back of my neck and eased her fingers out, stroking my clit as she passed it by. I was still so sensitive I came a second time, twitching and swearing at her. She laughed. When I could move, I turned and kissed her.

"Did you hear anything…odd…right at the end?"

"When I was coming?" Taylor regarded me incredulously.

"Uh-huh."

She tugged the towel from the hook and draped it around my shoulders. "No, but I'm pretty sure I saw God."

The next few days passed in a blur of pain and exhilaration. We fell into bed at nine o'clock and were up at six to start all over again. Once or twice I noticed the blonde who'd walked in on us that first morning in the bathroom staring at us in the cafeteria or during the rest breaks between training sessions. I thought at first she was cruising Taylor. Most femmes and not a few butches usually do. But then I saw her sitting on the sidelines while I was performing a tai chi form and Taylor was nowhere around. I swear she was fucking me with her eyes.

On the morning of the last day I woke Taylor an hour before everyone else usually got up.

"I've had enough of group living. Want to join me for a shower?"

She rolled onto her back and stretched, the muscles in her abdomen tensing as she bowed off the bed. She always looked just like that when she came with my lips fastened around her clit. I skimmed my fingers up the inside of her naked thigh and patted her cunt.

"Of course, you can always sleep an extra hour if you don't want to play."

"Fuck that," she said, jumping up.

We grabbed clean sweats, and I peeked out the door. The hallway was empty. I looked at Taylor's naked body.

"Race you."

We ran bare-assed naked down the hall and careened into the bathroom, trying to be quiet but laughing the whole way.

"We probably woke up the entire floor," I said. "Let's claim the showers before anyone else shows up."

We'd just stepped under the warm spray when I heard the door open. I looked at Taylor and grimaced.

"So much for our playtime."

"Says who," Taylor whispered and pulled me to her.

Her mouth was on mine before I could utter a protest. Then her tongue was in my mouth and her hands were squeezing my ass, and my crotch was doing a thing of its own, rolling and grinding over hers. Part of my mind was listening, but heard nothing. I hoped whoever had come in was only using the john, because Taylor knew exactly how to get me lethally horny in seconds. I heard another sound, like a half-strangled cough, and this time when I saw a flash of gold out of the corner of my eye, I saw the face that went with it. I pulled my mouth away from Taylor, who moved to kissing my throat, and stared into the eyes of the blonde who had been watching us all week. She was leaning against the wall just inside the shower. She was still watching us. And she was naked.

"Honey," I murmured.

There must have been something in my voice because Taylor left off sucking on my neck and followed my gaze. No one moved for an eternity. Then the blonde spoke.

"Please don't stop."

Taylor extended one arm and turned off the shower, then pushed me gently back against the wall. While she lowered her head and covered my nipple with her mouth, I kept my head turned toward the stranger. Her gaze dropped to my breasts and she unconsciously brushed her fingers over her own tight nipples as Taylor kissed and sucked on mine. The blonde's face was dreamy, her skin flushed a beautiful rose.

"Bite them," I murmured, loud enough for our audience to hear. When Taylor did, I cried out. The pain and the pleasure shot to my clit and I wanted to come. The blonde's breasts rose and fell rapidly, and she had both nipples clamped between her fingers now, tugging and tweaking them. My voice came out sounding breathy and thick when I spoke to her. "It feels so good. If I let her, she can make me come this way."

"Not yet," the blonde implored urgently. "Please don't come yet."

I laughed. "I'm taking requests."

Her face contorted for a second as she swept her hand down her belly and into the blonde strands between her thighs. So softly I could barely hear her, she whispered, "Come in her mouth."

My hips twitched and I was afraid I might go off just from the needy look on her face. Taylor must have heard her too, because she groaned and dropped to her knees. She wedged her face between my legs and lapped at my clit with long, hot strokes. Her arm was pumping between her legs, and I knew that she was jerking her clit in time to the movements of her tongue.

"Go slow, honey," I keened, my clit so hard I was afraid it would burst. "You're going to make me come."

Taylor flicked at my clit, dancing her tongue under the hood. I wanted to come so bad, but I wanted something else even more. I fixed my gaze on the stranger, staring at the slender fingers sliding through the blonde delta a few feet away.

"Let me see your clit," I gasped.

With a whimper, the stranger opened herself with one hand, pressing down so that her hard, deep ruby clit jerked upright, exposed and glistening with her juices. I felt Taylor turn her head for an instant, and then she was sucking me even harder. I rested my head against the wall. I was losing my grip on the terrible pressure building in my cunt. "I'm going to come soon."

"Me too," the blonde cried in a high, thin voice. She kept her clit visible with one hand, squeezed between two fingers like a bright shining stone, and rubbed it furiously with her other hand, pinching and tugging. "Oh, I'm going to co...me."

Taylor groaned, her hips jerking, and I flooded her mouth with hot come as my clit jumped between her lips.

When my belly stopped heaving, I smiled weakly at the blonde who had slid to a sitting position, her head lolling lazily and her hand still clamped between her thighs. I caressed Taylor's face where she rested her head against my stomach. "Get up, honey. Let's take a shower."

"Just turn the water on," Taylor murmured, her eyes half closed. "I'm good here."

I fumbled for the dial and turned it to hot, then beckoned to the blonde. After a few seconds' hesitation, she rose unsteadily and stepped close to us.

"You sure you don't mind?" she asked softly, suddenly shy.

I shook my head. "This is one time when three is definitely not a crowd."

BY THE LIGHT OF THE MOON

"Come on, J.," my best friend Trudy said. "We need a fourth."
I set a glass of wine by her elbow and glanced at the object
in the center of the card table, then at the three women eagerly studying
me. "I never heard there was a quota."

"Come on," she whined, half cajoling, half hurt. "You said you'd
play."

"No," I said with exaggerated politeness. "I did not say that. I said
you were all welcome to hang out here and watch the eclipse."

That particular night was one of those rare confluences of science
and superstition, when even ordinarily rational people surrendered to
mysticism. It was All Hallows' Eve, the moon was full and bright in an
otherwise inky-dark sky, and there was about to be a total lunar eclipse.
Everywhere around the world, I was certain, Wiccans danced naked
in tree-bordered glades and pagans prayed to the goddesses of yore.
That was fine with me, and I sincerely hoped that they had a magical
experience. My problem was that three of my good friends sat with
a Ouija board poised between them, waiting for me to join them and
summon a spirit from across the great divide. Presumably, the Ouija
board was the vehicle to open the gate between our world and the other
dimensions that some believed coexisted side by side with our own.
Trudy insisted that everything was conspiring to ensure our success.
Success at what, I wasn't entirely certain.

"You three go ahead. I'll light the candles."

I turned off the room lights and opened the drapes, exposing the
floor-to-ceiling windows in the French doors, beyond which lay the

gently rolling slope of lawn behind my house. The moon was a huge, shimmering globe above the treetops, and silver light immediately suffused the room with a warmth that was tangible. Even as I watched, a tiny sliver of midnight inched its way over the edge of the moon, marring its perfect beauty. I struck a match to the candles in several ornate silver candleholders that had been my grandmother's, knowing that in just a few moments, the room would be cast into total darkness. When I finished, I turned to find three sets of eyes still regarding me hopefully. With a sigh, I took the fourth seat at the table. I wasn't entirely certain of the source of my reluctance, and it seemed churlish to ruin their fun.

"Well," Trudy began with an eager note infusing her soft Southern accent, "y'all put your fingertips lightly on the planchette. Now remember, don't press too hard."

The instant my fingertips touched the smooth, varnished wood, I felt it. Some shift in the air. A faint tingle in the back of my throat. The barest stirring of blood deep, deep inside me. The sound of my own heart beating magnified inside my head. Of course I knew that it was only the involuntary rush of epinephrine prompted by my surprise as a faint breeze flickered the flames in the candles on the far side of the room. Breeze? It was early fall in New England. I didn't leave the windows open at night. I would have searched for the source of the cool breath against my face if all of my attention had not been riveted to the Ouija board. As I watched the planchette rock gently back and forth in a small semicircle, I heard Trudy's voice, muffled and soft, as if she were speaking from a great distance. For some reason, I could only catch every few words through the low hum in my ears.

"…friends…welcome…visit…lonely…"

One after the other, the candles guttered and went out. The moonlight, which moments before had illuminated the room nearly as brightly as sunshine, was quickly fading. I knew without looking that the shadow of the night now nearly covered the face of the moon. The planchette vibrated, sliding in an ever-widening circle on the board, jumping from letter to letter too quickly for my eyes to decipher. Was it spelling something in its frantic race from place to place, or merely reflecting the chaos of our own hidden secrets and desires?

"…waiting…"

My arms shook with the effort to keep the small pointer from flying into the air. Energy poured through my fingertips, along the avenues of my muscles and nerves, stirring anticipation in my depths. Anticipation that was surprisingly sensual, as if some memory of a touch long past had been awakened. The darkness was so complete I could see nothing, the silence so dense I could hear nothing, not even the shuddering breaths of the women beside me. And then, with crystal clarity, I heard her voice.

"Can you help me?"

The planchette stopped moving. Someone gasped. In the same instant, a dull thud registered in my overstimulated yet strangely sluggish brain. I froze, my heart seizing. Then the sound came again.

Knocking.

"There's someone at the door," I said in a surprisingly steady voice, lifting my fingers from the pointer.

"Don't answer it," Trudy said sharply.

One of the candles burst into flame, and I could see my friend's eyes, open wide with apprehension.

"Spirits don't use the door," I murmured as I rose.

For some reason, I felt no need to turn on the lights, making my way through the home of my childhood with the certainty born of having traveled the same path countless times before. Without hesitation, I pulled open the heavy wooden door and looked out.

"I'm so sorry," she said. "Can you help me?"

Can you help me? I recognized her voice, but I was certain I had never seen her before.

"My car…I'm afraid I've run it into a ditch. It was so dark…"

Her voice trailed off, and I realized that I was staring. There was almost no light reaching the tree-shrouded porch through a sky so black that even starlight did not penetrate. For some reason that I failed to comprehend and did not bother to question, I could see her face clearly. It was an ordinary face, if you could call simple beauty ordinary. Smooth, high forehead, wide, faintly almond-shaped eyes that even in the dark I knew with certainty were a pale shade of blue, prominent cheekbones tapering to her soft but well-defined chin. She was slightly shorter than I and somewhere close to my age. She regarded me with a quizzical expression tinged with doubt.

"I'm sorry," she repeated. "If I could use your phone?"

"Where is your car?"

"Just up the road there." She pointed over her shoulder, although there was nothing to be seen in the dark.

"I didn't realize it was raining."

For a moment, she said nothing, then glanced at the damp blouse that clung to her slender shoulders and full breasts. With a self-conscious laugh, she plucked the material away from her body.

"It started just before I went off the road. The sky just opened and the entire storm struck at once. I couldn't see a thing."

I nodded. My porch was dry. From behind me, I heard the faint hum of conversation from the living room. My unexpected visitor shivered.

"Why don't you come in and get warm. I'll take a look at your car."

"Oh, no," she said immediately. "I'll just call a garage."

"Even if you can find someone to come out here this late, it will take several hours. And you look like you're freezing." I held the door open. "There's a guest room at the top of the stairs on your left. If you want to get out of your wet clothes, there's a robe behind the door in the adjoining bathroom. You can get a hot shower, too, if you'd like."

"That would be wonderful."

As she stepped inside, she ran her fingertips lightly down my forearm and whispered, "Thank you." It was the kind of innocent touch that people exchange every day. Innocent and casual. The swift surge of desire that seared through me nearly dropped me to my knees. I caught my breath in surprise, but she didn't seem to notice. I watched until she had climbed the stairs and disappeared into the dark hallway above. Then I returned to my friends.

"Who was it?" Trudy asked curiously.

"Just someone who needed directions."

In my absence they had begun to gather their things, and I made no effort to convince them to stay. I didn't question why I didn't tell them about my visitor. I only knew that I didn't want one of them to offer her a ride into town. I walked with them to the front door, gave all the appropriate responses about getting together again soon, and watched until their cars disappeared from sight. Then I removed the large battery-operated flashlight from just inside the foyer closet and walked rapidly down my driveway to the road. Less than two minutes later, guided by the wavering yellow beam of light, I saw where the bushes lining the road had been destroyed by a careening vehicle. Nearly the entire car was in the ditch, and nothing short of a tow truck was going to get it out. The driver's door stood open and, when I shined my light inside, I saw that the windshield was cracked.

In less than five minutes I had returned to my house. I hurried upstairs, and then was strangely reluctant to enter the guest bedroom. Tentatively, I knocked on the partially open door and heard a soft voice call for me to enter. Once again, I had no trouble seeing although the night outside was still pitch black and the room lights were off. She stood by the window, her back to me, in a thigh-length white robe that appeared far sheerer than I remembered. The outline of her breasts and hips was unmistakable. She did not turn as I approached or move at all as I rested my hands gently on her shoulders.

"Are you hurt?"

She leaned infinitesimally back against my body, her head resting lightly against my shoulder. "No."

"From the looks of your windshield, you must have hit your head pretty hard in the crash."

She reached up for my hands and drew my arms down and around her waist, relaxing fully into my embrace. Her hair smelled of shampoo and autumn. She fit perfectly into the contours of my form, as if we were reciprocal sides of the same mold.

"If I did, I don't remember."

"What do you remember?"

"Knowing that you would answer the door, that you would invite me in."

She turned in my arms and slid hers around my neck. The robe fell open as her mouth found my neck. Her lips were soft, warm, as they traveled along the underside of my jaw, her tongue a teasing ribbon of heat. I arched my throat, offering her more. Her teeth grazed my earlobe, and she laughed quietly.

"I can feel how fast the blood is racing through your veins. I'm not a vampire, but I almost wish I were."

"What are you?" I whispered, smoothing my palms over her collarbones and underneath the now nearly translucent material of her robe. Even as I watched, the last tendrils of material drifted into the darkness and left her pale skin glowing in the light of the moon.

"Does it matter?"

Her words were a wash of heat against my ear that stirred my blood even more. With a groan, I closed my hands over her breasts. They were full and firm and hot to my touch. She was no spectre, no illusion. She was flesh, and I wanted her.

I had thought myself a sensitive lover, but I barely recognized myself as I drove her back toward the bed with the force of my hands on her body and my tongue in her mouth. When she struck the edge of the mattress and fell, I was close upon her. I had a fleeting thought that it was I who had become the vampire. I hungered for her, thirsted for her, ached for the taste and scent and wild glory of her. Vaguely aware of her hands fisted in my hair, I pressed my fingers high between her legs and found her wet and open, waiting for me. Her passion inflamed me, and with my teeth against the tender skin of her breasts, I entered her—not slowly, not with the gentle care of a new lover, but with the raging need of the long starved at the first glimpse of nourishment.

She uttered a victorious cry and arched beneath me, tilting her hips to take me deeper. Fully clothed still, I scissored my legs around her thigh, squeezing to ease the pressure building dangerously deep inside me. I claimed her, hard and fast, but I knew even as she closed around me in the first shock of orgasm that it was I who was owned. Her pleasure tore through me like a sweet drug, curling beneath my defenses to burn its mark forever upon my soul. As she came, over and over, pulling me with her into sweet oblivion, I knew with absolute certainty that I would never again ache for the touch of any other woman.

When I awoke, the first hint of dawn limned the room. The bed beside me was empty, and only the ache in my body and the persistent beat of desire in my depths assured me it had not been a dream. The robe hung on the back of the bathroom door, just as I had left it weeks before. There were no stray hairs on the pillow, no scent of love or lust lingering on the sheets. Weak limbed and faintly disoriented, I retrieved my flashlight and stumbled out into the early morning in search of her. I found the spot where her car had left the road, but the bushes were intact and there was no evidence of an accident. I scoured both sides of the highway for a mile in either direction and found no sign of her. Exhausted, I returned and fell into a troubled sleep plagued by the sound of her passion and the memory of her desire.

When I finally emerged from the torpor that had suffused me for most of the day, I showered and dressed with the efficiency of an automaton. As I started downstairs, my eyes were drawn to a small white card on the table just inside the door. With a rush of wild anticipation, I clambered down the remaining stairs and snatched it up. My heart leapt into my throat. The words were scripted in a clear, delicate hand.

Call me.

Eagerly, I turned the card in my fingers and stared in astonishment. There was nothing else—no number, no address. Nothing. Slowly, I sat on the bottom step, turning the card over and over in nerveless fingers. The house grew still and dark around me, and still I sat. At last, I stood and opened the front door, half expecting her to be there. The night was nearly as deep as the previous one, although this time the moon was bright and gave no sign of ever having been overpowered by shadow. I waited, calling to her in my mind, but she did not come.

Finally, I closed the door and made my way through the silent house, more aware of being alone than I had ever been before. When I reached the living room, I stopped and stared, remembering that I had taken time the previous night for nothing but her. Slowly, I sat down at the card table and rested my fingers on the planchette in the center of the Ouija board. Closing my eyes, I let her memory take me. I saw her face shimmer with passion, felt the softness of her lips on my neck and the smooth silken heat of her skin beneath my fingers. The planchette moved, but still I kept my eyes closed. I listened to her cries of ecstasy, felt my own body stir and surge toward orgasm, only to falter before the peak. Without her, I would perish from longing. I trembled, breathless, so hungry for her presence I feared I would bleed.

"Please," I whispered. "Please."

"I'm here."

Her words were a wash of heat against my ear. I opened my eyes and found myself in the bedroom again, my arms around her supple form, nothing between us now but desire.

"What are you?" I asked, knowing that the answer did not matter.

"Not what others have named me," she whispered with her mouth against my breast. She moved beneath me, stirring the hunger. This time, I took her inside me as I lost myself in her.

Reality was the dream; she was past and future. I emptied my mind of all that had been as the first surge of orgasm captured us both and I followed her by the light of the moon into the dark side of the night.

BLESSED BENEDICTION

Every morning I get down on my knees and thank the powers that be that my girlfriend likes to get down on hers. She just doesn't like it, she loves it. She loves to give head. She doesn't care who knows it, either. This I know because I've heard her announce it more than once in the middle of a party when girls always seem to end up talking about sex.

"Danny has a gorgeous cock. I luvvvv to suck her off," my girl Shelby purrs.

She doesn't let on that she notices the raised eyebrows, some in question and others in disdain. She just lifts her chin and thrusts out her great tits and dares anyone to challenge her. No one ever does, so I wasn't expecting it when I walked up while she was making her usual pronouncement to three or four femmes at a late-night bash, and one of them, a haughty redhead, looked down her nose at Shelby and scoffed, "Oh yeah. That I'd like to see."

Damn if one or two others didn't murmur in agreement.

"Hi, baby," I whispered, sliding up next to Shelby and nuzzling her ear. As I wrapped my arm around her waist, I nudged the stiff cock in my pants against her thigh. "Having a good time?"

She turned into me and looped her arms around my neck, rubbing against me the way she does when she wants to be sure she has my attention, while she pushed her tongue halfway down my throat. Being a few inches shorter, her soft belly molded to the ridge in the front of my jeans and when she rocked back and forth, she more than got my attention. She got my undying devotion and anything else she wanted.

"Unh," I muttered just to be sure she knew.

When she got done kissing me, she leaned back, her arms now draped loosely around my waist and her hips still slow pumping between my legs and said, "These girls are in need of a demonstration. Do you mind?"

They say when your dick gets hard your brain gets soft, but a hard-on sure as hell doesn't make me stupid. I cupped her tight little ass in both hands and rubbed my rod up and down in the sweet divide between her thighs. "Whatever you say, baby."

Her eyes got all soft and liquid the way they do when she's getting turned on, and I knew my dick was doing its job, bumping her clit and making her wet. She curled her calf around the back of my thigh and ground into me until my legs started to shake. She could get me to the edge faster than a New York minute.

One of her girlfriends hooted and another one called challengingly, "So, Shel, you gonna blow that cock, or fuck it?"

Shelby took a shuddering breath and pushed me backward until the back of my knees hit a chair and I flopped down. My dick stood up like a rocket between my legs and screaming hot blood beat a crazy tattoo beneath it.

"Why don't you gather round and see for yourselves," Shelby said, talking to the femmes but watching me as she knelt between my thighs.

Oh yeah, blessed, blessed be.

Now, the reason my girl is such a great cocksucker is that she understands that a blowjob is as much about the show as it is about her hot, wet mouth sliding up and down my cock until I come in her mouth. She doesn't go down on me like it's a chore, or penance, or a favor. She turns giving head into a work of art. Every move is designed to let me know she gets off on my cock, and that teasing my rod makes her cream.

"You want me to suck you, baby?" Shelby murmured, scraping her nails down my fly. The vibration hit me where I live and my hips twitched.

"Yeah," I croaked. Fuck, just thinking about what she was gonna do to me twisted my insides into a knot. "Take it out."

She smiled and jerked me a little, the tip of her tongue gliding slowly between her lips. "Sure?"

"Come on, babe. Suck my cock." I sounded pathetic now, but I didn't care. A hard-on leaves no room for pride.

She laughed and the show began.

I love to watch her take my cock out. She never hurries, in fact sometimes she works me around inside my pants for so long, by the time she gets me in her hand I'm ready to blow like a first-timer the minute she tongues me. She popped the button on my jeans and pulled my T-shirt out. With her eyes still on mine, she rubbed my belly and kissed my cock through my jeans. I gripped the arms of the chair and lifted my hips, pushing my cock against her face. One of her girlfriends leaned against the side of the chair and draped her arm over the back, her fingertips grazing my neck. Her breast just skimmed my shoulder. Another one in a skirt so short I could see a pale pink scrap of silk covering her pussy crowded up on the opposite side. The bitchy redhead leaned down from behind Shelby and skimmed Shelby's long blond hair back from her face so everyone could see as Shelby mouthed my cock. The faded denim over the head of my dick was soaked from her sucking on it.

"Are you getting nice and hard for me," Shelby asked, running her fingers up and down the bulge in my jeans.

I humped her hand, jacking myself up good. "Locked and loaded."

She gave my cock a swat and warned, "Don't even think about shooting until I tell you you can."

I just nodded dumbly as she tugged down my fly. My white briefs, stretched taut over my straining cock, heaved out through the gap.

"Ooh," one of Shelby's girlfriends said breathily, "I'd like to see you deep throat that monster, honey."

"Just watch," Shelby replied and slid her dainty fist inside my Jockeys.

"Uh," I grunted, my vision going double as she wrapped her fingers around me and gave me a couple of quick pumps just to be sure I was ready for her.

Then she twisted her wrist left, then right, and pulled my cock out into the air. A good three inches stuck out past her fist, which she kept wrapped around the base. With her eyes locked on mine, she kissed the tip and swirled her tongue around the head.

"The thing about boys," Shelby said to her friends, pausing every now and then to lick the underside of my cock, "is that all they think about is shooting that load." She slid her fist up my wet cock until only the head was visible. "A really good blowjob takes time, so don't let them rush you."

She made a circle of her ruby red lips and sucked the fat, shiny mushroom tip into her mouth. At the same time, she skimmed her fist down my rod. Pressure surged between my legs and I mumbled something stupid like, *oh yeah suck my dick*, like she wasn't already doing it. She hummed a happy sound and slid another inch or two in her mouth and my legs started a little dance. Up. Down. Up. Down.

"Fuck," I muttered, because I was about to embarrass myself in front of all these girls.

"Now," Shelby said, letting my cock pop out of her mouth, "if you jack their cock and suck at the same time, they'll last about thirty seconds." While she talked, she kissed and licked the head of my dick and jiggled the shaft back and forth over the spot where she knew I was stiff and pulsing. "That's fine if you're doing them while they're driving or you wake up with their hard-on in your face and you haven't even had coffee yet. Then a fast jerk and blow works great, doesn't it, baby?"

Just watching her tongue flick at the head of my dick was making my belly tingle and I was close to letting loose even if she wasn't jacking me off. "I want to come in your mouth."

Shelby laughed and looked up at her girlfriends. "See? One-track mind."

"Suck her cock," the redhead ordered, her voice all tight like something hurt her.

"Yeah, make her pop," the one in the short skirt standing next to me muttered, and I caught a glimpse of a wet spot in the middle of her pale pink panties.

"Be good, baby," Shelby murmured, and then she really got down to business.

Inch by inch, she sucked my cock into her mouth until her lips met the circle of her thumb and index finger around the base of my shaft. Then she slowly slid all the way back to the crown, following her mouth with her hand. When she got to the end, she circled her tongue around the head and toyed with the tip before sliding her lips and hand back down again. My cock was slick from the wetness of her mouth, making it easier for her to jerk me off.

"You like that, babe?" I whispered, clasping the back of her head with my hand. I knew better than to force her down on it, but I liked to feel her moving up and down me. She rolled her eyes up to mine, her mouth full of my cock, and I read her answer in her glassy unfocused gaze. Knowing she got off sucking me off is what really did it for me. "You like my big cock down your throat?"

She pulled off long enough to mumble, "I love your cock," and then she slurped me down again.

Watching her lids get heavy and her cheeks flutter as she sucked and licked and worked me in her fist stoked the fire between my legs. I felt that coiled-spring-about-to-snap tension deep down inside and I couldn't help it, I had to fuck her mouth.

"You're gonna make me come," I gasped, my stomach tight as a board. "Suck it, baby, suck it. Suck it."

She picked up her pace, her hand and mouth a blur on my cock, the sound of her wet tongue lapping at me like thunder in my ears. She knew just how to grind my cock over the hard center of my need and I grabbed her head in both hands, getting ready to shoot.

One of her girlfriends reached down and rubbed my belly. "Oh damn, girl, she's about to unload right down your throat."

Shelby whimpered, her mouth too full for anything else, and my cock and my clit exploded. I yelled and my hips jumped, and Shelby pulled back just enough so I didn't choke her. She didn't let up on me, though, sucking and stroking until I collapsed in the chair, my arms and legs limp and useless.

She sat back on her heels and licked her lips, still slow-stroking my cock. She gazed up at her girlfriends, who all looked flushed and hot. "The best thing about sucking her off," Shelby said sweetly, "is that now she's not in so much of a hurry." She stood, hiked up her skirt and twitched her panties aside, and straddled my hips. Her eyes shuttered closed for a second as she took me deep, then she shuddered and sighed. "So she can fuck me just as long as I need her to."

And me? Hell, after a blowjob like that, she can have anything she wants. Halleluiah.

BINGO, BABY

Honey, let's go in drag tonight."
I looked up from the newspaper and tried to suppress a grin. Shelby is a femme. Not ultra-ultra-femme—no super-long nails or heavy-duty makeup, but she doesn't leave the house without eyeliner, either. Plus, she's small. Okay, petite. Her head comes to my chest. But she's perfectly built—every part of her—from her pert, high breasts to her nicely rounded, squeezable ass. But no one, nohow, would take her for a guy. Not even with a twelve-inch dick. "Sure, baby, but we only brought one dick."

It's tough packing toys when you travel, and the security people at the airport in Provincetown check everything. But then I guess they've seen everything, too, and there's no way I was going on vacation without my equipment. Still, I couldn't bring a complete complement either, so we both wouldn't be able to dress in full gear.

Shel's lush pink lips parted, her tongue peeked out as she ran it lightly over the velvet surface, and my mind turned to oatmeal. "We only need one. For me."

I got hold of myself and dragged my thoughts away from what she could do with that tongue. "Huh? What am I going to wear, then?"

"This," she replied sweetly as she held up a tiny swatch of leather.

I paled. "That's a skirt."

"Uh-huh."

"It's yours."

"Uh-huh."

"I can't wear that." I started to sweat. I started to look for the exit. I was in boxers and nothing else. I couldn't run.

"You might be taller, but your hips aren't that much bigger than mine. It will just be a little short."

"A little?" God help me, I actually squeaked. Just the thought of the skirt was making my clit shrink. "That won't even cover my crotch!"

"This will."

She held up a black satin thong, and my clit fell clean off.

"Oh no—no fucking way."

"Please, honey?"

Not fair. Not fair, not fair, not fair.

"Then we'll both be in drag," Shel pointed out, twirling the thong around her index finger. "It is drag bingo, after all."

Ordinarily, Shelby within twenty feet of a thong makes me want to start at her toes and lick my way to the top of her head, but today all I could think about was how much that tiny triangle didn't cover. Especially on me.

"We don't have any drag clothes that will fit you. My jackets are all too big." I tried a different tack. Shel was very particular about her clothes.

"Don't worry about me. I'll manage something." She leaned over the sofa, cupped my crotch, and resurrected my clit as she squeezed. "Didn't fall off, now, did it?"

"Ha ha," I muttered as she stuck her warm tongue in my mouth. It was a few minutes before I thought about much of anything except how clever her fingers were. When she stopped doing that wonderful up and down, round and round thing she was doing with her thumb, I groaned in protest. "Hey—what—?"

"Later, honey." She gave me another little tug and kissed the tip of my nose. My clit gave a little jump right back. "I have to get dressed. And so do you."

That effectively killed my healthy, happy hard-on once and for all.

I dawdled. I balked. I downright stonewalled. Okay, okay—I mostly sulked. I showered but then I refused to get dressed. Shelby ignored me as I sat on the foot of the bed staring at the floor, naked, immobile—a pathetic rendition of the Thinker facing a firing squad.

"What do you think?" Shel asked softly.

I turned my head and found myself eye to eye with a pair of black silk boxers that tented out suggestively over the gently bobbing dick inside. Now I have to tell you, I think wearing a dick is about the sexiest feeling I've ever had—except, of course, fucking Shelby with one. But I've never particularly been interested in being on the receiving end. Fortunately, Shelby has never complained. So I'd never seen her strapped before. I couldn't take my eyes off her smooth, tanned belly encircled by the broad waistband of the boxers and the jutting prominence below. She is such a girl in every way, and I wouldn't have believed how hot she'd look with all that girl power dancing inches from my face.

"Jesus," I breathed in awe.

She made a little sound like a contented purr. And then she reached down and wrapped her dainty fist around the silk-sheathed cock and gave it a little shake. My mouth dropped open and my clit stood at attention.

"Does it always make you horny right away when you put it on?" she asked a little dreamily.

"Usually, yeah," I muttered, watching her hand action speed up a little bit. "Baby?"

"Hmm?"

"If you want to jerk off with that, come a little closer and I'll help."

"Oh no." She laughed knowingly, giving the dick one final tug before letting go. "You just want to distract me so we miss bingo."

"That was the furthest thing from my mind," I protested. It was true, too. In that moment, all I could think about was holding on to her ass and putting her dick in my mouth. *In my mouth? Jesus Christ. What's happening to me?*

"Come on, honey. Stand up. Let me dress you."

My brain was still a bit addled, and without thinking, I complied. The next thing I knew, I was wearing a sleeveless mesh top that was so tight my nipples nearly protruded through the tiny holes, the black satin thong that barely kept my clit covered, and the leather skirt that hit right at the bottom of my butt cheeks. I don't know why she bothered to put me into clothes at all. I took one look in the mirror and almost fainted.

"I can't go out like this."

"Sure you can. I promise your butch credentials will not be revoked."

I turned, ready to take a stand, and got a good look at her as she buckled a thin black belt around her waist. She'd gone for the simple *GQ* look, and it worked perfectly on her. She wore an open-collared black silk shirt tucked into tailored black trousers with dress shoes and the belt. She'd slicked back her short blond hair and wore no makeup. She resembled an androgynous Calvin Klein model, the ones that I always feel a little bit guilty about staring at. I glanced down. She looked like a handsome young man with a very substantial hard-on. *Oh baby*.

"You gonna walk around town like that?" I felt myself getting wet. This was so confusing.

"Why not?" She gave her hips a tiny bump. "You do."

"Well, yeah, but that's different."

She stepped closer, cupped my jaw, and stood on her tiptoes to kiss me. When she leaned against me, I felt the firm press of her dick against my thigh. Now I was wet and hard. I put my hands on her waist and moved to turn her toward the bed. To my astonishment, she pushed me gently away.

"Uh-uh. No touching."

"Oh, come on, baby. Let's just stay home."

"Nope." She slid a slim leather wallet into her back pocket and buttoned it. Then she held out her hand and gave me that smile that I've never been able to resist. "Come on, honey. Time to go to drag bingo."

We stood in line along with half the population of Provincetown to get through the white picket fence and onto the grass-covered front lawn of the Unitarian Universalist Church where dozens of metal folding tables had been set up for one of the highlights of Carnival week. Drag bingo. The space was crowded with tourists and townspeople, drag queens, and here and there, a drag king. It was a party atmosphere, and everyone was taking pictures of everyone else. We wended our way toward a free table, carrying our fat color markers and our stack of bingo cards.

I would have felt self-conscious in my less-than-flattering outfit, except no one was paying any attention to me. The drag queens were so flamboyant, so outrageously wonderful, that all eyes were on them. Except for the dykes who were unabashedly eyeing my girlfriend. I had a wholly unfamiliar urge to start scratching eyes out. Scratching eyes out? Who the hell am I?

"Can't you strap that thing down?" I said in an irritated whisper after the third time I spied some sexy femme staring at Shelby's crotch.

"It's as down as it's going to get," she said with a grin. "You ought to know."

"Well, I never get cruised the way you are when I'm packing it."

She gave me a fiery look. "Oh yes, you do. You just don't know how to stake out your territory. It's a girl thing."

"Then sit down," I hissed, indicating one of few free seats left, "and hide that before I have to hurt someone."

"I was wondering," she whispered, leaning close as I took the seat next to her, "if it always makes you want to come in your pants really bad, too."

I groaned. I would have banged my head on the table, but they were starting to call out the first of the bingo numbers, and everyone around me was in a frenzy to mark their cards. You didn't interfere with some of these people at bingo, not and keep your body parts.

It's not easy to sit very long in a skirt, I discovered. I tried crossing my legs, but my feet went numb. If I didn't cross my legs, I forgot to keep my knees together, and although I welcomed the breeze, I was afraid that I'd be advertising to all and sundry exactly the state I was in. Which, considering the fact that every few minutes, Shelby would run her fingers up the inside of my thigh underneath the table, was one of terminal arousal bordering on coming in my seat. When she casually picked up my left hand, moved it under the table and into her lap, and pressed it against the bulge in her trousers, I almost did.

"You're driving me crazy," I growled into her ear. "I'm going to the bathroom to stick my head under the cold-water faucet."

She laughed as I walked away.

I passed by the long lines for the Porta-Johns outside the church and walked around to the side entrance. Having been to more than one show in the church auditorium, I knew there was another small bathroom just inside. Fortunately, not many other people thought of it, and the line was short. Two of the three stalls were occupied, and as I stepped into the third—the farthest from the door—I felt a hand against my back and another person crowded in behind me.

"Shh," Shelby whispered before I could say anything.

I couldn't even turn around, we were pressed so close together, her behind me and my knees nearly up against the toilet. When she gave my shoulders a gentle shove, I reflexively reached out with both hands and braced myself against the wall in front of me. It's a good thing I did, because a second later she slipped her hand under the back of my skirt and between my legs, and my knees nearly gave out. For the first time, I appreciated the ingenious nature of a thong. With a practiced flick of her thumb, she swept the material aside and slid her fingertips between my labia.

I heard her groan as I drenched her hand, and I had to bite my lip to hold back a cry of my own. I think I mentioned how good she is with her hands, and I was already pushing my hips back and forth in an attempt to rub my clitoris against her fingers. I'd been so turned on for so long, I knew I'd come in seconds. To my surprise, she pulled away before I could get there. Then I heard it, and my heart stopped.

The unmistakable sound of a zipper slowly sliding open.

When I moved to turn around, she cupped the back of my neck in her hand to stop me with a whisper. "No."

Off balance, still braced against the wall, I had no room to do anything but wait. I felt as if my whole body were waiting, waiting to be touched, waiting to be filled, waiting to be taken. It was wholly unfamiliar and completely natural. With the first brush of the smooth, cool length of her dick between my legs, my clit jerked and I tightened inside and all I wanted was for her to make me come. I pushed back again, this time against the fat, firm head, and felt it slip inside. I moaned. I couldn't help it.

"Feels good, doesn't it, honey?" she murmured in my ear, her breath hot and ragged.

I knew what she was feeling, the pressure against her clit from the base of the cock, the sweet power of being inside her woman, the need to give and take at the same time. I could only whimper and nod. I wanted more, but I was afraid. Afraid to be other than I have always thought myself to be; afraid to be not less, but more. She knew, and she helped me.

She moved her hand from my neck around the front of my body and underneath the edge of the tiny skirt. She held my clitoris gently between her fingers and began to slide it back and forth the way she knows always makes me come. As soon as she started, I pushed back onto her dick and she slid deeper inside. As I stretched in body and mind to take her, the pressure surged into my clit, and I knew I was going to come.

She stroked me, I rocked against her, she pushed deeper. Once, twice, and then I felt it—the slow, rolling contractions in the core of me that in another minute would burst shooting from my clit.

"I'm coming," I cried softly. I felt her weight against my back, her body trembling as she worked herself inside me. I heard the quick, high-pitched sound she makes when she's nearing orgasm. Just as I crashed over the edge and lost all sense of anything but her, I heard her triumphant voice in my ear.

"Bingo, baby. Bingo."

THE LESSON PLANNER

"Hey, M?" called one of my four housemates from the bottom of the stairs leading to my tiny garret bedroom under the roof, "you busy?"

I looked at the paragraph I'd written—the grand total of three hours' work—clicked Save, and closed the file. "Nope."

I almost always worked in boxers and a tank top, which was what I was wearing, and I walked barefoot to the top of the stairs and leaned over the railing. Clare, a truly cute blonde with big blue eyes to die for and a really, really beautiful mouth, grinned up at me with mischief in her eyes.

"Gary's got a problem," Clare said, referring to the only guy in the house. Of course, Gary—slender, soulful-eyed gay boy Gary—was practically more of a girl than I was. Considering that I was the jock of the house, I guess that wasn't saying much.

"What's wrong?"

"He got a call-out and the client has a special request. But Gary doesn't know what to do."

"Like I can help with that?" Gary supplemented his graduate student stipend by hiring out to an escort service. I couldn't imagine what kind of request he couldn't handle, but I was absolutely certain I wouldn't be able to shed any light on it. The only cocks that interested me were the strap-on kind.

"The client's a woman," Clare said.

I started down the stairs, curious now. "Really? How come?"

"They're short on escorts tonight, and she's some kind of high-roller. They really need Gary to do it."

I hunkered down on the bottom step, trying very hard not to stare at Clare's breasts or any other part of her, which was pretty tough to do considering all she had on were pale blue silk bikini panties and a matching bra. When she wasn't studying law, she spent every minute in the clubs dancing, and her body looked it. Tight legs and a long, lean belly. She was also straight, and though I doubted she'd mind my appreciation, I didn't feel right leering at my friend.

"So what does she want," I asked.

"She likes to be jerked off while she's watching porn."

"Uh, that doesn't sound too complicated. What am I missing?"

Clare leaned against the wall opposite me and grinned. "Gary doesn't know his way around a clit. He's completely panicked."

I laughed. I had to. "Gary 'do anything anywhere' Smith is freaking out because he has to play with a clit?"

"Uh-huh." Clare fidgeted, curling a strand of long blond hair around her finger. She was actually blushing.

"What? What am I still missing?" I asked.

"I sort of volunteered us to give him a demonstration."

I stared, speechless. Partly because I wasn't sure I'd heard her right, and partly because my clit got hard so fast every single synapse in my brain fired at once.

"What?" I asked again stupidly.

"I told him we'd show him what to do."

"How?"

"Well," Clare said, finally meeting my eyes. "I thought he could watch and I could…you know…explain what I was doing while I masturbated you."

"You're going to make me come while Gary watches."

Clare looked away, almost shyly. I'd never seen her look shy before. She said, "Well, you could come if you wanted to, but you wouldn't have to." She rushed on as if to prevent me from saying anything else. "I just want to show him, you know, how to get started. He's really clueless."

The whole idea was nuts, totally nuts. That's what I was saying in my head. But my clit had already jumped right to the start line, because the idea of Clare playing with it, with or without an audience, seemed completely okay. Really okay.

"And you're not going to feel weird about this tomorrow?" I asked.

Clare frowned. "Why would I? It was my idea." She grinned, anything but shy now. "And I've always thought you were hot."

"Clare, you're straight."

"That doesn't stop me from thinking you're sexy." She sat down next to me, her naked thigh touching my naked thigh, her bare shoulder against my bare shoulder. She leaned ever so slightly into me. "So what you do you think? Will you be weird tomorrow?"

She smelled like that special girl smell. Flowers and rain and sunshine. My clit needed attention in a big way now and she'd already volunteered. If she didn't masturbate it, I was going to have to anyway. "I think if we don't do it now, I'll regret it forever."

She kissed my cheek and jumped up. "Awesome." She grabbed my hand and tugged me up. "Come on."

I followed her down the hall to her bedroom as she called, "Gary, we're ready."

Clare had the biggest bedroom in the house, and she'd pushed a love seat into the alcove in front of a set of bay windows. She motioned me toward the sofa and I stood in front of it, waiting.

Gary bounced in, wearing baggy sweats and a sequined tee. Sometimes when I wasn't really paying attention, I'd see him out of the corner of my eye and think, *God, she's really cute.* Then I'd realize I was cruising my gay housemate.

"Hi," I said.

"Oh, this is too cool," he said, dragging over the stool that Clare used to reach things on the top shelf of her closet. He plunked himself down in front of the love seat and put his chin in his hands. "Thanks."

"Oh, you're welcome," I said and rolled my eyes. I glanced at Clare. "What now?"

"Why don't you take off your boxers and sit down."

I did, spreading them out on the sofa under me. Clare sat next to me and rested her hand lightly on my thigh. She was half turned toward me and her breasts brushed my arm. I kept my legs closed, and I wasn't sure where to put my hand.

"Go ahead and put it on my leg. Get comfortable," she said like she did this every day. I leaned back, one arm stretched out along the couch, my other hand resting just above her knee. Then Clare looked at Gary. "Your client is probably going to be wearing something that'll be easy for you to get your hand into or under, or maybe she won't be wearing anything at all. But don't just jump on her. Let her get used to your hand on her skin."

While she talked, Clare brushed her fingertips rhythmically up and down my thigh, moving closer and closer to the inside of my leg with each stroke. I watched her fingers move on my skin and tried not to think about Gary, hunkered down just a few feet away. The more she stroked, the wider I opened my legs so she could reach farther, go higher.

"I got it," he said softly. "Don't shoot for the goal right away. But how will I know when she's ready for the next step?"

"Watch for the signals," Clare said. She drew her fingertip all the way up to the crease at the top of my leg, then skimmed around the outside of my sex—up over and down, barely missing the base of my clit with her short, rounded fingernail. My hips lifted to meet her finger.

"There," Clare announced with satisfaction. "You see her legs tense, her butt lift? She wants more."

I tried not to groan, because hearing her talk about it was getting me majorly excited.

"Where?" Gary asked eagerly. "Where do I touch her first?"

"Maybe we need just a little bit of an anatomy lesson." Clare leaned close and whispered in my ear. "Are you okay if I show him what you look like?"

My harsh breathing sounded loud in the still room. I gripped the top of the sofa with my free hand, the one that wasn't on Clare's leg, and dug my fingers into the worn fabric. Still looking down at her fingers just a few inches from my clit, I said, "Go ahead."

Clare placed two fingers at the top of my sex, on either side of my clit, then spread her fingers, pulling up a little at the same time, opening me and drawing the hood back to expose the head of my clit. The air felt cool, and sweet as a kiss, and I knew I was wet. Clare made a little sound of appreciation in the back of her throat.

"Huh," Gary murmured. "I didn't think it would be so big."

"She's excited. That's why her clitoris is swollen and dark red like that." Clare's voice was husky and low. "Your client's probably going to be just like this right away, too, because she's going to know what you're going to do, and she's probably been thinking about it all day."

Clare pressed the shaft of my clitoris with one finger and my hips jerked again. She laughed and I felt her leg shake next to mine. "She's probably not going to be quite this big, though."

"Hey, M," Gary said seriously. "How does it feel? I mean, are you pretty turned on already?"

"Yeah," I murmured. "It feels great. Getting me hot."

"Like how hot?"

"Like I want her to make me come."

"Okay," Clare said a little breathlessly. "Now here's where you're going to have to experiment a little, Gare, because every girl is different. How she likes to get off, I mean. Some like it fast and light, others slow and hard, others fast and hard. But everyone likes to be teased for a while first." She bumped my shoulder with hers. "Right?"

"Uh-huh. Teasing is good." I didn't think I should tell her that all I really wanted her to do was work me over good and fast right now, because screw foreplay, I just wanted to come. I wasn't sure if Gary could see it, but she had to feel it. My clit jumped every time my heart beat.

"I'm guessing," Clare said, continuing to keep me exposed with one hand, "that she'll like this."

Then she gripped my clit between her thumb and index finger, way down at the base, and squeezed while stroking all the way up to the end, dragging the hood with her. Up and down, up and down, slow and steady. I couldn't look away from her fingers milking me, forcing the blood to fill my clit.

"Wow," Gary whispered. "It's getting purple."

"Is that good?" Clare whispered, her mouth almost against my neck. Her breath blew quickly across my damp skin, short fast bursts of warm air. "Is it what you like?"

I pulled my gaze away from her fingers pulling my clit and turned my head to meet her eyes. They were soft, the pupils flickering. Her lips were parted, pink and moist. "Unbelievable." I imagined her lips closing around my clit.

Clare gasped. "Oh my God, you just got really really hard. What just happened?"

"I thought about you sucking me," I whispered too low for Gary to catch it.

She swayed toward me, and for a second, I thought she was going to kiss me, but she blinked and straightened. Looking down into my lap, she said, "Hold yourself open for me."

I made a grab for my clit and forked my fingers wide on either side. I couldn't help it. I vibrated it a little and my legs danced. "Oh fuck."

"None of that," Clare chided, and she dipped one finger low between my lips, pulled the slick come up and over my clit, and went back to stroking. The hood slid back and forth over the wet head, and it felt like she was licking it. I whined and she picked up speed. When she spoke, her throat sounded dry. "Can you see that, Gary?"

"Yeah. It's really standing up. Does that mean she's gonna come?"

"Are you?" Clare asked. "Are you going to come if I keep doing this?"

"Won't be long," I croaked. "If you don't stop soon."

Clare eased up on my clit and slowed her strokes. I hung on the edge, panting. She lightly traced the edges of my lips, the top of my shaft, the underside of my clit. Not hard enough or fast enough to make me come.

"God, it feels so good," I moaned, closing my fingers down on it while she caressed me. Clare's fingertip glistened. Round and round my clit. "God, Clare."

Gently, she kissed my cheek, the way she had earlier in the hall, moved my hand off my clit, and let me go. "You get the idea, right, Gary?"

I sagged back, my stomach cramping, my clit pumping just short of orgasm.

"What about, you know, going inside?" he asked.

"If she wants you to, she'll show you where and how." Clare drew back, her hand on my thigh now. She massaged the trembling muscles. "Let's give this one a couple minutes to catch her breath, okay?"

Gary jumped up. "Right. Okay. Hey, thanks." He hurried toward the door, then turned back at the last minute and smirked at me. "You *are* going to jerk off, aren't you? Because you've got a wicked case of blue balls."

"Not anatomically correct," I muttered, standing on shaky legs with my boxers clenched in my hand. I knew my clit was poking straight out from my body and that they could probably see it. "But close enough."

"Two minutes to blast-off!" Gary called as he headed into the hall.

"One minute." I bent to pull on my boxers.

Clare gripped my forearm. "Don't put those on just yet." Then she followed Gary to the door, closed it, and turned the lock. From across the room, she met my gaze. "Sit down again."

"I gotta go, Clare." I had to get to my room so I could masturbate. I couldn't think of anything else. I tried to step around her, but she caught my arm.

"You are a really good sport," Clare said, pushing me back toward the couch. My knees hit and I fell onto it.

I didn't know what to say. *You've got amazing hands. You made me so hard I can't stand it. Please, just let me go so I can jerk off.*

"Are you okay?" Clare knelt and pushed my legs apart. She made a purring sound and framed my sex with her hands, opening it again. "Look at you. God, you're beautiful."

My clit jerked rapidly up and down. "I need to go."

"You were close a couple of times, weren't you."

"I really need to go now."

"So you can masturbate?"

"Yes. Yes. I'm sorry. I have to."

"I want to do it." She pressed both thumbs on either side of my clit and rocked it back and forth.

"You don't have to." Tears leaked from my eyes, I needed to come so bad. "But I really need to…" She kissed it. One quick feather-light kiss. "Oh fuck!"

"There you go," she whispered. "You just got totally hard again. That felt good, didn't it?"

"Like you wouldn't believe."

"Tell me what to do to make you come."

I stared helplessly at my clit sticking up between her thumbs. "Stroke it between your fingers like you did earlier."

She did. "Fast enough?"

I bobbed my head, my mouth open, my ass clenching and releasing. My clit swelled.

"You feel like you're going to come. Are you?"

"A little faster," I gasped, bending forward so I could watch her fingers make me come. "Up and down. A little faster. Just like that. You'll make me come if you keep doing that."

"I'm not stopping," Clare said fiercely. "I want you to come so bad." She looked up, her eyes glassy. "So bad, baby. Please."

I couldn't help myself. "I'm going to come. Right. Fucking. Now."

"Oh," she cried, losing her rhythm but it didn't matter. I was already going off. "I can feel it."

I tried to keep my eyes open, but the first wave hit me so hard I flopped backward, blind. I knew I was making pathetic whimpering sounds, but I couldn't stop those either. Then I heard Clare give a sharp little yelp of surprise and I managed to open my eyes. Her head was thrown back, and her hand whipped between her legs. Seeing her coming set me off again.

I wasn't aware of anything much after that until I realized I was lying on the sofa with Clare in my arms. Her head was tucked under my chin and she was murmuring softly, little sounds of pleasure and contentment. I stroked her hair.

"You okay?" I asked

"That was amazing." She kissed my collarbone. "You're really beautiful when you come."

I laughed. "So are you."

She pushed herself up, brushing strands of hair away from her face with one hand. "So if Gary needs pointers on oral sex, are you up for another lesson?"

"Absolutely." I skimmed my finger over her lips and she kissed the tip. "But can I be the teacher next time?"

"It's an advanced course. We might have to run double sessions."

"Then maybe we should work on the syllabus, just to be sure we're ready."

Clare straddled my chest and twitched her panties to one side. She was wet and full. "Lesson two."

CHARACTER STUDY

"Hi, love, what are you doing at work so early?" Hayden Palmer asked.

"Reading through the slush pile." Auden set aside the manuscript she'd been reading and swiveled her chair to look out the window behind her desk. The sun wouldn't be up for another hour, and Rittenhouse Square, the historic park below her office building, was illuminated by streetlights on wrought-iron poles set around its two square block perimeter. She imagined it had looked the same for two hundred years. The Palmer building was at least that old, and the publishing house that bore her lover's name had been creating books for all that time. And now she was the senior editor. "How did you know I'd be here?"

"I called the house and you didn't answer," Hays said.

"It's the middle of the night where you are, darling. What are you doing awake?"

"The signing went late and I had too much coffee at the reception."

"But you're feeling all right?" Even after five years of remission, Auden still worried. In the midst of a busy day, she'd pass Hays's office and glance in to see her behind her desk, her sleeves rolled up, one trousered leg crossed over the other, the phone in one hand and an elegant arm draped over the chair. Auden would catch her breath at how beautiful she was. How vibrant and strong and alive. And for just an instant, she'd remember the endless days and countless sleepless nights when they hadn't been sure if Hays would ever leave the hospital. For those few seconds, her heart would break all over again. "Hays?"

"Don't worry, love. I'm fine. As fine as I can be in the middle of a book tour."

"You're not overdoing? This is the longest tour you've done in a while. Six cities in three weeks and still another week to go."

"Believe me, I know how long it's been. That's why I'm calling. I'm not tired and I'm not sick. I miss you." Hays's voice dropped. "A lot. And it doesn't help that Gayle decided to come with Thane on the tour."

Auden laughed. "Are they misbehaving?"

"When aren't they? You'd think they'd just met." Hays sighed. "It's not that I'd exactly object to watching, but somehow when it's your best friend…"

"I should have come with you."

"The timing is bad. Right before the holiday season, one of us needs to be sure production stays on schedule."

"Are you getting any writing done?" Hays was a talented publisher, but her passion was for writing. When she was on the road this long, she often couldn't find time to write, and that was never good for her.

"I just put in a couple of hours."

"Good." Auden envisioned Hays working at the desk in the hotel room, her dark hair disheveled, her pale elegant features remote as she slipped into another world. Auden loved to watch Hays transform into Rune Dyre, the author. Still hers, but a darker, more dangerous version of Hays. "What did Rune wear to the signing tonight?"

"Well, it is San Francisco and I was reading erotica." Hays laughed. "Black jeans, boots, and a black silk shirt."

"How many buttons did you leave open?"

"On my pants or my shirt?"

Auden caught her breath, imagining the women watching Rune, dark and sexy and mysterious, while she read to them in her deep, sensuous voice. While she seduced them with scenes of women claiming, taking, pleasuring other women. Some of the women listening must fantasize about her, how could they not. Auden knew Rune had more than a few offers for company when she wasn't around, and even when she was. But Rune was hers, just as Hays was. "What have you been writing?"

"Not much. Trying to get a feel for the new book."

"The erotic romance?"

"Mmm-hmm." Hays sounded distracted. "Working on a few scenes. Still can't get a grasp on the character."

"Have you been writing sex?"

"Bits and pieces. Hoping I'd find her that way."

"Bits and pieces. For how long?"

Hays hesitated. "A few hours."

"Is that why you can't sleep?" Hays always needed to make love after she'd been immersed in sex for hours like that. She'd come to Auden aroused, wound tight, already wet, already distended and tense. Sometimes she'd orgasm the instant Auden caressed her clitoris. Sometimes she'd want to make love to Auden, devouring her as if starved. Making her come over and over until they were both exhausted.

"I'm okay. Just edgy."

"This character?"

Hays sighed. "Yeah. Under my skin but I can't quite get to her."

Auden glanced over her shoulder at her office door. It was closed. No one would arrive for at least another few hours. She lifted her hips and slid her skirt up her thighs. "There's someone knocking on your door."

"Do I know who it is?"

"You will." Auden brushed her fingertips over the silk covering her sex. "Open the door and let her in."

"She's here," Hays announced, her voice slipping into that low, seductive range she used when she read to her audience. Her other lovers.

"What does she have to say?"

"There's a big overstuffed chair in front of the windows, by the desk," Hays said. "She wants me to sit there."

"You should finish unbuttoning your shirt and open your pants before you do." Auden pressed down on the swell of her clitoris, imagining Hays's pink-tipped breasts framed by the open folds of black silk. "She's kneeling down between your legs. Running her hands over your chest, your stomach. Caressing your breasts, circling your nipples."

"She's rocking against my crotch. Makes my clit ache," Hays said, the words heavy and slow. Her pants would be open now. Her hand sliding lower.

"Your nipples are hard and she licks them." Auden pinched her clitoris lightly through the silk, her breath coming faster. "Sucks them. First one, then the other."

Hays groaned quietly. "She nips at my nipple and my clit twinges. Like she has her mouth on it, biting me."

Auden swept the silk aside and flicked the tip of her clitoris with her fingernail. "She draws her nails down your belly to your pants. Lift up so she can work them off."

Hays's breath rasped over the line, uneven and harsh. Auden pictured her squeezing her nipples while she rolled her clitoris rhythmically between her long, supple fingers—her dark eyes hooded, her brows creased in concentration. Coiled tight already, imagining the mouth on her breast, the fingers on her fly, the lips skimming down her abdomen.

"She kisses your clitoris," Auden whispered, using three fingers to massage the sensitive spot at the base of her core against the bone underneath. The ache spread deeper and she bit her lip to hold back a whimper.

"Her lips are so soft." Hays groaned. "Feels so good."

Listening to Hays's voice catch, knowing what she was doing, Auden gushed. Hays would be hard, so very hard now. Wet and rigid, swollen, pulsing. Her lean thighs tight, her pelvis tilted up to the mouth devouring her. She'd be so lost in it now, so desperate for the next word, the next phrase, the next image to carry her one step higher. Auden fluttered her clitoris between her fingers, teasing her orgasm to the surface.

"She brushes her lips over the top, back and forth. Ever so lightly."

"More. Jesus. Suck me," Hays panted. "Jesus, suck me."

"Her mouth is warm and wet. She circles her lips around you, closes down on your clit." Auden circled the tip of her clitoris with one finger, spreading the satiny fluid over the tingling nerve endings. Carefully, carefully. Close now. "She teases along the ridge with the tip of her tongue, back and forth underneath the hood. Mmm, tasting you. She sucks. Kisses. Sucks."

"She'll make me come," Hays warned sharply. "In another minute, she'll make me come."

The ring tone on Auden's computer sounded and she swirled

her chair back to face her desk. When she saw the number, her hand trembled and she clicked the mouse over the phone icon on her monitor. The image filled her screen. Hays in a chair, her head tilted back, her shirt open, her breasts exposed. Her lips were parted, her eyes narrowed and intense as she stared down at the woman out of sight between her legs.

"She sucks you down deep. Swirls her tongue." Auden's voice shook. "And then she pulls off and kisses your clit all over."

Hays's eyes flickered up to Auden, then down again. "I'll come in her mouth the next time she does that."

"She licks you underneath, on the sides, around and around the tip. She teases your ass and your lips with her fingers." Auden felt her orgasm gathering force in the base of her clit, twisting through the muscles in her pelvis, pulsing in the core of tissue between her legs. "She's playing with her clit. Moaning while she sucks you. She wants to come too."

"She's sucking hard now, not letting go. Her lips are so damn tight around my clit. Jesus, she's going to make me come!" Hays grimaced, her shoulder vibrating, and Auden knew she was whipping her clit into an orgasm. She stroked hers faster, feeling the floodgates open.

"Oh, oh God," Auden moaned. "She's sucking you and her clit is exploding and she's spilling everywhere, everywhere, all over her fingers, down her thighs…" She lost her breath and could only whimper as her belly clenched again and again.

"I'm coming," Hays said through gritted teeth, her glassy gaze holding Auden's. "I'm coming in her mouth, and she's sucking me, she's sucking me and I'm coming on her face and…" Hays's neck strained and her chest arched off the chair. "Oh Jesus. Oh God. She's so good."

"Oh my God," Arden sighed, holding herself tightly as her sex pulsed. "Oh my God."

Hays laughed shakily. "What did you say her name was?"

Auden managed enough energy to grin at Hays. "I didn't. You're the author, remember. You pick a name."

"Whoever she is, she's definitely got the lead in my next book."

"Then I'm very glad I'm your editor." Auden straightened her clothes and checked her watch. "I should go home and shower. Are you going to try to sleep?"

Hays brushed her hand over her chest and stretched. "I'm a little jazzed right now. I think I'll write some more."

"Then I think I'll work at home this morning. Call me when you get done." Auden touched her fingers to her lips and sent Hays a kiss. "We'll see which character shows up at your door then."

About the Authors

Radclyffe is a retired surgeon and full-time award-winning author-publisher with over thirty lesbian novels and anthologies in print. Five of her works have been Lambda Literary finalists including the Lambda Literary winners *Erotic Interludes 2: Stolen Moments* ed. with Stacia Seaman and *Distant Shores, Silent Thunder*. She is the editor of *Best Lesbian Romance* 2009 and 2010 (Cleis Press) and has selections in multiple anthologies including *Best Lesbian Erotica* 2006, 7, 8, and 9; *After Midnight*; *Caught Looking: Erotic Tales of Voyeurs and Exhibitionists*; *First-Timers*; *Ultimate Undies: Erotic Stories About Lingerie and Underwear*; *Hide and Seek*; *A is for Amour*; *H is for Hardcore*; *L is for Leather*; and *Rubber Sex*. She is the recipient of the 2003 and 2004 Alice B. Readers' award for her body of work and is also the president of Bold Strokes Books, one of the world's largest independent LGBT publishing companies.

Her forthcoming 2009 works include *Justice for All*, *Secrets in the Stone*, and *Returning Tides*.

Books Available From Bold Strokes Books

Sistine Heresy by Justine Saracen. Adrianna Borgia, survivor of the Borgia court, presents Michelangelo with the greatest temptations of his life while struggling with soul-threatening desires for the painter Raphaela. (978-1-60282-051-7)

Radical Encounters by Radclyffe. An out-of-bounds, outside-the-lines collection of provocative, superheated erotica by award-winning romance and erotica author Radclyffe. (978-1-60282-050-0)

Thief of Always by Kim Baldwin & Xenia Alexiou. Stealing a diamond to save the world should be easy for Elite Operative Mishael Taylor, but she didn't figure on love getting in the way. (978-1-60282-049-4)

X by JD Glass. When X-hacker Charlie Riven is framed for a crime she didn't commit, she accepts help from an unlikely source—sexy Treasury Agent Elaine Harper. (978-1-60282-048-7)

The Middle of Somewhere by Clifford Henderson. Eadie T. Pratt sets out on a road trip in search of a new life and ends up in the middle of somewhere she never expected. (978-1-60282-047-0)

Paybacks by Gabrielle Goldsby. Cameron Howard wants to avoid her old nemesis Mackenzie Brandt but their high school reunion brings up more than just memories. (978-1-60282-046-3)

Uncross My Heart by Andrews & Austin. When a radio talk show diva sets out to interview a female priest, the two women end up at odds, and neither heaven nor earth is safe from their feelings. (978-1-60282-045-6)

Fireside by Cate Culpepper. Mac, a therapist, and Abby, a nurse, fall in love against the backdrop of friendship, healing, and defending one's own within the Fireside shelter. (978-1-60282-044-9)

Green Eyed Monster by Gill McKnight. Mickey Rapowski believes her former boss has cheated her out of a small fortune, so she kidnaps the girlfriend and demands compensation—just a straightforward abduction that goes so wrong when Mickey falls for her captive. (978-1-60282-042-5)

Blind Faith by Diane and Jacob Anderson-Minshall. When private investigator Yoshi Yakamota and the Blind Eye Detective Agency are hired to find a woman's missing sister, the assignment seems fairly mundane—but in the detective business, the ordinary can quickly become deadly. (978-1-60282-041-8)

A Pirate's Heart by Catherine Friend. When rare book librarian Emma Boyd searches for a long-lost treasure map, she learns the hard way that pirates still exist in today's world—some modern pirates steal maps, others steal hearts. (978-1-60282-040-1)

Trails Merge by Rachel Spangler. Parker Riley escapes the high-powered world of politics to Campbell Carson's ski resort—and their mutual attraction produces anything but smooth running. (978-1-60282-039-5)

Dreams of Bali by C.J. Harte. Madison Barnes worships work, power, and success, and she's never allowed anyone to interfere—that is, until she runs into Karlie Henderson Stockard. Eclipse EBook (978-1-60282-070-8)

The Limits of Justice by John Morgan Wilson. Benjamin Justice and reporter Alexandra Templeton search for a killer in a mysterious compound in the remote California desert. (978-1-60282-060-9)

Designed for Love by Erin Dutton. Jillian Sealy and Wil Johnson don't much like each other, but they do have to work together—and what they desire most is not what either of them had planned. (978-1-60282-038-8)

Calling the Dead by Ali Vali. Six months after Hurricane Katrina, NOLA Detective Sept Savoie is a cop who thinks making a relationship work is harder than catching a serial killer—but her current case may prove her wrong. (978-1-60282-037-1)

Dark Garden by Jennifer Fulton. Vienna Blake and Mason Cavender are sworn enemies—who can't resist each other. Something has to give. (978-1-60282-036-4)

Shots Fired by MJ Williamz. Kyla and Echo seem to have the perfect relationship and the perfect life until someone shoots at Kyla—and Echo is the most likely suspect. (978-1-60282-035-7)

truelesbianlove.com by Carsen Taite. Mackenzie Lewis and Dr. Jordan Wagner have very different ideas about love, but they discover that truelesbianlove is closer than a click away. Aeros EBook (978-1-60282-069-2)

Justice at Risk by John Morgan Wilson. Benjamin Justice's blind date leads to a rare opportunity for legitimate work, but a reckless risk changes his life forever. (978-1-60282-059-3)

Run to Me by Lisa Girolami. Burned by the four-letter word called love, the only thing Beth Standish wants to do is run for—or maybe from—her life. (978-1-60282-034-0)

Split the Aces by Jove Belle. In the neon glare of Sin City, two women ride a wave of passion that threatens to consume them in a world of fast money and fast times. (978-1-60282-033-3)

Uncharted Passage by Julie Cannon. Two women on a vacation that turns deadly face down one of nature's most ruthless killers—and find themselves falling in love. (978-1-60282-032-6)

Night Call by Radclyffe. All medevac helicopter pilot Jett McNally wants to do is fly and forget about the horror and heartbreak she left behind in the Middle East, but anesthesiologist Tristan Holmes has other plans. (978-1-60282-031-9)

Lake Effect Snow by C.P. Rowlands. News correspondent Annie T. Booker and FBI Agent Sarah Moore struggle to stay one step ahead of disaster as Annie's life becomes the war zone she once reported on. Aeros EBook (978-1-60282-068-5)

Revision of Justice by John Morgan Wilson. Murder shifts into high gear, propelling Benjamin Justice into a raging fire that consumes the Hollywood Hills, burning steadily toward the famous Hollywood Sign—and the identity of a cold-blooded killer. (978-1-60282-058-6)

I Dare You by Larkin Rose. Stripper by night, corporate raider by day, Kelsey's only looking for sex and power, until she meets a woman who stirs her heart and her body. (978-1-60282-030-2)

Truth Behind the Mask by Lesley Davis. Erith Baylor is drawn to Sentinel Pagan Osborne's quiet strength, but the secrets between them strain duty and family ties. (978-1-60282-029-6)

Cooper's Deale by KI Thompson. Two would-be lovers and a decidedly inopportune murder spell trouble for Addy Cooper, no matter which way the cards fall. (978-1-60282-028-9)

Romantic Interludes 1: Discovery ed. by Radclyffe and Stacia Seaman. An anthology of sensual, erotic contemporary love stories from the best-selling Bold Strokes authors. (978-1-60282-027-2)

A Guarded Heart by Jennifer Fulton. The last place FBI Special Agent Pat Roussel expects to find herself is assigned to an illicit private security gig baby-sitting a celebrity. Aeros Ebook (978-1-60282-067-8)

Saving Grace by Jennifer Fulton. Champion swimmer Dawn Beaumont, injured in a car crash she caused, flees to Moon Island, where scientist Grace Ramsay welcomes her. (Ebook) (978-1-60282-066-1)

The Sacred Shore by Jennifer Fulton. Successful tech industry survivor Merris Randall does not believe in love at first sight until she meets Olivia Pearce. Aeros Ebook (978-1-60282-065-4)

Passion Bay by Jennifer Fulton. Two women from different ends of the earth meet in paradise. Author's expanded edition. Aeros Ebook (978-1-60282-064-7)

Never Wake by Gabrielle Goldsby. After a brutal attack, Emma Webster becomes a self-sentenced prisoner inside her condo—until the world outside her window goes silent. Aeros Ebook (978-1-60282-063-0)

The Caretaker's Daughter by Gabrielle Goldsby. Against the backdrop of a nineteenth-century English country estate, two women struggle to find love. Aeros Ebook (978-1-60282-062-3)

Simple Justice by John Morgan Wilson. When a pretty-boy cokehead is murdered, former LA reporter Benjamin Justice and his reluctant new partner, Alexandra Templeton, must unveil the real killer. (978-1-60282-057-9)

Remember Tomorrow by Gabrielle Goldsby. Cees Bannigan and Arieanna Simon find that a successful relationship rests in remembering the mistakes of the past. (978-1-60282-026-5)

Put Away Wet by Susan Smith. Jocelyn "Joey" Fellows has just been savagely dumped—when she posts an online personal ad, she discovers more than just the great sex she expected. (978-1-60282-025-8)

Homecoming by Nell Stark. Sarah Storm loses everything that matters—family, future dreams, and love—will her new "straight" roommate cause Sarah to take a chance at happiness? (978-1-60282-024-1)

The Three by Meghan O'Brien. A daring, provocative exploration of love and sexuality. Two lovers, Elin and Kael, struggle to survive in a postapocalyptic world. Aeros Ebook (978-1-60282-056-2)

Falling Star by Gill McKnight. Solley Rayner hopes a few weeks with her family will help heal her shattered dreams, but she hasn't counted on meeting a woman who stirs her heart. (978-1-60282-023-4)

Lethal Affairs by Kim Baldwin and Xenia Alexiou. Elite operative Domino is no stranger to peril, but her investigation of journalist Hayley Ward will test more than her skills. (978-1-60282-022-7)

Word of Honor by Radclyffe. All Secret Service Agent Cameron Roberts and First Daughter Blair Powell want is a small intimate wedding, but the paparazzi and a domestic terrorist have other plans. (978-1-60282-018-0)

In Deep Waters 2 by Radclyffe and Karin Kallmaker. All bets are off when two award winning-authors deal the cards of love and passion… and every hand is a winner. (978-1-60282-013-5)

The Lonely Hearts Club by Radclyffe. Take three friends, add two ex-lovers and several new ones, and the result is a recipe for explosive rivalries and incendiary romance. (978-1-60282-005-0)

Winds of Fortune by Radclyffe. Provincetown local Deo Camara agrees to rehab Dr. Bonita Burgoyne's historic home, but she never said anything about mending her heart. (978-1-933110-93-6)